Why was Josh interested in his arresting officer?

There was a softness in Violet's eyes, a compassion, and that made Josh pause. Made him think. And feel things he hadn't felt in a really long time.

Josh had spent most of his adult life chasing the next win. He hadn't stopped to consider what he really wanted.

"Belonging."

The word rushed out of him like a riptide from the bottom of his heart. To be important to just one person. What would that be like? What would it be like to walk into a room and have Violet's face light up just because he was there? Not the blaze of fame like he saw in a fan's face, or the need in those dependent on him, but love.

Was that what he wanted?

Love?

Dear Reader,

To all of you who are returning to the Shores of Indian Lake series and who read *Family of His Own*, you might remember Violet Hawks. For those of you who are new to Indian Lake, welcome. Indian Lake is a lovely and loving smallish town located in Northwest Indiana. The town is noted for its close community of involved, concerned and caring people. I have been fortunate in my life to grow up in a place like Indian Lake.

Violet Hawks is a rookie police officer. She dreams of becoming an investigative detective one day, but when she sees an expensive Bugatti Chiron shooting down a country road, she pursues. The Chiron is driven by handsome, famous and wealthy race car driver Josh Stevens. Josh is shocked when the feisty and pretty Violet actually arrests him!

The judge orders Josh to do community service, which keeps him tied to Indian Lake and to Violet. When Josh is injured in a Memorial Day race, Violet realizes that her concern for Josh has turned into something deeper.

I hope you enjoy *Hers to Protect*. It was interesting and challenging to delve into the law enforcement world as seen through Violet's young, ambitious eyes. Josh clearly burrowed into my heart.

I love hearing from you as I delve into more Shores of Indian Lake stories. Follow me on Facebook; Twitter: @cathlanigan; catherinelanigan.com; Pinterest; YouTube; heartwarmingauthors.blogspot.com; and my book tours at prismbooktours.com; and see my Hallmark movie, *The Sweetest Heart*, based on the book *Heart's Desire*, on the Hallmark Channel.

God bless,

Catherine

HEARTWARMING

Hers to Protect

Catherine Lanigan

HARLEQUIN® HEARTWARMING™

ISBN-13: 978-1-335-51066-2

Hers to Protect

This edition published by arrangement with Harlequin Books S.A.

For questions and comments about the quality of this book, please contact us at CustomerService@Harlequin.com.

Printed in U.S.A.

Catherine Lanigan knew she was born to storytelling at a very young age when she told stories to her younger brothers and sister to entertain them. After years of encouragement from family and high school teachers, Catherine was shocked and brokenhearted when her freshman college creative-writing professor told her that she had “no writing talent whatsoever” and that she would never earn a dime as a writer.

For fourteen years she did not write until she was encouraged by a television journalist to give her dream a shot. That was nearly forty published novels, nonfiction books and anthologies ago. To add to the dream, Hallmark Channel has recently released *The Sweetest Heart*, based on the second book in her Harlequin Heartwarming series, Shores of Indian Lake. With more books in the series and more movies to come, Catherine makes her home in La Porte, Indiana, the inspiration for Indian Lake.

Books by Catherine Lanigan

Harlequin Heartwarming

Shores of Indian Lake

Family of His Own
His Baby Dilemma
Rescued by the Firefighter

Visit the Author Profile page at Harlequin.com for more titles.

This book is dedicated to my husband and hero, Jed Nolan, who died October 21, 2015. I love you to the moon and back and throughout all the galaxies forever. I am ever grateful to you for watching over me.

ACKNOWLEDGMENTS

My heartfelt thanks to my editor Adrienne Macintosh for guiding me through this fast-paced relationship between Violet and Josh. We had so much fun sitting in the grandstand while these two jockeyed for positions in their rocketing romance. Your insights and brilliance continue to polish my creativity and make my work turn to "play."

To Dianne Moggy, my editor and friend. We've racked up another one and we're heading into even more fun! Thank you for being there for me over twenty-three years. That time went fast.

To Kathleen Scheibling, Kathryn Lye, Deirdre McCluskey, Dana Grimaldi and all the creative Heartwarming team who work endlessly to make every Heartwarming story the superlative novels they are, my deepest gratitude. You all continue to amaze me.

And to my agent and dear friend, Lissy Peace, our journey has been decades in the making and the speedway to our futures is certainly filled with thrills and triumphs. The race has only just begun.

CHAPTER ONE

VIOLET PEERED THROUGH her binoculars at the shower of apple blossoms fluttering onto the hood of her unmarked Ford Taurus squad car. Though she listened to satellite radio through an aux jack, she was waiting anxiously for a call from her superior, Detective Trent Davis. This was Violet's first stakeout—though only an innocent-looking old farmhouse, it represented her superiors' trust in her.

After six months on the ILPD force, she'd been handed every rookie assignment the chief couldn't pawn off on one of the veteran cops. She was the greenie kid fresh out of the academy. Every one of her superiors had dodged giving her a real assignment. Until today.

She'd been walking past the chief's office—okay, she'd been purposefully loitering there, eavesdropping on the conversation between Trent Davis, Sal Paluzzi and Chief Williams about a Chicago-based drug dealer moving into the area. She heard Chief Williams say, "All I've got is that this guy is in the area, drives an expensive sports car and a name. Miguel Garcia."

Violet choked on the coffee she'd been nursing. Trent looked up and saw Violet on the other side of the open door. "Officer Hawks?"

Violet didn't shy away. "Yes, sir." She boldly walked across the threshold, but as she opened her mouth, an image of being fired for her impertinence invaded her thoughts. Risks were something an officer of the law faced every day. She took the shot. "It's likely an alias. Miguel Garcia is a very common name. It would take more than searching databases to get a bead on this guy. Which would be the reason it was used."

Trent folded his arms over his wide chest. The chief narrowed his eyes, while Sal sought refuge in his coffee mug. He was waiting for her to trip up. Again.

"You're correct on that, Officer Hawks," the chief said. "Any suggestions?"

Fast thinking, intuition and the ability to piece together unrelated clues and fragments of information had served her well since the first time she played board games, or watched television mysteries with her siblings. "Over Easter dinner at my mother's house, which is out on the north side of the county, Mom said she'd seen an expensive sports car racing down 1000 North. She said it came out of nowhere and had to be going over one-fifty. It was so fast she didn't remember the color. For my mother, an architect and designer, who sees every tone and hue of color, that's fast."

"Your point?" Trent challenged.

Her thoughts fell into place like lightning strikes. "It's been ILPD experience that drug dealers around here tend to have fast, expensive cars. They also comb the county roads around Indian Lake because that's how they traffic their shipments and avoid us. Er, the authorities. I've lived in the north of the county all my life. I know every road, farmer's access road and gully. I've picked strawberries at Paulson's Farm and peaches at Brown's Orchards. The tourists don't usually head out that way. Superfast cars aren't the norm out near my mother's house. It wouldn't be much of a stretch to say that speeding car belonged to someone who was up to no good, someone who might be part of this new dealer's network or even the dealer himself."

Her mouth had gone dry. Had she done the right thing? This wasn't her meeting. She'd been hired as a traffic cop, though all she'd ever dreamed about was becoming an investigative detective on a major city's police force such as Chicago or New York.

The truth was, Violet wasn't good enough

for big city forces. She'd applied in Indianapolis, Evansville and South Bend. They'd all turned her down. Being the second youngest Hawks kid, she'd wanted to get out of Indian Lake and make her mark elsewhere. Anywhere. But since drug use and trafficking in small towns and rural areas throughout the Midwest was on the rise, towns like Indian Lake needed cops. Trent Davis knew her sister, Isabelle, and Isabelle's husband well, so he recommended Violet to the chief. She got the job.

Violet knew she had dues to pay. She was okay with that. Still, she would have rather done so in Los Angeles or Chicago where her detective skills would have been tested nearly every day and advancement would have been faster. Or so she thought. Trent Davis's Drug Task Force had made significant inroads and arrests last year. Isabelle's husband, Scott, had written a prize-winning newspaper article on his eyewitness report to Davis's bust bringing down the notorious and elusive Le Grand gang. Now a new gang was taking over. If she could contribute to this investigation, she could become a permanent member on Davis's team. After that? The possibilities were endless.

Trent rubbed the pleased smile off his face and turned to Violet. "Did your mother have an idea what kind of car it was?"

"She said Maserati. My brother Eric always had posters of Italian race cars in his room. She said it was something like that."

"It could be anything," Sal interjected.

Trent unfolded his arms. "How many Maseratis have you seen around here? Even in tourist season, Sal?"

"None."

Chief Williams pointed at Violet. "Hawks, I'm ordering you on a stakeout. Davis, you get her outfitted with what she needs. If something is going on up there on or around 1000 North, I want to know about it. This makes sense. It's close to the Michigan state line. The interstate is a stone's throw away. Those county roads up there are a spiderweb. I can't tell you how many times I've missed my turn and ended up in Three Oaks, Michigan." He cleared his throat.

Trent rose and walked toward Violet. Sal was behind him. He lowered his voice as they headed toward Trent's desk. "Congrats, Hawks. But, while I'm ordering up a car for you, I want you to search that database." He pointed to the computer on his desk. "Don't look for Garcia. Look for Maserati sales in the tristate area."

AS SHE SCANNED the early May orchards, she savored the sweet taste of satisfaction on her lips. She'd stepped up to the plate, and finally, she felt she was part of a team.

The radio chirped.

"Hawks?"

She grabbed the square shoulder mic. "Sir?"

"What have you got?" Trent asked.

"Nothing." She sat up straighter. Her ears pricked as she heard the sound of an engine. This wasn't a tractor or a slow-moving old truck taking fruit saplings out to plant. It was something she'd never heard before.

Holding the binoculars again, she saw a streak of blue through a blind of windbreak trees to the far south.

"Are you still there?" Trent asked.

"I got something."

"What?" His voice pitched with interest.

"I don't...know...but it's moving like a bullet train."

"Use your radar gun. How fast?"

She snatched the radar gun from the passenger seat, aimed and tagged the vehicle, whose make she still couldn't identify. "Holy crap. Sorry, sir." She turned on her car's engine already anticipating the chase. "Two zero two."

"Talk later. Go!"

"Roger. Out."

She flung the radar gun and binoculars to the passenger seat, stomped on the gas pedal and shot dirt from under her tires. The blue bullet was streaking down the country road as if the devil was on its back. As Violet sped the Taurus over seventy, then eighty miles an hour, she knew she'd never outrace her prey.

She'd have to outsmart him.

Knowing that Jasper Brown had bisected his enormous orchard years ago with a dirt path wide enough for his truck, she headed for that familiar dirt alley that separated the apple trees from the pear trees.

Turning sharp right, she tore down the bumpy trail that seemed a lot more hazardous today than it had ten years ago when she used to ride her bike home from apple picking. She tightened her seat belt and hit the gas. From the right, she could see the blue sports car approaching. It would pass her, but she'd have it within her sights.

As she burst out of the farm's dirt path and up the slight bank, the blue bullet screamed past her. The driver was a blur.

"Oh, no you don't." Violet's squad car nearly leaped onto the pavement and made chase. She turned on her light bar and siren. "Officially, you're mine."

Expecting the blue sports car to slow down now that her lights and siren were on, Violet was shocked when it kicked up its speed. Convinced she had the drug dealer dead to rights, she wasn't about to let up. She plunged the gas to the floor. The Taurus could do up to one-fifty, but this sports car was out of her league.

Just then she heard Trent's voice. "Officer Hawks, keep this line open."

"Sir. Yes, sir."

"Report."

"I'm coming up on 350 East. I'm in pursuit. I've never seen this car make. I'll shoot the license. It's over two hundred miles an hour. I can't overtake. I need backup."

"County deputy sheriffs are on their way."

"Ten four."

"Stay with him. You got something."

In the background over the radio, Violet could hear Trent speaking to the county sheriff's dispatcher.

Trent's voice was stern. "County is close. They're forming a barricade two and a half miles from you. Back off."

She smiled. "Ten four." She turned off her radio. Violet kept her foot depressed. This was her perp. Her collar. She was going to see it to the end. When the county sheriff barricade stopped this drug dealer, she would be there and she would make the arrest. Glory was within her reach. And possibly a promotion.

Gold-and-brown Indian Lake County sheriff

cars and SUVs were strung across the county road with lights flashing. The blue bullet slammed on its brakes, tires squealing and black rubber smoking streaks across the concrete. Violet let off the gas and braked, bringing the Taurus to a quick but safe stop. She couldn't unbelt herself fast enough. It was all she could do not to run up to Miguel Garcia and drag him from the luxurious sports car. If her brothers were here, they'd be whistling over this car. She still had no idea what it was, but she was sure "expensive" didn't come close to describing its price.

Before she got to the blue bullet, the door was flung open and a tall, lean, blond man exited. Violet halted. He was killer handsome, dressed in expensive black slacks, a dark blue knit shirt that stretched over his broad chest, its fine material lying over cut muscles. The long sleeves were shoved up to his elbows, exposing taut forearms. He clenched and unclenched his fists. He glared at her. She noticed his eyes were sky blue.

"Aw jeez. A country cop." He spat the word from between pursed, angry lips.

"ILPD. City cop."

His anger vanished as he flashed her a blazingly charming smile. "What a coincidence."

"Excuse me?"

"I'm from Indianapolis. It was a joke."

"I'm not smiling." This man was likely guilty of nothing more than speeding. And her reaction to him vied with the realization she'd left her stakeout, where the drug dealer might even now be driving by.

She felt she was right back where she started, giving out speeding tickets on Highway 35.

"Sir, I clocked you at over two hundred miles an hour."

He glanced behind him at his car. He patted the hood. "That's all?"

Violet gaped at his audacity. Who did he think he was?

The scuffle of boots against the pavement alerted her to the audience of four county sheriff's deputies watching the scene.

Violet reached to her back pocket for her ticket pad. She pulled a pen from her breast pocket. "I'm citing you for speeding and reckless driving."

"You're kidding. Right?"

She glared at him. "Do I look like I'm kidding?" She lowered her eyes to the pad and wrote. "The speed limit here is fifty."

"I never saw anything posted."

"Well, it is," she replied, still not looking into his startling blue eyes. "But then you were going so fast, how could you see it?"

"I see a lot of things. If there was a sign posted, I would have seen it. I've been all over these country roads."

"You have."

"I know people here. Austin and Katia McCreary."

Violet also knew Austin and Katia. A little. Some said Austin was the wealthiest man in town. He owned the antique car museum, and, according to Isabelle, he'd been a recluse for years until he married Katia. Violet had worked a couple charity events with Katia.

How did this guy know Austin?

She heard the deputies snickering at her, so she pressed on. "It doesn't matter who you know in town. I need your driver's license and registration." She held out her hand.

At that point the deputies broke into guffaws.

This was too much. She took a step away from the car and shot a laser look at the tallest of the four deputies. "What?"

He broke from the barricade as the other deputies walked back to their cars hooting to themselves. "You don't know who this is, do you, Officer…?"

"Hawks," she replied officially. "I'm about to find out once I get his driver's…"

"Josh Stevens," the deputy sheriff said. "He's

just about the most famous race car driver to come out of Indiana. I saw him race."

Violet felt herself flush. She imagined she'd gone from red to crimson to deep purple. Of course she knew who he was. You couldn't grow up in the Hawks house and not know names like Danica Patrick, Fernando Alonso and Josh Stevens. Violet's brothers had spent nearly every Memorial Day weekend in college seated in the bleachers in Speedway, Indiana, watching the Indianapolis 500.

All she could do was follow through with her job. If she didn't, the deputy would report it to the county sheriff, who would report her to the chief. She may have egg on her face, but she was in the right and she knew the law. Violet wrote Josh's name on the top of the ticket.

"I still need your license."

Josh looked at the sheriff, who shrugged.

"Apparently, you don't need us anymore, Officer Hawks."

"No. I don't."

Josh pulled his wallet from his back pocket. "I don't believe this." He pulled the license out along with the car's registration.

It was all Violet could do to keep her hands from shaking as she finished writing the ticket. "Court is two weeks from Friday. Be there."

"I will not. I'm in training."

"Excuse me?"

He waved the ticket at her. "This is ridiculous and so are you for giving it to me. I'm not a criminal, and I won't be treated like one."

Violet felt her ire sail to the top of her skull.

"You broke the law," she countered.

"You don't want to take me on, Officer Hawks. I'll have your job for this."

"Is that a threat?"

"A promise."

"You're under arrest."

"I refuse."

"I'll gladly add resisting arrest to the charges."

"This isn't happening," he spat.

"It is," she replied, feeling that same rage she'd once felt when she was bullied at school, the day Billy Pope had knocked her to the ground. Violet had vowed never to look up into the face of an assailant and feel powerless again. "You have the right to remain silent..." She began reciting his Miranda rights.

Before Josh could say another word, Violet had flipped handcuffs around his right wrist and had spun him around to clasp his hands behind his back. She tightened the handcuffs.

"You can't do this to me!" he snarled. "This is ridiculous. I won't let you arrest me. My lawyer will tear you apart."

She continued reciting. "…and if you have no lawyer, the court will appoint one to represent you."

"Trust me, I have the best." Josh cracked a harsh chuckle. His smile spread across his face, but his eyes glinted icily.

The remaining deputy sheriff had stopped walking and was recording the scene on his iPhone. He stopped, lowered the phone and asked, "You need help?"

"I got this," Violet said.

Josh shook his head and laughed. He turned his back to the deputy sheriff and flipped his keys onto the pavement at the man's feet.

Josh was still laughing as he said, "Drive my Bugatti back to town, will ya?"

"Don't mind if I do," the deputy said with a grin, then picked up the keys and gave Josh a little salute.

Violet rolled her eyes. The admiration she saw in the deputy's eyes was killing her. She steered Josh toward her Taurus, putting her hand on the top of his head. "Watch your head. And those long legs of yours are going to smash up against my seat."

Josh spun to face her. They were nearly nose to nose as his angry eyes bored into hers. "You have no idea what you've just done. You're going to regret this till your dying day."

"I doubt that seriously. The way I see it, you're a danger to others." Violet somehow managed to keep her voice steady, despite her rage. She'd come out here today to gather information on a drug lord. She despised drug dealers, pushers and the traffickers who preyed on kids.

So Josh wasn't a drug dealer, but he had been a danger. It wasn't merely the fact that Josh Stevens had been speeding, it was his attitude that he could get away with his infraction that kicked up her ire. People like Josh Stevens felt they could wheedle, bully, intimidate and charm their way through all their actions, legal and otherwise.

Violet was just one cop, and she knew that sometimes, all it took was one person to make a difference.

CHAPTER TWO

Josh inspected the ink on the pads of his fingers. When he was photographed, he was wise enough to drop his indignation and flash his celebrated smile for the camera. As he was escorted from area to area, desk to desk, he watched Officer Hawks carry out her duties with by-the-book efficiency.

She typed her report like a demon and asked him only requisite questions. He thought of dozens of smart-mouthed barbs he could shoot her with, but she appeared impervious to his taunts. She treated him like a bug. He was a perp. A wrongdoer.

"I get a phone call," he said.

"You're entitled to several calls, actually. However, the station cannot allow you to tie up our phone lines talking to your, er, 'people.'" She kept her eyes on the computer screen as she typed.

"I'll use my cell."

"Not for now you won't."

"Fine. So, when can I make my calls?"

"When I feel like it."

"I'm not answering another question until I talk to my lawyer. That's the law, Officer Hawks," Josh said bluntly. He'd already figured out that threats didn't dent this woman's disposition. Neither did his charm. She was a rock. A government robot. She was the kind of powerless bureaucrat who validated her position by exercising her influence on innocent citizens.

Like me.

He'd seen plenty of people like her. His parents had been killed when their car had been hit head-on by a drug addict. As an only child and with no other family, he'd been shuffled by state officials from one foster home to another.

This cop made him think of his best friend back then. Diego Lopez had had such a severe distrust of authority. He'd also barely spoken English, but Josh had enjoyed teaching him.

"Give me your attorney's number and I'll place the call for you. What's his name?"

"Paul Saylor."

"In Indianapolis?"

"Yes. You know him?"

"I went to a seminar he gave when I was at the police academy in Indianapolis."

"And that was when?"

Her eyes narrowed. She was instantly on the defensive.

Josh had guessed she was young, twenty-three or twenty-four. She carried herself stiff, like a rookie. She was out of her league with him. That was for sure.

"I can look up the number if you forgot it."

"Actually, he's in Europe..." Josh checked his watch. "Just my luck. He's back tomorrow. He's always around for my time trials and the race Memorial Day weekend." He smiled pleasantly, without too much force.

She glared at him.

He dropped the smile. Nothing worked on this woman. "I'll call Harry instead."

"Harry?"

"My manager."

Silence.

Josh swallowed and then rhymed off Harry's cell number, and Violet dialed.

Once it started to ring, she handed Josh the receiver. She went back to typing, but she didn't leave him alone.

Josh turned his back to her and held the receiver close. His manager answered on the fourth ring. "Harry. It's Josh. I need your help."

"Sure. What's up?"

"I need you to find Paul Saylor when he gets back tomorrow."

"Why would you need Paul?"

"To bail me out of jail."

The long pause segued into a low groan. "What for? Drugs?"

"For Pete's sake, Harry! You know me better than that. I was ticketed for speeding."

"Where are you?"

"Indian Lake. I told you. I was here to see Austin and Katia McCreary."

"Right, the antique car guy. Did you buy anything?"

"Harry. Focus. I'm in a jam here."

"No big deal. Paul can clear this up...wait. You said jail. Why jail for speeding?"

Josh lowered his voice to a whisper. "They've got me for threatening the officer. I resisted her arrest."

"Her? Well, that explains it."

"Thanks a lot," Josh retorted. "Look, I want to get out of here."

"I want you out, too. Mainly so I can wring your neck!" Harry blasted him. "Has anybody seen you?"

"Seen me?"

"Yeah. Like the press. Some kid on social media? This kind of thing can really hurt us. Bad publicity only weeks before the Indianapolis race. Just what I need, Josh."

"Hey, this is *my* career we're talking about here."

"Precisely. And your career affects my career and my life. You have responsibilities, Josh. To the sponsors, the crew, the advertisers. You've been on a glory roll for nearly three years. No crashes. No bust ups. Not a glitch. Now you go out joyriding in some backwater town. Who knows what the locals think of you."

Josh's head inched downward with each of Harry's accusations. He was right. Josh was a man of duty and massive commitments. His sponsors put up hundreds of thousands of dollars for him to spend his life screaming around a raceway in some of the most expensive cars on the planet. His entourage depended on him to do everything right. Eat right, exercise, train and make lightning-quick decisions on the track. His job was to stay alive and be a good guy while doing it.

Today, he'd let everyone down.

"I'm telling you, Josh. This may have been fun for you, but it can cost us. If that cop has you on resisting arrest, that tells me you let your mouth run away with you. Again."

"It wasn't that bad," Josh muttered.

"Yeah? Tell it to the judge. And believe me, you will. In the meantime, shut your trap. You got that?"

"Got it."

"Good. Be as polite as you know how. I

don't know anything about this Indian Lake, but I'm going to find out. These little towns take small infractions seriously. It's not Indianapolis where you can buy or autograph your way out of just about anything."

"I'm seeing that." Josh's eyes tracked up to Violet. He watched the hard set to her jaw as she banged away at the computer. She scrolled the mouse over a section of writing and cut it. Then she licked her bottom lip and went back to work. The harsh light shone on her heart-shaped face, and he noticed the long, dark lashes that cast shadows over naturally pink cheeks. She had expressive dark brows that pinched at the bridge of her pert nose when she found another section to cut. Until this moment, he hadn't thought about what she must think of him besides the fact that he was a criminal. He was curious to know her thoughts. And that surprised him.

To Harry, he said, "So, how do I get out of here?"

"I can post the bail for you. Is there anyone there who can tell you how much?"

"Hold on." Josh turned around, put his palm over the receiver and asked, "Officer Hawks, how much is my bail going to be?"

She stopped typing and pointed to a poster on the far wall. "Five hundred dollars."

Josh went back to his call. “Five hundred.”

“Great. I’ll get in touch with the bail bondsman there in Indian Lake. Just chill. Make the best of your afternoon.”

“Easy for you to say,” Josh replied, and hung up. He handed the receiver to Violet. “You do realize this is costing me a lot more than a few hundred bucks.”

“How’s that?”

“I’m missing an interview with the *South Bend Tribune*’s sports writer. A radio program and television interview, as well. Interviews translate to tickets sold to the race. These things are important to me.”

“You shoulda thought of that earlier.”

“I was thinking...” His voice trailed off. “Oh, what do you care?”

She rose from her chair. “Until your bail is posted, I have to take you to a cell.”

“A jail cell? I can’t just stay here? Harry said it won’t take long to post bail.”

She cocked her head to the right, indicating a heavy metal door with a small wired-glass window. “Through there.”

“I don’t believe this. Sure you don’t want to put leg irons on me?”

“I can do that if you wish,” she bit out.

Josh remembered what Harry had said about

being polite. "No. You've gone to enough trouble for me, Officer Hawks."

They went to the hall that led to four jail cells. Officer Hawks spoke to the young officer just inside the hall. "Cell three has been assigned to..."

"Josh Stevens! Officer Trey McLaughlin. Glad to meet you," he said, holding out his hand to Josh. "I've seen or heard nearly every race. How's it lining up for the Indianapolis race?"

Josh shook his hand exuberantly. "You follow the races?"

"I do. I'm a huge fan."

"Thanks, man." Josh felt his grin grow. Two minutes ago he'd felt dirty. Now he felt whole again thanks to his fan. He would go back to his world, and his life would return to normal. It would. It had to. "Trey, I promise you, it's looking great."

Officer Hawks took Josh's arm. "In here," she barked.

Josh entered the cell, turned and put his hands on the bars. He was in jail. He'd fought all his young years to make the right choices, even when others lobbied with very persuasive skills for him to go down another road. The quick road. The road of drug deals and stunning amounts of cash. Hot cars. Expensive clothes. Tropical resorts where women would flock to him.

But Josh's parents had taught him that his integrity was what mattered. With integrity and honesty, he would win the respect of even his critics.

Right now he had to remember that.

As he looked through the iron bars at the startlingly and surprisingly compassionate green eyes of his captor, he couldn't help wondering what it would take to win her respect.

With his gaze locked on hers, Josh said humbly, "Thank you, Officer Hawks."

CHAPTER THREE

"DO YOU KNOW what a Bugatti Chiron costs?" Trent Davis asked as he paced his office while Violet stood near his desk. Many times in the past she'd felt like running from confrontation, but this time wasn't one of them. Deep in her belly, as much as Chief Williams and Detective Davis believed she'd bungled this assignment, she knew she was right. Josh Stevens might be a celebrity—he had fame, fortune and influence—and she was barely more than a traffic cop, but Josh had questioned her authority. She'd clocked him speeding. Anything over a hundred miles an hour was considered "reckless driving." She was in the right, and she would stand her ground.

"A lot, I presume."

"It's so expensive, Officer Hawks, that I had a difficult time finding the price."

"Sir?"

Frustrated, he said, "I don't care about the car or its cost. My point is that you left your post at the stakeout farmhouse."

"Sir, I was told that Miguel Garcia was known to drive a very expensive sports car. The Bugatti fits that bill. I thought I was chasing Garcia."

"That's your first mistake, Officer. You assumed before you had the facts. Sal was working the database and had found that Garcia drives a Maserati 2016. If you had checked in with him, you would have known that."

Violet remembered how fast the Bugatti had streamed past her. She knew what a Maserati looked like. But she'd never seen a Bugatti Chiron. They were both fast cars. It was an understandable mistake.

She promised herself that over the weekend she'd comb the internet for images of every expensive car made. She'd log them into her brain and the next time a Bugatti sailed past her, she'd know what she was looking at.

Trent was still pacing.

"What color is the Maserati, sir?"

Trent halted, lifted his head and cleared his throat. "Blue."

Violet's eyebrow cranked up in surprise, and she quickly corrected her expression. Blue. Well, she had that one right.

"The bottom line is that I'm disappointed in your work. The next time I give you an assignment, you carry it out."

"Sir. Yes, sir."

"Dismissed."

Violet turned sharply and left the office. She went straight to her desk, avoiding Sal's and Trey's eyes. Trey was getting coffee, which was odd, because he didn't drink coffee.

Violet halted like someone kicked her in the back. It was probably for Josh.

She couldn't forget the look in his eyes when she'd put him in the cell.

Josh was her first lockup. Her first arrest.

As she'd ushered him into the cell, she'd felt her heart squeeze in her chest. Two steps inside the cell, his broad shoulders had slumped and his face had gone ashen.

Shockingly, he'd thanked her.

Why?

What kind of man thanked an officer for showing him his limitations? His vulnerability?

The unique kind.

When he'd looked at her, his blue eyes weren't malicious. They actually held gratitude.

Every assessment she'd made about Josh Stevens from the second of his arrest was shattered in that moment.

Suddenly, she wanted to comfort him, but she didn't know why. He was her prisoner. He was in the wrong.

Yet she'd nearly reached for the bars to touch his hand, to reassure him.

A jangling phone on Sal's desk broke through her thoughts. "Paluzzi here," he answered, then checked his watch. His eyes meandered over to her, checking to see if she was working.

Violet quickly scanned her computer for the photographs she'd taken of the farmhouse. With her thumb and forefinger, she enlarged a particular photo of the white clapboard house. It looked like it had been recently painted. Sure enough, she picked out three paint cans near a fenced-off area with garbage cans.

She moved her fingers over the photo and the image of the side of the house. She could see a For Sale sign against the side of the house. She sat up straight. "But the sign isn't in the front yard. It's been put away. Which can mean that they took it off the market, or it's recently sold. But to whom?"

Miguel Garcia? she thought. *And was this where he intended to headquarter his gang?*

Enlarging the picture even more, she was able to read the Realtor's phone number. She jotted down the number on a notepad, then picked up her phone and dialed.

A pleasant-sounding woman answered. "Indian Lake Realty Company. This is Heather. How may I direct your call?"

"This is Officer Violet Hawks, of the Indian Lake Police Department. I understand your company recently sold a farmhouse out near 1000 North?"

"Let me check."

"I need to speak to the listing agent, please."

"Sure," Heather said. "That would be Roy King. He's out for the day. Funeral. May I take your number and have him call you back?"

Violet left the station number and her extension. "I appreciate your help, Heather." Violet hung up.

Now that her call was over, she heard the phones in the booking area ringing. She glanced over to the dispatcher's area. She was putting calls through to various extensions without taking a breath. Another phone rang and Trey grabbed a call. Then Sal took a call.

"Busy day," she mumbled as she looked at the farmhouse photo. She rubbed her forehead. Trent Davis's wife, Cate, was a Realtor. There was a good chance Cate would know about the recent sale.

Violet watched as Trey rushed past her desk toward the front door. "What's the rush?"

"A delivery."

"Oh," she replied. Trey was known for his pizza addiction. The slender guy could eat pizza three times a day and never gain an ounce.

She logged in to the database, looking for more information on Miguel Garcia and the blue car. If she could track down the Maserati dealer where Garcia bought the car, there might be an address, and it might even be legitimate.

She scrolled through more information as Trey bounded back through the room toward the jail cell area. But he wasn't carrying a pizza carton. Instead, it was a brown bag with the Indian Lake Deli logo on it as well as a pink-and-white-striped sack from Cupcakes and Coffee Café. She could only guess the food was for Josh.

She started to stand, and as she did, she came face-to-face with her brother-in-law.

"Violet." Scott greeted her with a wide anticipatory grin. "Trent tells me you have Josh Stevens in lockup. Is that right?"

"Word travels fast."

"Can I see him?" Scott asked, looking toward the metal door.

"Scott, you're drooling," she said sarcastically.

"I should be! An interview with a real celebrity never happens in Indian Lake."

Violet dropped her chin to her chest. "Not you, too."

"What?"

"In all these years you've hung around my family, you never told us you were a race car enthusiast."

"I keep it on the down low. Besides, Vi, c'mon. How can you live in Indiana and not go just a little nuts over Memorial Day weekend when you hear the announcers call the race? It's in our blood." He leaned closer. "And it's certainly in my readers' blood."

"I don't have the authority to grant you that interview. You have to talk to Trent."

"Piece of cake." Scott smiled widely.

"Hey, a word to the wise. Friendship may not get you this one. Detective Davis isn't all that happy that Stevens is in a cell. Anyway, he'll be out before sundown. His manager is arranging bail as we speak."

Scott's expression sobered. "You don't like him, do you?"

"The manager?"

"No, Josh."

Violet pursed her lips. "I don't like his entitled attitude. He thinks he can come here and do as he pleases. Race his car through our roads at over two hundred miles an hour."

Scott whistled lowly. "Seriously?"

She nodded. "I clocked it. I wish I hadn't."

"Why not?"

"Because these celebrity types don't care if their publicity is negative, as long as they stay in the limelight. It's the juice they need. Take this guy. He's got a need for speed. For what? What's he trying to prove? Or gain? More fame? He's got that. Obviously, he's got money to burn. Detective Davis says that Bugatti of his is so expensive that until recently, a price wasn't even posted. Dealers negotiate the price quietly. His success isn't a result of hard work and sacrifice. It's all luck. He hasn't earned it. And he sure hasn't earned my respect."

"I see that," Scott mused, keeping his eyes on her.

Violet wanted to squirm under Scott's introspective gaze. "What?"

"Nothin'. Just that I never heard you talk like this about anyone before."

"Yeah? Then you never watched a Cubs game with me in the room, have you?"

"Bad?"

"Brutal." She paused. "Scott, take my advice. If you want a story about Josh Stevens, wait till he's in court and I'm testifying against him."

Scott peered at her, his right eyebrow hitched and his jaw slowly opening. "You're going to testify against this country's most famous race car driver? The current winning driver of the Indianapolis race? The guy who's in a half-dozen ads on TV? The guy who just signed with Breitling to model their watches?"

"I am."

"You do realize he'll pull in some high-powered and totally brilliant lawyer from Chicago…"

"He's in Indianapolis…" she interjected.

"And that doesn't give you cause for caution?"

"No."

Scott blew out a breath. "You are one tough cookie, sister-in-law."

"I'm in the right," she replied adamantly.

"Who cares?"

"I do! It's the law. He broke the law and then resisted arrest."

"Oh, this is good."

"Don't write anything until we're in court, please?"

"Violet, today this story is a scoop. In a couple weeks, half the country will know about it and I'm just another guy covering the beat. I'll lose my edge."

Sal Paluzzi slammed down his phone and sprang out of his chair. He rushed past Violet's desk. "Where's the fire?" she asked.

"Be right back," Sal said with a wave over his shoulder as he headed to the doors to the front hall.

A moment later, Sal was back with his wife, and five young children. The kids were chattering excitedly. Sal's wife was wearing a particularly lovely spring sweater, a floral dress and kitten-heeled shoes. Her dark hair tumbled down her back in perfect curls. Being a hairdresser, Patrija always looked her best, but today Violet guessed she was on her way to a party. Since Sal and Patrija had only one child, eight-year-old Antony, Violet guessed the other kids must be friends.

They walked toward the cell-block door. It was then Violet noticed that each child held a notebook.

"Autographs?" She started toward Sal. Scott reached out and touched her forearm.

"Vi, let it go."

"He's practically holding court in there," she said. "This isn't punishment for him in the least."

"No," Scott replied. "But why is it killing you so much?"

She jerked her head back to Scott. "I… I'm… It's not. In fact, this just goes to prove my earlier evaluation of him. People who live with that kind of notoriety and influence use it to their own advantage."

"That can be true."

"Believe me, it's very common." Again, she thought of her childhood bully, Billy Pope, and how he used his father's power as the town mayor to go after other, weaker kids. "What I do know is that I'll be very glad when Josh Stevens leaves town. He's precisely the kind of person I would avoid," she said as her eyes strayed back to the cell-block door and lingered.

"Yeah, right," Scott replied.

When Violet's phone rang and she glanced back at Scott, she realized he was watching her closely. She picked up the receiver. "Officer Hawks."

She listened as Josh's manager, Harry Wilcox, explained that the bail bondsman would post bail within thirty minutes. He hoped Violet would have all the necessary paperwork ready. She assured him that everything was in order.

As she ended the call, the chief walked up. "Hawks, I just got off the phone with Harry Wilcox. I'm giving the newspaper permission for an interview." He nodded at her brother-in-law. "I trust you'll be, er, complimentary, Scott?"

"Absolutely, sir."

The chief walked away. Scott smiled at Violet.

"Looks like you'll get your scoop, Scott," she said. "Why don't I give Josh your card? He may not want to be interviewed in or near the jail."

"You're probably right. Here ya go," he said, reaching in his wallet. "I appreciate it, Violet."

Scott kissed her cheek.

"Hug Isabelle and the kids for me," she said.

"Officer Hawks," Trent Davis said, standing in the doorway to his office. "Do you have your report ready?"

"Yes, sir. I'm printing it out now."

"Good. Bring it in." He smiled faintly. "Then go down to the cell and get Josh Stevens's autograph for me before he leaves. Have him sign it to my son, Danny."

Violet gaped as he closed his door. "Not you, too?"

CHAPTER FOUR

VIOLET HANDED THE document to the bondsman, who scribbled something illegible on it and handed her the cash.

She stapled the paperwork together and went to the cell block, unable to help the wave of incompetence that swept through her veins. Deflated and riddled with guilt for the disappointment she'd caused Detective Davis, she was in no mood for gloating from Josh Stevens.

She squared her shoulders as she tucked in her shirt and smoothed her uniform slacks. It was the end of the day, and all she wanted was a hot bath. But first, she had this duty to perform.

She handed the paperwork to Trey as the metal door closed behind her.

"He said his manager would pull through," Trey said, smiling.

"Had a nice chat, did you?"

"Oh, we did. Josh has the most amazing stories. You know he's raced in Europe and…"

"Not now, Officer. I'm here to release him."

Josh was sitting on the bare bench inside the cell. He looked up at her. "Nice jail you have."

"This isn't the jail. We use this room to house criminals we know will only be here a few hours. Like you."

He rolled his eyes. "I'm not a criminal."

"Fine." She motioned to Trey. "You can open it up."

Josh stood. "I'm being released?"

"Yes. It's my duty to inform you that you will have to return to Indian Lake in ten days for a hearing. At that time, I will give my testimony to the judge. You will give yours or your lawyer will speak for you. That's your call. What happens next will be up to the judge."

"What's typical in cases like mine?"

"There aren't many cases like yours."

"Okaaay. Similar cases."

"He or she may give you a fine. And the speeding ticket will be reported on your record as well as the charge of resisting arrest."

Josh walked to the open jail door. "And the endangerment to others?"

"That, too."

Violet struggled to remain calm. She took a step back from him, wondering how he could smell like clean soap and spicy cologne after most of the day in lockup.

Just looking at him reminded her that she'd bungled her job, and badly. All her life, she'd prided herself on her instincts and her intuition. She'd relied on those instincts when she'd started the chase after Josh, believing him to be the drug lord. She had wrongly mistaken his Bugatti as Miguel Garcia's car.

She handed Josh his release papers.

"Well, Officer Hawks, I can tell you that my attorney is not only smart but effective. This speeding ticket and the other trumped-up charges you've brought against me won't fly. As far as I'm concerned, you stole a day of my life. My agent has been dodging calls all day about my whereabouts. And the fallout I'm going to face once the story gets out that you, Officer Hawks, chose to incarcerate me to make yourself look good to your superiors..."

Violet opened her mouth to speak, her words coming in an indignant squawk. "Mr. Stevens," she managed, "this disruption in your life is your fault. Not mine. Apparently, you haven't learned there is a price to pay for your behavior."

"Behavior? Your hot-headed reaction is to blame here. My guess is that because you're so young, you haven't been doing this long. So, I'm going to give you that, Officer Hawks. I've told my attorney I won't sue you, the city or the county. But trust me, this bust you made is gonna go away."

Violet's nerves jangled from the tip of her skull to her toes. She had to remember that Josh Stevens was the kind of person who thought he had the upper hand—always. And she'd had just about enough.

Instead of losing her cool, she smiled as charmingly as she could. "I appreciate your position, Mr. Stevens. In ten days we'll see how it all falls out. In the meantime, please understand. You aren't the only one with responsibilities. I have people who depend on me and my judgment, as well. They aren't my entourage as you label your people. I call mine family."

She turned to Trey. "Please see Mr. Stevens to the front door, Officer. Make sure he has his cell phone and belongings upon his departure."

She turned and walked out of the cell block.

CHAPTER FIVE

TRUE TO HIS WORD, the Indian Lake County deputy sheriff had brought Josh's Bugatti to the police station. Josh walked out looking at his blue baby with its C-shaped sides, the curves that acted to redirect and optimize the airflow into the side intakes. Twin pipe exhaust. Low front aerodynamic hood. The car was masterfully designed. There were only 750 or so sold worldwide. What he had was unique. The engine was a beast at 1,179 horsepower.

"She thought she could outrun me?" He snorted as he walked to the car, opened the door and climbed into the luxurious leather cockpit. "Officer Hawks, you are such a rookie."

And just then he saw Violet walk out of the station, her uniform as perfectly pressed as if she hadn't worn the darn thing all day. Her dark hair had been clipped back all day, but now, she'd pulled out the clip as she walked. Her hair fell well below her shoulders, like a veil of dark satin. It shone, and a gentle spring breeze lifted long locks around her face. He held his breath.

He hadn't expected that.

She didn't look at him or his amazing Bugatti. She simply got in her squad car and backed out, pulling away like anyone leaving work after a long day.

He'd half expected her to give him the finger.

But this—ignoring him—showed him she saw him as the criminal she said he was. He stared at the finely stitched leather-covered steering wheel that he knew the finest artisans had skillfully sewn. He turned on the engine and heard it hum, promising adventures unimagined.

Some adventure today. When he'd braked at the police blockade, he'd lost his temper. People like Officer Violet Hawks, cops with guns on their belts or licensed authority figures who swooped into an orphan's life and put him in a stranger's house, jacked him up something fierce.

He had to admit that he'd been a real jerk to her. It wasn't Violet Hawks who ran up his blood pressure. It was the authority figures she symbolized. Since the day his parents died, Josh had battled every apathetic or on-the-take social worker and fraudulent foster parent. He'd met a ton of cops who thought all foster kids had chips on their shoulders and "should appreciate what the state gives them."

"Authority" to young Josh had meant lies, abuse and torment. And then he'd found his calling. *Cars.*

It was always about the cars.

When he was very young, he thought he could drive himself away from his awful, abuse-filled life. He believed that once he could drive, he'd never feel powerless again.

By the time he was eleven, he'd taught himself how to fix everything on a car that could be fixed. Through high school he learned more by hanging out with mechanics in garages. He worked his way through tech college to learn electronic and computer systems in cars. Then, one day, while test-driving a new Mercedes engine he'd put in an attorney's car in Indianapolis, his life changed.

Paul Saylor was the man who had caused that change. Paul had been a car buff and he was rich. He saw Josh's driving skills that first day. Paul was influential and he represented many of the race car owners, some drivers and even pit crew bosses. Paul was Josh's entrée into the racing world.

Today, Paul was his attorney. Josh would

always be grateful to the man for everything he'd done for him.

Paul was family to Josh.

"Family."

Josh looked down Maple Boulevard in the direction Violet had driven. Her comment about having family hit him hard. Josh had been very young when his parents died, and even now he could remember the smell of lavender on his mother's skin when she held him close. He could hear his father's wing tips on the wood stairs when he came home late from work and came to check on Josh.

"But they left me," he whispered, feeling wrenched again straight across his midsection.

He would give the world to feel his mother's hug again. And hear her voice telling him that she loved him. Even his father's seldom-heard laugh would be a gift. Just one more time.

That was why he drove so very, very fast. He felt closest to them when he pushed the limits of speed. As if he could almost touch them. He had no intention of crashing, but he also couldn't resist the urge to go just a little faster.

Today, when he'd been racing down the country road, he'd been thinking about his mother. He owned a car that went nearly three hundred miles an hour, but it was no Rolls-Royce turbofan engine that could hit supersonic speeds of over seven hundred miles per hour.

Josh hung his head, refusing to believe he was teary-eyed, but it had been happening a lot lately. He didn't want anyone to see his tears. Especially no one in his employ. Not Paul. Certainly not Harry.

Officer Hawks had been right. He didn't have family and very few real friends, except for Austin and Katia McCreary, and when he was younger, his foster brother Diego.

He pulled out of the police station parking lot and turned south on Maple Boulevard, suddenly curious about what exactly Officer Violet Hawks had meant by family. Did she have a husband? Kids?

The other side of the beautiful boulevard was planted with flowering pear trees, daffodils, tulips and irises. He hadn't paid much attention to its beauty when he'd driven down it last time he was in town to visit Austin and Katia who lived at the end of the street. It was too late to drive the three hours back to Indianapolis now.

He was more than exhausted. He couldn't think all that straight. He'd go to Austin's house and beg a room for the night.

Across from the station was a huge Victorian house. He quickly hit the brake and moved the Bugatti to the curb.

Was that a squad car in the drive?

He couldn't believe it.

Slowly, he backed the Bugatti so that he could see down the driveway.

"I'll be..."

Sure enough, Officer Hawks's squad car was parked at the very end of the drive.

"So this is where you live? Nearly across the street from the police station? Keeping your head in the game, Officer? Always on call? Ever ready?"

Josh hadn't the first clue why he was interested in his arresting officer. Other than the fact that she'd brought back memories of his parents. Like an old song that played strong and melodic in his head. As much as Violet was focused on her career, Josh sensed that same kind of big heartedness and warmth he remembered his mother having. There was a softness in Violet's eyes that he read as compassion, and that look made him pause. Made him think. And feel things he hadn't felt in a really long time.

Josh had spent most of his adult life chasing the next win. He hadn't stopped to consider what he really wanted.

"Belonging."

The word rushed out of him like a riptide from the bottom of his heart. To be important to just one person. What would that be like? What would it be like to walk into a room and have Violet's face light up just because he was there? Not the blaze of fame like he saw in a fan's face, or the need in those dependent on him, but love.

Was that what he wanted?

Love?

Josh saw lights on the third floor flip on. More lights on the main floor as if the inhabitants had come alive due to Officer Hawks's coming home.

Did Violet have love in her life? Josh imagined a man kissing her. Perhaps a child holding out its arms for her.

Josh turned the steering wheel and pulled away from the curb, the images in his mind becoming bothersome. He headed to Austin's, then dialed his friend's number.

"Austin! It's Josh! Hey, man. I need to beg a favor."

Austin chuckled. "Anything."

"I'm still in town. Can I bum a room?"

"Absolutely. Where are you?"

"Outside your front window."

"Sweet. I'll open the second garage. You can park next to my vintage Bugatti."

Josh drove up the drive, and the back gate opened electronically. There was a short concrete drive around to the second garage. That door opened automatically. Sure enough there was a blue 1926 Bugatti roadster sitting in the bay.

Josh pulled the Chiron inside.

Austin came walking out with a glass of white wine for them both.

Josh exhaled and smiled. "Bro, you are the very best."

"I think you need this more than I do."

"Oh, jeez. You heard," Josh groaned.

"It's a small town. Come on, Katia and Daisy are making a seafood dinner. I told Katia we'd sit on the terrace. I have the wine in an iced cooler. We can talk." Austin slung his arm over Josh's shoulder. "I'm here for you, man."

"Seriously, I need this. I need you."

"Yep, friends are the best," Austin said. "Unless you have family."

They sat at a glass patio table.

Josh stared at him. Austin's parents were dead, too. Just like Josh, he was an only child and had no aunts, uncles, nieces or nephews. No wonder they were close.

Just then Katia came out onto the terrace carrying a glass tray of appetizers decorated with tropical flowers. "Josh! How are you?"

She placed the tray on the patio table. She bent and kissed his cheek.

"Katia, you are a vision," Josh said. Then he slid a glance to Austin. "You don't mind me saying that, do you, dude?"

"It's the truth. And she's my vision."

When Katia looked at Austin, Josh knew she wouldn't have known if a cyclone blew into town. He'd seen the look of love before, but theirs was so intense, he felt he was interrupting.

"Listen, guys, I know you have a lot to talk about," Katia said. "Daisy and I are still cracking crabs for dinner. So, take your time. Josh, seriously, always know this is your haven. Okay?"

Josh felt a lump the size of a speed bump in his throat. "Thanks."

"You okay?" Austin asked as Katia went back inside.

"You're a lucky man, Austin."

"I know that. But so are you. I saw that photo of you in *Racing People*. That girl. What's her name? Joycelyn? She's a knockout."

"Who?"

"Joy—"

"Austin." Josh shook his head. "She's an infield girl. That's for publicity. I don't have anyone."

Austin's eyes widened. He took a long slug of wine. "I thought…well. That you had your pick."

"There's never been anyone special. Certainly no Katia."

Austin's gaze went to the wide kitchen window where they both could see Katia and Daisy laughing and poking each other with crab legs. "I've loved her all my life."

Josh felt chills down his back. He'd give anything to say that. To know there was a special someone for him. He didn't know what it was or why this was happening to him now. Was it being in this small town? Was it the shock of finding himself behind bars? Or was it Officer Hawks? He couldn't stop thinking about how she looked at him when the jail cell door had clanged shut. If a gong had been struck in his head, he couldn't have been more affected. He felt derailed, on a new course, and he hadn't the slightest idea where he was headed.

As much as he daydreamed about a different life, the reality was he'd been living as the image Harry and he had concocted for the media years ago. He was a winner. Women came and went. He was successful, rich and alone.

Quite alone.

Yeah, his dreams were mirages. A life like Austin had would never be possible for Josh.

CHAPTER SIX

VIOLET DUMPED SOME vegetable soup into a bowl and shoved it into the microwave. Her thick black belt, holster, handcuffs and gun were methodically arranged on the sofa table her mother had given her when she moved into Mrs. Beabots's apartment. Though she'd picked up her clean uniforms from the laundry, Violet had re-pressed the shirt, taking out the tiny crease she'd seen on its back.

She chuckled as she extracted a soup spoon from her organized flatware drawer. Her mother, Connie, often kidded Violet's compulsive need for order and cleanliness had finally found a purpose in her "spit-shine" world of law enforcement. Violet didn't think she was all that obsessive. There was right and wrong. Good and evil. Black and white. "And clearly, clean and dirty."

The microwave dinged. She took out the soup just as her cell phone rang.

"Hello?"

"Violet," Mrs. Beabots said, "don't think

about eating that sodium-laden canned soup. Come downstairs for dinner. I have pasta and chicken in a pesto sauce. Homemade."

Violet narrowed her eyes. She'd known Mrs. Beabots since she was a child, and the woman always made her think she had eyes in the back of her head. "How did you know what I'm having for supper?"

"I'm a detective."

"You saw the cans in my trash bag."

"That, too. Now come down here for dinner. Sarah and Maddie are coming over. And Liz is bringing wine. Oh! I hear Liz's truck now. She really does need to get that muffler fixed."

"See you in a sec." Violet looked down at her skinny jeans, sky blue high-top sneakers and powder blue turtleneck cotton shirt. She was comfortable and had planned to go for a walk after dinner. Now that it was May, the evenings had finally warmed to a brisk fifty degrees, and she loved the flowering Bradford pear trees and forsythia. Having grown up in the country, she'd never appreciated town living, but after six months living on Maple Boulevard, she'd found it had innumerable charms.

Violet tucked her cell phone in her back pocket and walked down the long staircase to the main floor landing. She heard voices and laughter, and she could smell the aroma of garlic and basil coming from under the door. Her stomach growled. “Guess I do need more than soup.” She knocked on the back kitchen door.

“Come on in, honey,” Mrs. Beabots said. “Door’s always open.”

Violet entered the kitchen to find Sarah Bosworth, the next-door neighbor, architect and mother to Luke Bosworth’s children Annie and Timmy. Sarah and Luke’s toddler, Charlotte, looked just like blonde, cornflower blue–eyed Sarah.

Sarah hugged Violet. “It’s great to see you. Where’re the kids?”

“Luke got pizza and a movie. Need I say more?”

“Nope.”

Next to Sarah was Maddie Barzonni, owner of Cupcakes and Coffee Café, and married to Dr. Nate Barzonni. Maddie was breaking up romaine lettuce leaves into a huge wooden salad bowl and giggling with Liz Barzonni, owner of Crenshaw Vineyards. Liz was removing a cork from a bottle of wine.

“Hi, Maddie.” The women hugged. “Hi, Liz. That a new wine?”

Liz held up the bottle. “Very special pinot noir.”

“Special?” Violet asked.

Mrs. Beabots winked. "Violet. You're just in time for our toast."

"Oh? What are we toasting?"

Sarah beamed. "I just beat out the rock star of all Chicago design firms for a new medical complex on the east side of town."

"I never doubted your design abilities, Sarah," Maddie said as she took a glass of wine from Liz.

"I know and I love you for it, but there were days..." Sarah looked across the kitchen to the window that looked out on the adjoining yard to her house.

"Hey," Liz said. "That was after your mother died. Before Luke. Before the kids. You got your juice back."

"And then some," Mrs. Beabots said, handing Violet a glass.

They clinked their rims and said, "To Sarah!"

"Congratulations, Sarah," Violet said. "I know the relief and satisfaction that comes from winning those contracts. Whenever my mother would win a design bid, she'd make us all a nice dinner just like this." She smiled at them all. "You should be proud."

"Thanks, Violet," Sarah said.

Maddie lowered her glass. "Gosh, Violet. Your mom wasn't one of the other bidders, was she? Connie is so talented, I'd feel terrible if she lost." Her eyes tracked to Sarah.

"No. She's working on a high-rise residential tower in Indianapolis."

"Oh." Maddie's relief was audible.

Violet stared at the wine. Indianapolis. Where Josh Stevens lived.

Where had that thought come from and why would she be making that connection? "Um, can I help with any of these preparations? I always made the herbed butter for the bread."

"Sure," Mrs. Beabots said, handing Violet the bread knife. "I set the table earlier. This was supposed to be a think-tank dinner and a meeting for the fund-raiser for a new foster child care center I want to spearhead."

"Really?" Violet unwrapped the silver paper around the Italian bread. "Tell me about it."

"I want a privately funded and operated family center. No government funds or grants. That way we don't fall under their jurisdiction, though we will comply with all state and federal regulations. But in the end, our arms will be open to whatever needs there are. Drop-in day care. Possibly a temporary shelter until a family gets back on their feet. I envision job-placement service. Even job training."

"That's…an enormous undertaking," Violet replied, knowing the massive amount of organization and money it would take to create such a center. But it had been done before. The Star of Hope in Houston had been doing it for over a hundred years.

"I'll need help, of course, getting it off the ground."

"Did you call Isabelle? Since she and Scott have adopted Bella and Michael, I would think she'd be all over this."

Smiling, Mrs. Beabots answered, "She was my first call. She's my committee chair. But little Michael was showing signs of the flu, and she didn't want to leave him."

"That flu can be bad," Sarah said.

"Especially for a toddler," Liz, the mother of two-and-a-half-year-old Zeke, said. "I hope he's okay."

"I didn't talk to Isabelle today," Violet said. "I was on a stakeout."

Sarah stopped grating Parmesan cheese. "Seriously? A stakeout? Isn't that dangerous?"

To Violet, not apprehending a criminal was dangerous to the entire community, and that motivated her more than any harm she would encounter. Her exemplary training would see her through. She would count on her skills. Bank on her instincts.

She winced.

Except for today.

She could only imagine what Detective Davis was thinking about her performance today. In the morning she might have to face Chief Williams.

Violet slid the bread into the oven and set the timer.

Maddie helped with the angel-hair pasta, draining and rinsing it in a red plastic colander under cool water in the sink. “Olive oil?”

“Middle of the island,” Mrs. Beabots said, adding finely chopped sun-dried tomatoes to the pesto.

They continued prepping the food. Maddie had brought her delicious and beautifully decorated cupcakes for dessert. Violet set up two French presses with decaffeinated coffee while Sarah poured cream into a small pitcher and Maddie found the raw sugar.

“I think we’re about ready. Liz, would you take the wine to the table?”

The timer dinged, and Violet took out the bread and placed it in a woven basket. She followed the group to the dining room. “I see you’re setting for yet another. If I’m taking Isabelle’s place, who’s missing?” Violet asked, sitting to Mrs. Beabots’s right.

“Katia,” Mrs. Beabots answered. “She had something come up. I’ll call her tomorrow with the details.”

Sarah acted as the server and ladled the pesto sauce over the pasta. "So, Violet. Can you tell us about the stakeout you were on or is that top secret?"

"Well, I can't discuss all the details. But I was excited because, as Mrs. Beabots knows, I've been stuck either in a patrol car or behind a desk since I came to work for the ILPD. Handing out traffic tickets, which there aren't that many of in Indian Lake, was a highlight of the week."

"Sounds boring," Liz said.

Maddie elbowed her. "Don't mind her, Violet."

"No, she's right. It was beyond boring. What I really want to do with my career is work my way up to detective."

"And you'd be really good at it." Mrs. Beabots smiled. "I have a way of knowing these things."

"Thanks for your confidence in me," Violet said.

"So, did anything happen?" Sarah asked.

"Uh..." She searched for the right words. "Not with the perp we're hoping to find."

Maddie stared at Violet. "That was a hesitation. Something happened."

As Violet looked around the table, she realized that all four women had moved to the edge of their seats.

"Are you after a murderer?" Sarah asked.

"Drug dealer?" Liz asked, holding a forkful of pasta.

"I'm not at liberty to say. At this juncture, we don't know about murder, but it wouldn't be outside the realm of possibility."

"It *is* a drug dealer," Liz said. "Listen, Violet. After what Cate and Trent went through, and poor Mrs. Beabots being the victim of a drive-by shooting in this very house, you can't shock us."

"That's true," Mrs. Beabots said. "You know all those security lights and cameras I have outside on the house?"

"Yes. It was the first thing I noticed when I came to inspect the apartment. I thought you were smart to protect yourself so well."

Mrs. Beabots shook her head. "I didn't do it. The cops did. Sorry. It was Trent's idea when he was trapping that drug dealer, Le Grand. Now, I've inherited all this equipment."

"That happens. And it's good protection. Anyway, the perp didn't show up." Violet toyed with her pasta. "I did make an arrest, though."

"Who?" they asked in unison.

"I can't say. I wouldn't be surprised if his publicity manager kills the story."

"Publicity?" Mrs. Beabots stared at Violet. "This wouldn't be about Josh Stevens, would it?"

Violet's hand went numb and she dropped her fork. The silence at the table was deafening. "How. Did. You. Know?"

"Katia told me. Josh Stevens is the reason she couldn't be here. Josh is staying with Austin and Katia tonight. She's making crab." Mrs. Beabots beamed.

Violet was glad she'd already dropped her fork. She had to close her mouth. Josh had said he knew Austin, but she hadn't believed him. She simply assumed Josh was grasping for anything that would aid in his release. Lots of people knew Austin. Now that she had a chance to think about it, it made sense. Austin was a huge antique car collector. She'd heard stories that Austin's grandfather had been a designer with the Duesenberg brothers at the turn of the last century. Austin's father had collected cars all his life. Josh and Austin probably met at an auction or something.

She took a sip of wine.

Just my luck.

Bad luck at that. She'd arrested not only a

celebrity, but one who was friends with her friends. *Terrific.*

Violet couldn't have been more embarrassed. She'd only been doing her job. "He was speeding," she said without a trace of emotion. "I ticketed him."

"Speeding? Isn't that what he does?" Maddie joked.

"Uh, not going down the county road in front of my mother's house."

"Oh, that's not good," Liz added.

"It's not. I can't tell you exactly how fast he was going."

Silence.

"It's a confidentiality issue," she continued.

They continued to stare at her, like hungry baby birds.

"Well, we'll read it in the newspaper tomorrow," Maddie said.

"Yeah." Violet remembered Scott's visit to the station. Resigning herself to the inevitable, she said, "It was over two hundred miles an hour."

All four gaped at her.

"Good for you!" Sarah exclaimed. "What if some kids were out bike riding now that the weather's nice? They could have gotten scared, lost their balance." She dropped her forehead to her palm. "It could have been disastrous."

Mrs. Beabots's eyes narrowed. "He was driving that blue Bugatti Chiron, wasn't he?"

"I believe so."

Sarah cranked her head up. "How do you know about Bugattis?"

"I used to own one." Mrs. Beabots grinned. "I like to keep up. And I read in *Race Car Driver Magazine* that Josh bought one."

Violet rolled her eyes. Was everyone she knew a Josh Stevens fan?

Liz sank her fork into the pasta. "It may not seem like much, Violet, but thank goodness you were there in the right place at the right time today."

"Thanks, Liz. I needed that."

Mrs. Beabots took a thoughtful sip of wine. "You know, this gets me to thinking about my fund-raiser. What I'm proposing is ambitious for Indian Lake," she said. "Violet, you certainly are aware of the situation with the many foster children in the system, what with Isabelle and Scott adopting their foster children."

"I do. And I applaud you for taking on such a task. How much do you want to raise?"

"Oh, it's not just the money we need, Violet. Sophie and Jack Carter helped to get the Alliance Recovery Center for addiction support and rehabilitation started. They've made incredible progress, and their efforts are working. Though addressing the drug problem is vital, this town has to deal with the abandoned children and homeless families that are the fallout. We need a facility with day care and programs for the children and the parents. I want more than counseling. The children need activities and learning experiences. And so do the parents. Their backs are against the wall, and they're desperate."

"They need options," Violet agreed.

"Yes," Mrs. Beabots said. "We will staff it, and I personally will award an endowment so that the shelter can go on for years."

"You will?" all four women chorused.

"Sarah, I told you I was the ambitious type." Mrs. Beabots smiled proudly.

"Yes, but..." Sarah looked from Violet to Maddie and to Liz.

Mrs. Beabots wagged her forefinger at Sarah. "Now don't go thinking because I'm older that I can't do this. I can and I will. I want to leave something that will go on—after I'm not here."

Violet reached over and touched Mrs. Beabots's hand. "You are all heart."

"Look who's talking. You don't fool me, Violet Hawks. If you weren't trying to eliminate crime in our town, you'd be the first to take in these children and you know it."

"Well, I'm not sure about that. I don't have much experience with kids." Violet felt a pinch in her heart thinking about the infants that were abandoned by addict mothers and fathers. She pushed her emotions aside. "So, Mrs. Beabots. Exactly what are you thinking? To build this kind of shelter will take millions. And just as much to staff."

"I understand that. I have philanthropic friends all across Indiana. It's about time I talked to them. And Maddie, I could have a chat with that friend of yours, Alex Perkins, who helped you get the investor for your café."

Maddie folded her hands and rested her chin on them. "You have been thinking about this, haven't you?"

"Ever since I started volunteering at The Alliance. But this idea came to fruition when Beatrice Wilcox and Rand Nelson took in those two foster boys of theirs. If more people stepped up to the plate like they did, think of the lives that would be changed forever."

She picked up her linen napkin and dabbed her eyes.

Maddie said, "I think this is a great idea. I want to help."

"Me, too," Liz chimed in.

"You know I'm at your beck and call," Sarah said.

"I'll help in any way I can," Maddie said. "I could organize food pantry donations at my café."

Liz nodded. "I can help with that as well at the vineyard. In fact, we should double our efforts during harvest when we have so many tourists to the vineyard. With the holidays after that, Thanksgiving donations tend to soar."

"That's a wonderful idea," Mrs. Beabots said.

Maddie snapped her fingers. "It should be an annual event. Maybe we could have a harvest dance and donation at the vineyard. I'll donate cupcakes, doughnuts, cider. The tourists will love it."

"So would I," Liz said.

"Mrs. Beabots," Violet said slowly, "this is a monumental task. You're going to need more than just us. What if I were to talk to my chief? Perhaps the Indian Lake County Sheriff's Department. Both have resources and connections we could use."

"That's a fine idea, Violet." Mrs. Beabots placed her hand over Violet's. "I've thought of everything from taking on one of the old mansions that needs renovation and starting there. I've toyed with the idea of asking Gina Barzonni to donate a tract of her farmland to build on, too."

Maddie looked at Liz. Gina was mother-in-law to them both. “What do you think? Would Gina do that?”

“Gina adores children. I think if we presented it to her the right way, she just might. Rafe is managing the farm now, but Olivia said that he’s got two Thoroughbreds he’s been racing all spring and they are winning race after race. If he keeps this up, he won’t want such a large farm to manage. His heart is still with his horses.”

Violet caught their enthusiasm. “You know, I grew up in the country north of town. I loved it. We had neighbors, an Amish family, who let me ride their horses. Mother didn’t know, but I was always very careful. I loved working our little vegetable garden, and Isabelle planted a million flowers every spring, claiming they were magical. I thought it was the best place to grow up. If those kids had a whole farm to learn skills and play and just be in the clean air and sunshine…”

“Violet, you are so right!” Maddie said. “We have to talk to Gina about this.”

“But remember, girls,” Mrs. Beabots cautioned. “The land is only the beginning. It’s going to take a lot of money. For that, we need one huge extravaganza of a fund-raiser.”

“You can’t steal my summer festival idea,”

Sarah said. "St. Mark's still needs the profits every year."

The edges of Mrs. Beabots's mouth cranked up. "It's Violet who gave me the idea."

"I did?"

"What was the biggest gathering you all have seen since we've been doing fund-raisers together? Not counting Sarah's Summer Festival."

"The opening of Austin's car museum," Maddie replied.

"Exactly!" Mrs. Beabots's eyes grew wider with excitement. "And Violet, I'm going to take you up on your offer to help."

"What can I do?"

"Austin McCreary is sponsoring an event at his car museum. Wine and appetizers. I was thinking if you would ask Josh Stevens to make a personal appearance that night, we could sell so many tickets, people would be out the door. Better still, ask him if he'll bring that fancy Bugatti of his for photographs of him and the donors."

"Why not ask Austin to ask Josh?" Violet asked uncomfortably.

"Because I've asked Austin for a great deal more than a simple event at his museum."

"Like what?" Violet asked.

"He's donating a million dollars. And that,

ladies, is information that remains in this room."

They all stared at Mrs. Beabots.

"Pressing Austin for more after his generous donation might not be prudent," Mrs. Beabots said.

"Well," Maddie interjected, "I think this is all fabulous. And this upcoming event is perfect. I know Olivia would be happy to take photographs. She's so talented. Maybe she can get them printed in the Chicago papers."

"The Indianapolis newspaper would run anything about Josh Stevens," Sarah said.

The enthusiasm was electric. But Violet felt her hands grow clammy and her mouth go dry.

She hadn't told her friends all the truth. She hadn't told them that in ten days she would be testifying against their hope for this project's success.

They didn't know anything about him other than that he was a friend of Austin and Katia's. And how strong was that relationship?

Violet was a bit surprised that reclusive Austin would have a celebrity like Josh for a friend. Though Austin was wealthy, he came across as an ordinary kind of guy, running his father's auto parts manufacturing company, and now a new cell phone parts manufacturing company. Austin was a hardworking entrepreneur. Violet just didn't see the connection between status-hungry Josh Stevens and Austin.

What she did see was that there was no talking her way out of helping her landlady and her friends with this very worthy fund-raising endeavor.

Her biggest fear was that once Josh Stevens discovered that Violet was part of the fund-raiser, he would decline. Mrs. Beabots would be without a celebrity to bring in ticket sales, and Josh Stevens would race out of town so fast he'd break the sound barrier.

CHAPTER SEVEN

JOSH WALKED UP the steps of his manager's brownstone near the South Side of Chicago. It was a three-story 1920's building that had been gutted, re-bricked, and re-roofed. Josh guessed that all that remained of the original building, which sat close to the sidewalk across from the University of Chicago, were the Tudor stained-glass windows and transoms. Med students, interns and residents dressed in scrubs sat in the wide grassy boulevard under leafing maple and oak trees. It was spring in the city, and the buzz of life was everywhere.

"Josh Stevens to see Harry Wilcox," Josh said to the young over-processed blonde with false eyelashes.

She gushed before she spoke. "Oh, I'd know you anywhere, Mr. Stevens! We have your posters all over the hallway." She pointed to the left. Josh glanced up. He hadn't been to Harry's office since before last year's race in Indianapolis. He was familiar with his most famous poster, which Harry had orchestrated and paid for, then begged and borrowed markers to get published in every racing magazine.

He noticed that rather than the victory photo in which his pit crew jubilantly hugged him, or the one in which he held the trophy, three of these posters were of him grinning broadly and surrounded by four gorgeous models, two of whom were kissing his cheeks. The way they were posed, Josh could see how the onlooker would think each one was his newest girlfriend, when in fact, he didn't remember one of them. Models were brought in for photo shoots, and the minute the shot was taken, they went off with their managers or agents to get paid and move on to the next photo shoot.

It was all part of the biz.

Especially the kisses.

It had been a long time since Josh had received a meaningful kiss.

If ever.

The receptionist was still babbling about something, but he hadn't heard a word. "Mr. Stevens?"

"Sorry."

"Would you like coffee or water?"

"Coffee. Black would be great."

She rose. "Harry's off the phone and will see you now. I'll show you in."

"I know the way," he said.

"Great. Then I'll get your coffee."

Josh walked down the hall to the austere, contemporary corner office where Harry sat at a chrome-and-glass mega-sized desk. There were two laptops on the desk, a cordless phone and not a scrap of paper anywhere.

Harry was forty-four years old, prematurely gray at the temples and dressed in a tailored suit, blue shirt and navy silk tie, his ever-present Bluetooth in his ear. Harry looked up from the computer and, seeing Josh, he smiled, but the pinch between his brows put there by concern remained.

"Josh." Harry stood and shook his hand. "Glad to see you."

"No, you're not."

"Yes, I am. I just wasn't up to the drive to Indiana." Harry sat back down, motioning to the leather slipper chair for Josh.

The receptionist came in with Josh's coffee and a chai tea for Harry. She deposited the tray on Harry's desk.

"Thanks, Madison," Harry said. "No calls while Josh is here."

"Sure," Madison replied, taking her time moving out the door.

Josh could feel her lingering gaze on him. He lifted his coffee mug off the tray and drank.

"Harry, it was no big deal."

"Trust me, when it comes to small-town cops, they believe jaywalking is an infraction. They would take parking ticket violations to the Supreme Court if they could."

"Don't exaggerate." Josh smiled and sipped the coffee, hoping the caffeine would lift his spirits. "Besides, I asked my friend Austin McCreary to talk to the local paper and keep it out of the daily police report, which he did."

Harry clapped his hands together. "Thank heaven you know a guy." Then he leaned closer over the desk. "You listen to me, Josh. That report could have been picked up by the Associated Press. What a nightmare this could have been. If this does get out, and your mug shot goes viral—" Harry groaned theatrically. "We're talking YouTube. Twitter..."

"Stop." Josh held up his hand. "This is gonna go away."

"Nobody, and I mean nobody, can know about this. Not your pit crew. Not the sponsors. Not the advertisers. We're only weeks from the Indy race."

"I know that."

"Yeah? Then what the blazes were you thinking when you were driving down a country lane at two hundred freaking miles an hour?" Harry shouted. "What's gotten into you lately?"

"Lately?"

"Just last week, if you remember, we were going down Lake Shore Drive, granted at two in the morning when traffic was scarce, but you zoomed through a red light! I was terrified, Josh. And as a rule, not much scares me."

"Would you calm down?" Josh looked down at his hands. The same hands that had expertly held the steering wheel of his Bugatti. How could he tell Harry that he hadn't known how fast he was going…only that it wasn't fast enough? All he'd seen was his mother's face. "I'm fine."

But Josh knew Harry was right. Something *was* happening to him, had been for the past six months. Something was changing. It was as if his perspective was off-kilter. Always serious about his career and his driving—Josh almost didn't know himself anymore.

His wins on the track weren't enough. He wasn't feeling victory the way he had a few years ago. If anything, he felt the burden of the win. More would be expected of him. He was responsible for more people in his entourage.

Harry wiped his face with his palm. "I'm gonna have arrhythmia before this is over. I'm too young for this stress."

"I'm handling this…"

"You? Oh, right. Sure. Do you have any idea what I've been going through?"

Josh cocked his head, his eyes on Harry. "Tell me."

"I knew we had to deflect the situation. I planted those interview stories you did for me a few months back all over the internet. I've had Madison out there tweeting photos of last year's win every fifteen minutes. I've got our social media team going after new podcasts, YouTubers, newspapers and posters on abandoned playgrounds…anything to keep the spotlight away from this Indian Lake fiasco and focused on your attributes. But it's still not enough. I need to show you're more than a driver… I need to show your humanity."

"My what?"

"You know, concern for the community. Involvement. We should attach you to a charity. I need to show a different face of Josh Stevens."

"I'm not going to start kissing babies."

Harry snapped his fingers. "Great idea! Kids are good. Forget the models."

"Harry—" Josh dropped his chin to his chest with a sigh "—please. This is nothing. I'll talk to the judge and get the speeding ticket and the resisting arrest thing expunged."

Harry's eyes narrowed; his face grew grim. "You listen to me, Josh. I've been with you from nearly the beginning. You're a smart guy. This blaze of fame can be extinguished in a heartbeat. One screw-up like this could end your career."

"Harry..."

"No matter how you paint this, you were wrong. You're lucky you didn't hit someone. Even a dog or cat. They would rake you over the coals for that. There is no way I'm letting you go into that traffic court without Paul."

"Is that really necessary?"

"It's all-important. Maybe I haven't been clear. The stakes can be high for you. If this goes down badly, or the press gets away from us, painting you as a reckless driver, you could be cut from the race."

"But I've qualified. All we're doing now is vying for our positions on the track."

"Josh, you know as well as I do everyone has a camera on their phones and tablets. Any celebrity can be caught at any moment in embarrassing situations. Cops, cars and race car drivers are a recipe for disaster, promotionally speaking."

"I know that, Harry. I do. But being cut..."

"'Josh Stevens' is no longer just you." He flapped his hands in front of Josh, the gesture erratic and displaying Harry's frustration and fear. "Josh Stevens is a corporation. Multimillion dollar business. The last two years you're one of the top three Formula One drivers in the world. You killed at Bahrain International Circuit and in the German Grand Prix. And… and… Monaco—!"

"Is like riding a bike around my living room," Josh interjected.

"Abu Dhabi Grand Prix. Not to mention Italy…"

Josh held up his palm. "I get it."

"Good," Harry barked. "This corporation can't afford any hiccups." Harry picked up the phone and hit a button. "Is Paul in? Great. I have Josh here."

Harry put the call on speaker. "Paul, thanks for taking our call."

"Paul, how's it going?" Josh tried to smile through his greeting, but failed. He knew he had to listen to both Harry's and Paul's advice.

"Fine, Josh. I'm glad you're with Harry. We had a long talk yesterday while you were…visiting Indian Lake."

So, Harry's angst was driven by legal counsel? Josh sat up straighter in his chair. "I'm listening, Paul."

"Once you get a hearing date, you call me. I'll drive up and represent you. Make no statements about anything in regard to the speeding charges or the arrest to a single soul. Obviously not the press. It's too easy for you to say something that can be misconstrued as condescending or even detrimental to our case."

"Paul, you know I wouldn't do that."

"Is that right?"

Josh didn't like the brittle edge to Paul's words. "Why do I get the feeling there's more going on here than just my traffic ticket?"

Harry avoided Josh's gaze.

Not good.

"Because there is, Josh. I've been on the phone most of yesterday and half the night. I spoke with Chief of Police Williams there in Indian Lake. Seems he and his detectives have gathered a great deal of intel he wanted to share with me."

"And?" Josh felt the hairs on the back of his neck prickle and chills shoot down to his tailbone. He didn't like Paul's tone. And why would Paul feel the need to talk to the chief of police over a traffic ticket? Was his "resisting arrest" charge that worrisome?

"Do you remember when I defended Diego Lopez, your friend from that foster home, on a marijuana possession charge a few years ago?"

"Yeah. Sure. He was very grateful. So was I. I mean, I am."

Paul cleared his throat before he began. "Apparently, you haven't kept up with Diego lately."

"No, I haven't, now that you mention it. I've been—" his eyes tracked to Harry, who made certain Josh didn't have more than an hour to himself that was not productive in either advertising, training or promoting the next race or product "—busy."

"Well, Diego has been busy, too. When was the last time you saw him?"

"I dunno..."

Harry held up two fingers.

"Two years ago. His birthday."

"That's when you gave him the Maserati?" Paul asked.

"It was. How...did you know that?"

"Skill."

"What?"

Paul continued. "One of my many talents, I like to think anyway, is investigation. I haven't dealt with criminal law for some time, but as rusty as I am, I found out plenty."

Josh moved to the edge of his chair to be closer to the speakerphone. "Cut the crap. Why would the Indian Lake police divulge information to you?"

"Because I'm your lawyer. Because they're hoping you have information about Diego that will help them. That's why."

"Go on."

"Diego Lopez calls himself Miguel Garcia now. The word on the street is that he's trying to take over the remainder of the Le Grand gang. That's not confirmed, however. The stakeout that Officer Hawks was on when she spotted you was all about your pal Diego."

Josh shot to his feet. "This can't be true! Diego was wild, but not like this." He raked his hair. "Seriously? You're telling me that my Maserati is helping to ship illegal drugs to an offbeat, quaint little town like Indian Lake?"

"I am," Paul replied.

"This is not good." He thought for a moment. "Paul, do these Indian Lake cops think I'm involved with Diego—er, Miguel's drug business?"

"When I spoke with Chief Williams, I made it clear to him that you have never done drugs or dealt them. I reminded him that you are very outspoken against drugs in the media, and have personally donated money to the Indiana Addiction Hotline.

"Chief Williams clearly stated that they do not think you are involved with Miguel's drug traffic business. But they're curious as to why he is driving a car that you still own title to. I intend to be there for your hearing. There is no way I'm going to let you stand in front of even a traffic court judge with Miguel Garcia's shadow looming over you."

"But I haven't heard from him since that party two years ago."

"I believe you. But I know you, Josh. All I can say is that from now until the time of that hearing, you keep your nose clean. Be sweet as you know how to be. Help little old ladies across the street. Buy a case of Girl Scout cookies. And stay out of sight."

"I understand."

Harry leaned toward the speakerphone. "Paul, Josh has to go back to Indy for training until the hearing. Is there a problem with that?"

"I don't see any. But if for any reason you hear from Miguel, you call me no matter what time it is. Day or night. You got that?"

Josh could feel ropes of stress constricting his chest, imprisoning him. All because he'd tried to be the big brother to Diego once again. He'd wanted to share his good fortune with the closest person he had to family. Never had Josh thought that Diego would literally take the car and run. It wasn't so much the car, it was the fact that Diego discarded Josh, his overture of a renewed friendship, his affection. Worse, Diego hadn't straightened out his act at all. He appeared bent on making a name for himself and finding his own fame—in the criminal world.

Paul interrupted Josh's thoughts. "I mean

it, Josh. These cops may be small town, but they're highly trained and smart."

"I see that. But why do you think Diego would contact me now?"

Harry rolled his eyes.

Paul said, "That, my friend, is one of the rules of the universe. When things start going haywire, lightning strikes, electrifying those wires and creating destruction."

"And I thought I was paying my attorney to reassure me. Give me confidence," Josh moaned.

"You pay me to protect your interests. That's what I'm doing. You've never caused me a single night's lost sleep."

"Until now."

"Look, Josh. I believe in preparation. If we know the players and what's at stake, we can deal with the blows as they come. But when a rookie cop is on a stakeout for a known drug dealer whom you happen to have known for years, and then charges you with resisting arrest near said known drug dealer's possible location, it doesn't look good. Quite frankly, I'm surprised the ILPD didn't put a tail on you. Are you certain you weren't followed to Chicago?"

Josh walked to the end of the room where Harry kept a thermal pitcher of ice water, sliced limes and glasses. He poured himself a glass and rolled it over his sweaty forehead. "How did this happen?"

"You were driving too fast in the wrong place," Harry said.

I was thinking about my mother.

"I know," Josh replied softly, looking down at the ring of lime in his water. He hadn't been thinking. He hadn't looked at the speedometer. He'd been lost in memory. "I'm sorry."

"Let's keep our eye on the ball here," Harry said. "What's done is done."

Josh turned around and looked at Harry. "But it's not over."

Paul spoke over the speakerphone. "Josh, when you get back to Indy, come into the office. I want to go over our courtroom strategy."

"Fine." Josh downed the rest of the chilled water. "I'll do whatever is necessary."

"You'll let me do the talking. Call me when you get back here."

"Thanks, Paul," Josh said. "I really do appreciate everything—"

Paul cut him off. "I know you do. Drive carefully coming back."

"Done," Josh said as they both hung up.

Harry stood up. "You want to get some lunch?"

"Not really." He put down the glass and looked at Harry. "I didn't know about Diego or whatever his name is now. I thought he was straightening out. I thought if I helped him with his back rent and the Maserati, he would see the value in working toward a goal."

Harry's dour expression said it all.

"You're worried."

"I've been worried," Harry admitted. "But that was just about a speeding ticket. I had no idea Diego was vying to be some drug kingpin."

"Nor did I."

"That changes things. All I can say is that Paul is right. You need to stay as squeaky clean as possible."

"Meaning?"

"Do something that would make those folks over there in Indian Lake want to erect a monument to you."

"What would you do?"

"That's easy. I'd stay away from rookie cops who want to build a reputation by slapping your butt with citations, and drug lords who could pull you down at any minute."

Josh didn't know why he instantly thought of Officer Hawks's probing green eyes. Why his mind went to the image of her blazing righteousness when she'd argued with him as she arrested him. But he found himself admiring her sense of duty.

Josh wouldn't have any trouble staying clear of Diego. He hadn't been in touch with him for years.

Officer Hawks was another matter. He'd be seeing her in court.

What puzzled him most was why that thought made him smile.

CHAPTER EIGHT

VIOLET FACED BLACK-ROBED Judge Sandra Lewis, whose stone-faced expression matched her own. This wasn't her first time in front of a judge bringing a witness to a traffic violation, but this was her first time to defend her actions as an arresting officer. She knew that if she'd been the last officer called up, instead of being the first case to be heard as she and Josh Stevens were, her shoes would be full of nervous sweat.

As it was, she had plenty to be nervous about. Josh was accompanied by his attorney, Paul Saylor. Chief Williams had informed Violet of his conversation with the attorney.

It didn't help that several deputy sheriffs had shown up. From their admiring glances toward Josh and their overzealous smiles, Violet couldn't help wondering if they'd shown up to get Josh's autograph or photos with him. Deputy Sheriff Amswell, who had driven Josh's car back to town from the scene, was also present. He tipped his head in her direction.

She nodded back. Amswell had been instrumental in her strategy for today's appearance.

"Officer Hawks. Present your case for the State."

"Yes, Your Honor," Violet began, her mouth full of cotton. The words came slowly as she struggled to keep all emotion out of her statement. "On May 3 of this year, I clocked the defendant's vehicle, a 2018 Bugatti Chiron, at two hundred and two miles per hour. The driver did not slow down or pull over. Instead, he forced me to chase him."

"That's not true!" Josh blurted.

She glanced at him just as his attorney elbowed him. Josh closed his mouth and tore his eyes from her and back to the judge.

Violet went on to describe the ticketing. The judge showed no emotion, not even a raised eyebrow when Violet described Josh threatening her job.

Judge Lewis looked at Josh and his attorney, Paul Saylor. "What say you?"

As Josh parted his lips, Paul cocked his shoulder enough to nudge Josh behind him.

"Your Honor, we plead guilty to the speeding ticket. My client was in the wrong, but as this is his first offense in this matter, we throw ourselves on the mercy of the court. As to the second charge, we respectfully disagree with

Officer Hawks's, er—" he glanced dismissively at Violet before continuing "—rendition of the encounter. We believe Officer Hawks, who was in the area on another assignment from ILPD, acted unprofessionally. We plead not guilty on the charge of resisting arrest, Your Honor."

"Your Honor," Violet interrupted as she reached in her back pocket and pulled out Sheriff Amswell's smartphone. "May it please the court, I have a video, recorded by Indian Lake County Deputy Sheriff Douglas Amswell at the scene of the ticketing incident and the threat that was made to me by the defendant."

Though she didn't look at him, she heard a muffled groan from Josh. Paul Saylor took a half step forward. "Your Honor, I object. Counsel was not informed of this evidence. I request this video not be admissible."

Judge Lewis's eyes tracked to Paul Saylor. "So noted." She lifted her hand to Violet. "Officer Hawks…"

Violet stepped forward and handed the smartphone to the bailiff, who gave it to the judge.

Judge Lewis played the scene. Violet could hear the dialogue. She knew Josh and his attorney could hear it, as well.

"Your Honor," Paul began. "I wish—"

Judge Lewis cut him off. "Objection overruled."

Before Violet could process what was happening, the judge passed her ruling. She fined Josh one thousand dollars, the limit of the law for speeding, and another three thousand dollars and forty hours of community service for a misdemeanor resisting arrest charge. The misdemeanor would remain on record. Judge Lewis banged her gavel and called the next case.

Violet walked to the far left of the courtroom where the bailiff handed her the phone. She thanked him and went over to Amswell.

"Thanks for your help, Deputy."

"Call me Doug," he said. "You did great for your first time in court."

She looked over at the group of cops and deputy sheriffs who were making their way to the door. She could tell by their smiles that they didn't care if Josh had been found guilty; they wanted to meet their racing hero face-to-face.

"Yeah? I don't think it's going to help my career in the least."

Doug whispered, "Let's hope Chief Williams isn't a racing fan."

Violet cringed as she and Doug walked out of the courtroom.

In the vestibule, Josh was crowded by fans,

cops, deputy sheriffs and kids all wanting pictures and autographs.

Paul Saylor noticed her, eased away from Josh and the crowd, and walked toward her. He was a handsome man in his mid-fifties. He wore an impeccable suit, the kind she'd only seen on Austin McCreary.

Probably has the same tailor, she thought.

"Officer Hawks."

"Mr. Saylor." Violet braced herself.

Paul put his hands in his pockets. "This isn't going to go away. But I guess you know that."

"You mean you'll appeal," she offered.

"Absolutely." He cocked his head toward Josh. "He's never been on the wrong side of the law. You may not know this, but this has been hard for Josh."

Violet looked over his shoulder at Josh as he beamed at his fans. "Yeah. I can see he's crushed."

"It's an act. He knows how to handle fans. It's part of his job."

"And I was doing my job."

"I know. Josh knows it, too. He wanted me to tell you that."

She stared at him. Why would Josh care what she thought of him?

"Tell him—thank you," she said.

Paul withdrew a silver case from his breast

pocket and removed a business card. "I'll do that." He took out a pen and wrote on the back of the card. "This is my private number on top. Below it is Josh's number."

He handed her the card.

She stared at it. "Why would I need this?"

"My client feels badly about the consternation he caused you and the good people of Indian Lake. When the time is right, he wants to apologize to you personally. Off the record." Paul's smile was genuine. He touched her arm. "You have a good day, Officer Hawks."

"Thanks," she said as Paul walked over to the ever-growing crowd around Josh.

She saw Katia and Austin in the group now. Austin whispered something to Josh, who nodded. Then Paul walked up to Josh and put his arm around his client's shoulders. Josh looked up.

His eyes caught Violet's.

She didn't know what happened, but it was as if everyone else had vanished. Violet could have sworn she was suddenly standing inches from Josh. His gaze held hers, and she had to consciously remind herself that she could not hear his thoughts.

Contrition filled his eyes and his smile was tenuous, where only a second ago, he'd beamed at his fans as they jostled each other for his autograph or a photo. Paul had been correct. Josh with his public was all performance.

What she was seeing was the real person. She felt his regret, and a pang of conscience told her if she ever had a chance to get to know the real Josh Stevens, she just might wind up liking him.

CHAPTER NINE

JOSH CRANED HIS neck over the heads of the crowd around him.

"Can I get a selfie with you, Mr. Stevens? It's for my boy. He wants to be a race driver."

"Josh Stevens." A chubby teen girl giggled. "I never thought I'd actually get to meet you in person. Mind if I take a photo of you?"

"Sure," Josh replied, keeping his smile in place while watching Violet walk out of the courthouse.

He was in the middle of a crowd. His best friends, Austin and Katia, were here to take him to a late lunch. Paul was with him. Yet, Josh had the oddest and very unfamiliar feeling of emptiness.

Harry had been right that something had changed in Josh over the past months. Maybe a year. He'd become aware of how lonely his life was. Perhaps that was another reason for the chances he took on the racetrack. And for his desire to reunite with his parents.

It was an impossible obsession—wanting to

see them again. It made no more sense than this sensation of loss watching Officer Hawks walk away.

Harry had managed to keep the story out of the papers, but now the verdict was in. He was guilty. Paul and Harry had been right. Small towns took every infraction very seriously. They didn't make exceptions for anyone. *Especially* not celebrities.

Paul would eventually find a way to get the arrest expunged. There might still be community service hours, his lawyer had said. Curiously, Josh didn't mind. That would mean he'd have to come back to Indian Lake to fulfill those hours.

Didn't it?

The thought lifted his spirit.

Why was that?

"Thanks, Mr. Stevens. I'll keep this autograph next to my poster of you," a young boy with freckles said as he rushed over to his parents.

Josh signed another dozen and a half autographs, and the crowd dwindled. Finally, there was only Austin, Katia and Paul left.

Austin slapped his back. "I gotta say, Josh, if this is losing, winning for you must be awesome."

Paul laughed. "You got that right, Austin."

He turned to Josh and shook his hand. "I gotta run. A copy of that video will be emailed to me."

"How'd you do that?"

"Chief Williams and I had a discussion. That video was not properly entered as evidence. Granted, this was only a hearing. It was a bold move for Officer Hawks. It worked, but I can get a higher court to overrule Judge Lewis's verdict."

Josh blinked, and in that moment of hesitation, he saw things clearly. "Don't do it."

"What?"

Josh looked at the closed courthouse door through which Violet had left. "Leave it. I'll pay the fine and do the community service."

"You can't. You're scheduled over half the map until the end of autumn."

"I'll figure it out."

"Fine," Paul said reluctantly. "I know better than to argue with you." He shook Josh's hand.

Austin clapped his hands together as Paul left. "You gotta be starved. Katia and I want to take you to one of our favorite hangouts in town. I guarantee Lou can serve up the best burger you ever had."

"Austin, for real? I've had plenty of great burgers." Josh grinned at Katia, who slipped one arm through Austin's arm and one through Josh's.

"Humor him, Josh." She chuckled. "But, honestly, Lou's Diner is unforgettable."

VIOLET CHANGED INTO a pair of skinny jeans, a pink long-sleeved blouse with a V-neck and pink espadrilles. After court, she'd been given the rest of the afternoon off.

Then Saturday she'd be back on stakeout.

Violet couldn't believe it. She was still pinching herself as she put on mascara, lip gloss and a wisp of blush. She ran a brush through her long hair and fastened the right side back over her ear with a black plastic clip. Sticking small gold hoops in her ears, she grabbed her cell phone and purse and left the apartment.

The cell rang. She checked the ID and smiled as she answered. "Mom."

"Honey," Connie said. "I heard the news. You did great. And you were so worried."

"Thanks, Mom."

"Isabelle said you're meeting for lunch. Give her a hug for me. And your brothers called to check on you."

"I'll call them all later. Love you, Mom."

"Love you, too."

As she walked down the stairs, she stopped

at the landing and knocked on Mrs. Beabots's kitchen door.

"It's open, sweetie," Mrs. Beabots said.

"I'm going to Lou's with Sadie, Isabelle and the kids. You want me to bring you anything back?"

"Sweet potato fries. Lou makes the best," she said, sifting flour into a red ceramic bowl.

Violet paused. "What are you making?"

"Pies. For Sarah, Luke and the kids. I've frozen four so far this morning."

Violet rolled her eyes. "Do you ever take a break?"

"No, why? Should I?" She laughed. "You're going to be late."

Violet looked at her watch. "Oh, right. See ya later."

"See you."

Violet backed out of the drive in her squad car. She drove to Main Street and headed up toward the train station. As she pulled into the last angled parking space, she waved to her sister, Isabelle, who was taking toddler Michael out of his car seat.

"Hey, sis!" Isabelle took six-year-old Bella's hand as she scrambled out of the SUV.

"Hey, yourself. You need any help?"

"No," Bella answered before Isabelle could

respond. "She's got it." She lifted her head to look at Isabelle. "Dontcha, Mom?"

Isabelle smiled happily. "I do." She walked over to Violet and kissed her cheek. "You look good. I heard court went well."

"How'd you know about that?" Violet asked, walking alongside her sister.

"Mom told Sadie. Sadie told me," Isabelle said.

"I shoulda known."

"No secrets in this family," Isabelle replied. "By the way, Sadie had to cancel for lunch. She said she'd stop by the station and see you later."

"She always says that and then doesn't show."

"She's busy. Law school is like that, you know," Isabelle replied as she looked closely at Violet. "You look almost, well, radiant. I don't think I've ever seen you like this."

Isabelle's eyes scoured Violet's face. "You were worried about this, weren't you?"

"Yeah. I was. I didn't know how it would go, what with Josh Stevens bringing in a powerful lawyer from Indianapolis."

"But, Vi. You were in the right. How could it go wrong?"

Violet shook her head. "I've never been in court like this before. In fact, I'm learning so much every day on the job, I feel…"

"Overwhelmed?"

"Yeah."

The 1940s railroad dining car that Lou had transformed into a diner was jam-packed with people. The red plastic-covered stainless-steel stools at the long serving counter were full. The din of clattering plates, silverware and sizzling burgers from the open window grill and kitchen was underscored by an Elvis Presley song on the jukebox. Except for the new appliances, the decor was authentic vintage.

Violet loved it.

Friends waved to her and Isabelle. Even little Bella fell into the companionable atmosphere and waved around to just about everyone in the diner.

"There's not a seat left," Violet said.

"Oh, yes, there is. C'mon," Isabelle replied, waving to someone at the six-top table in the corner.

"Who?" Violet followed Isabelle, who was carrying Michael in a way that obstructed her view. Violet peered around her sister and saw Austin stand up and greet her with open arms. He happily took Michael from Isabelle.

Just as Isabelle leaned down to hug Katia, Violet saw him.

"Josh?" she gasped.

"Hi." He rose slowly from his chair, though his eyes never left her face. "It's you."

"Yeah. It's me. No uniform," she said uncomfortably, wondering why she should feel awkward.

"Hey, you guys!" Katia gushed. "Come sit with us. It's practically standing room only around here. We got the last table in the place. Josh promised the waitress we'd eat enough for six, so we got the big table." Katia swept her hand over the large array of onion ring towers, plates with burgers, fries and Lou's famous malts.

"Thanks!" Isabelle replied quickly. "The kids are starving."

Violet had wanted to stop her sister, but Isabelle slid in next to Katia. The waitress brought booster seats for Michael and Bella.

Bella scrunched her nose. "Oh, thank you, but I don't need one. I'm a big girl." She sat in the chair next to Isabelle, apparently satisfied that she was not classified as a baby like her brother.

Since Austin was sitting next to Katia, that left Josh on the end and the only seat open was the chair next to Josh.

He grinned at her. "It's okay. Really." He moved the chair out for her.

"Thanks," Violet said, placing her purse on the floor under her seat where she could feel it with her foot.

"I can't believe our good luck," Isabelle said, sparkling with that same idol-admiration Violet had seen on the faces of the crowd around Josh earlier that day. "Running into you like this, Josh, is, well, what can I say, kismet."

"Really." He reached for his strawberry malt.

Isabelle went on. "You met my husband, Scott Abbott? The journalist. He's very grateful for the interview you gave him. He hasn't finished the piece, however. He was waiting till the trial was over."

"Hearing," Violet and Josh corrected in unison.

"Sorry. Hearing."

Violet turned her head to see Josh watching her. His smile was small but appreciative. Something pinged in her heart.

"My brother-in-law will write a flattering piece, I'm sure. Don't worry," Violet said. Why had she felt she should give him reassurance? He was the almighty and powerful Josh Stevens. He could have anything he wanted.

"I'd appreciate any kind words at this point."

"Mom, I'm hungry," Bella whined.

Michael slapped the table. "Me, too."

Isabelle put her arm around Michael and kissed his cheek. "They're very busy here today. We have to wait our turn."

"But I need food now, Mom," Bella countered.

Violet looked around the diner. It was true. The three waitresses, dressed in pink and white with pink striped aprons, were dashing from table to table. The woman behind the counter couldn't make malts and shakes fast enough.

Bella started toying with her silverware and flipped the spoon onto the floor. "I'll get it!" She scrambled off her chair and onto the floor, crawling under Michael's chair. He started giggling and laughing as she pulled on his leg.

"Bella, get up," Violet ordered.

"I don't have the spoon yet."

"Then get it," Violet said.

Violet looked under the table and saw the spoon was easily within Bella's reach. The child was actually inching the spoon away from her so that she could crawl farther under the table.

"Bella!" Violet scolded.

Bella jerked and knocked the table.

"Whoa!" Josh grabbed the table to steady it.

Isabelle reached under the table and pulled Bella up and onto her lap. "Behave, Bella. Or no ice cream for you. Now tell me what's really wrong," Isabelle cooed.

"Mom, I just wanted to be by you."

Isabelle kissed the top of her head and

hugged her close. "Katia, could I have a couple of those fattening French fries you wouldn't think of eating?"

"Of course." She lifted the plate and let Bella pick the ones she wanted. "You know me too well, Isabelle."

Just then the waitress came and took their order.

Michael picked up a spoon and banged the table. Isabelle was still talking to Katia and Austin. She reached over, without looking, and placed her hand firmly on Michael's hand. He started to cry, and Isabelle simply took the spoon and then kissed his forehead and smoothed his baby-fine hair from his face. All without missing a beat of conversation.

While Austin, Katia and Isabelle chatted, Josh said to Violet, "I'm not very good with kids."

"Me, either, though Isabelle's great with them. Honestly, she was forced by circumstances to raise me, my sister and all three of my brothers."

"Oh?"

Violet turned her gaze from Isabelle to Josh and found his face was close. Very close. "My dad died."

"I'm sorry. I know just how rough that had to be."

"You do?"

"Both my parents died when I was six."

"That's how old I was. Isabelle was eleven."

The waitress brought their drinks, and boxes of animal crackers for Bella and Michael, explaining that their order would be a few minutes. The crackers were complimentary.

Violet leaned back in her chair. Josh propped his elbow on the table, cradled his head in his hand and stared at her. "Looks like we have some things in common."

Violet was unused to being scrutinized. This wasn't a date, but it was beginning to feel like one. She fidgeted with her napkin. It made no sense that he made her nervous. Just this morning, they'd been adversaries. Now they were hanging at lunch like friends did.

"Not all that much," she said finally. "After all, you live a very dangerous lifestyle."

"Me? What about you? You walk around with a gun on your hip, and you think I'm living dangerously?"

"There's a big difference, Josh. I'm sworn to protect the people in this town. There's honor and...and, well, even nobility in the choice of my career."

"Whereas, I—"

She interrupted. "You risk your life for other people's entertainment. You spend hours signing your name to countless pieces of paper and autograph books that will be lost or thrown out in a few weeks or months. You smile for a camera and hope these people will buy a ticket to your next race. And when that time comes, you may or may not die. How many chances do you think you'll spend before you lose?"

His eyes were unblinking as he reached behind him to the jacket hanging on his chair. "Thanks."

He stood. "Austin. Katia. I'll give you a call from the road." He took out his wallet and tossed a one-hundred-dollar bill on the table. "Isabelle, nice meeting you." He looked at Bella and Michael. "Kids, too."

"You're not leaving?" Austin said. "What about tennis this afternoon?"

"Paul wants me back in Indy ASAP. I should get going."

He folded his jacket over his arm and leveled his eyes on Violet. "Officer Hawks. Good day."

Josh walked out of Lou's Diner as another couple walked in.

"Vi," Isabelle said, "what's going on? Is he still upset about the verdict?"

"No," Violet replied. "He's leaving because of me."

"Because you're the cop who arrested him?" Katia asked.

She'd wanted to knock the arrogance out of him. She'd put him in the basket with other borderline criminals and lawbreakers. The truth was she didn't know all that much about him. And she'd been rude.

Austin and Katia, obviously, knew a different Josh Stevens.

Maybe the person they knew was the one she'd glimpsed when their eyes had met in the courthouse vestibule. Maybe if she'd allowed him to reveal more of himself to her, she might not have made her rash assessment.

Maybe she wouldn't be feeling such deep regret.

No matter who he was, it wasn't her place to hand down judgment.

She looked from Austin to Katia to the concerned look on Isabelle's face. "Not because I'm the cop, Katia, but because I was wrong."

CHAPTER TEN

"JOSH!" VIOLET CALLED as she ran after him.

He was half a block from Lou's Diner, and he kept walking.

"Josh, please." She rushed up to him.

He kept walking. "Why? You made it pretty clear what you think of me. Frankly, you were easier on me when you arrested me."

"Stop." She tugged on his sleeve.

He halted at the street corner. "Look, I'm leaving town. Okay? Believe me, I'm better off in Indianapolis, or Dubai for that matter. Anywhere but here."

"I was wrong," she blurted.

"When?"

"Just now. I shouldn't have said what I did."

He snorted. "Oh, but you thought it, right? Your low opinion of me still stands."

"That's not what I'm saying."

"Then just what is it, Officer Hawks?"

"Stop. Again. Call me Violet. All my friends do."

"And now I'm your friend?"

Her forced smile faded. "I don't know you, Josh Stevens. But I'd like to. I was harsh in there, and what I said was rude and uncalled for. I want…you to forgive me."

He dropped his chin to his chest, his bluster dissipating. He raised his head and his eyes probed her face. "Okay."

"Is that a 'yes'?"

"Uh-huh. If you'll forgive me."

"For what?"

"I've been on edge for weeks. I overreacted in there. I shouldn't have walked out in a huff. It's just that this race is important for my sponsors and all my crew. They count on me."

"But you'll win. You always win."

"It's not like that, Officer… Violet. I barely made the time trials, and we're still vying for post positions. There's a lot of drivers coming up who are really good. And some others who would like to clean my clock."

"Rivals?"

"Exactly like that. One in particular, Chuck Crain."

Violet looked at him thoughtfully. "I've heard that name. My brothers call him 'Crash' Crain. That the same guy?"

"One and the same."

"And he's a threat to you?"

"Absolutely."

"Was it the race you were thinking about when you were speeding?"

"When you caught me, you mean?" His smile was fleeting. He shoved his hands in his pockets.

"Yeah."

"No, something else. When I'm driving, I'm always focused. But every once in a while, my mind goes to a place..." He looked down at the sidewalk. He swept the toe of his shoe over a Bradford pear blossom. "Actually, you brought it up in there." He jerked his head back toward the diner.

She sighed. "I think I know. Your mom and dad."

"Yeah."

"You still miss them? I know I miss my dad."

"I do. Guess that's another thing we have in common."

"You were only six. I still had my mom and family. Who took you in after that? Your grandparents?"

He shook his head and looked away.

Violet saw sparkling tears in his eyes.

He took a moment before answering. "Naw. No family. I was put in a foster home."

"Where?"

"Indianapolis to start. Then Carmel. Then Zionsville. Then..."

She touched his hand. "Josh, I'm so sorry. Can I ask? How many were there?"

"I stopped counting after twelve. But there were plenty more before I was on my own. Luckily, I met Paul. He saw potential in me because I could fix just about any car engine you put in front of me. Antique, electronic. Foreign. Domestic. I made it my business to know them all."

"I'm impressed."

He slid his forefinger under his eye, rubbed the corner as if making sure she didn't see the fissure in his composure. "Then Paul introduced me to big players in the racing world. I was a natural, and I worked my way up to Formula One like I was born to do it. The rest is history."

"Hmm." She tilted her head as she looked at him. A warm feeling spread inside and lingered around her heart. "I think there's a lot of pages missing. Especially the ones that explain why you drove so fast that day."

"I'm not quite ready to share those pages yet."

"You don't trust me, you mean."

"Well, do you blame me?"

"I don't. I know I was right to ticket you for speeding, but I shouldn't have arrested you."

"Yeah? Tell that to the judge." The side of his mouth cranked into a half smile.

She knew he was thinking of the ramifications that judgment could make on his record. If his attorney couldn't get it expunged, the press would pull it up in the future whenever they wanted to demean him.

"Maybe I will."

"Will what?"

"Talk to the judge. If I tell her I want to retract the arrest, and explain to her that I misjudged the situation…"

"But the video…" he reminded her.

"I know," she replied, looked down and slowly back up to him. It was hard for her to admit her mistakes. It took courage. "Josh, what I'm trying to say is that I let my emotions run away with me. I got angry and reactionary."

"Same."

"Okay. So, we were both a bit hot-headed." She chuckled, and her heart urged her to do the right thing. "I'm not saying I can get the charge dropped, but I'm willing to give it a try."

Josh was thoughtful for a long moment. "And what will your chief say?"

"He's not all that happy with me as it is. I've made no secret about wanting to make detective someday. That stakeout I was on was my very first. I'm being given a second shot at a stakeout. I have to earn anything more than that." She drew in a breath. "There is the possibility that if I tell the judge I made a mistake and the chief doesn't approve, I might even lose my job."

"Then don't do it."

"If I'm wrong, I say I'm wrong. I have to make the chief understand that. If he has a problem with it, then I should go. I'll find another job."

"Oh, yeah, sure. But not right here in your hometown where you know everyone."

"Indian Lake wasn't my first choice. It was precisely because this was my hometown that I wanted to leave. I was aiming for the sky."

"The sky? As in…"

"New York. LA."

"Fine metropolitan centers." He chuckled. "Lots of crime in both places."

"I know. I like to think they need me," she joked.

He touched her upper arm. "Seriously, Violet. I don't want you to risk your job for me. It's not worth it."

"Perhaps the chief will be reasonable, keep me on and cite me for an infraction."

"What's that? Ten days in the brig?"

"That's the navy," she laughed.

"Oh, sorry. I'll have to learn the lingo."

Violet swallowed her laugh. "Why would

you do that? Take time to learn about my job, I mean?"

His hand had moved to her shoulder. She started to reach to touch his hand and then lowered hers.

"Because..."

Just then Katia and Austin came out of Lou's Diner. Isabelle and the kids hugged the couple and walked in the opposite direction toward Isabelle's car.

"Hey!" Austin yelled, turning and seeing Josh. He waved.

"You're still here!" Katia grabbed Austin's hand. They walked up to Violet and Josh.

Katia hugged Josh and kissed his cheek. "We wish you all the luck in the world with your post-position trials, Josh."

"Sure do, man," Austin said, hugging Josh, as well.

"Thanks, guys. You're both the best." Josh beamed. "You'll be there, right? For the race?"

Katia leaned her head against Austin's shoulder. "We wouldn't miss it for the world."

"What are friends for but to take you up on free tickets and those after-race parties?" Austin laughed.

"See you soon," Katia said. "And Vi, come over some night for dinner, huh? I'll call Mrs. Beabots. You both come."

"Thanks, Katia."

Austin and Katia walked arm in arm toward Austin's Ferrari convertible.

Josh shoved his hand in his pants pocket and took out his keys. "Well, it's getting late. I should be going, too."

"Right. You have a long drive."

"It's not so bad. I go the old route through Kokomo."

"Good thinking," she replied, watching him walk backward.

"Well, take care, Officer Hawks," he said, then turned and slowly jogged away.

He didn't look back.

She put her arms around herself, turned and walked back to her car.

Josh had hugs for Austin and Katia. There were smiles and promises of seeing each other very soon.

"That's what friends do," she said as she hit the remote on her squad car.

"I would like it very much if you were my friend, Josh."

She got in the car and turned on the engine.

"Very much."

CHAPTER ELEVEN

VIOLET DUNKED A bag of orange pekoe tea into a Styrofoam cup of steaming water. She needed to stay awake because she was on to something regarding Miguel Garcia. She'd been at the computer running through the National Crime Information Center database for hours. In addition to criminal history and basic information like birthdate and physical description, she found prison records.

Trent had a source in the Chicago Police Department who'd told him that Josh knew Diego Lopez, aka Miguel Garcia, and that Lopez had been a former inmate at the Illinois State Prison. She opened her desk drawer and withdrew the *Indian Lake Herald* newspaper article Scott had written two years ago about the police bust on the Le Grand gang that Detective Davis had spearheaded.

A zing of excitement rushed through Violet as she hovered over the keyboard, her fingers racing. "Is it possible?"

The Miguel Garcia she was researching

might have met up with Le Grand. The king-pin drug lord had targeted Indian Lake as his next "way station" for his highway to traffic drugs up from Mexico to Chicago, up to Detroit and then on to Toronto and the rest of Canada.

If her suspect had known Le Grand in prison, it was highly possible Miguel was carrying out orders to set up distribution centers in Indian Lake.

The next tab came up and revealed that Miguel had been released the previous year. "The timing would have given Miguel a year in which both he and Le Grand were in the same prison." She dug further into the records and found both men had been assigned the same cell block. She'd call the prison in the morning and verify her findings. But her hunch clutched her gut.

Out of 319 Miguel Garcias she'd found, one had been arrested outside a coffee house in Evanston, Illinois. He'd been followed by Chicago Drug Task Force undercover officers for months. After a particular drug deal, Garcia sought to elude police by switching vehicles as many as four times during a two-hour period after the drug deal. Unfortunately, the cops didn't find a gram of drugs when they finally caught up with him. Garcia was let go.

Violet moved the mouse up several lines and paused as she read about the different car makes he'd driven. "What's a GranTurismo?"

She did a Google search and as the photo came up, her back slammed against the office chair. "Maserati."

Clamping her hand over her mouth to stifle both glee and surprise, she looked around at the empty station. Nearly everyone had gone home. The dispatcher was still on duty, doing crossword puzzles. She looked up at the clock on the wall over the door.

"How can it be nearly midnight?"

She'd been so intent on her search, she'd lost all track of time.

"But it's paid off..."

Violet keyed up the particular Miguel Garcia, and pulled his mug shot and searched for background history.

He was born in Indianapolis, tall, black hair, brown eyes. His face was angular. Again she sat back, looking at the noticeable determination in his expression. There was no regret, not even anger. This was a man who knew what he wanted and would fight to get it.

Violet continued reading.

"Born Diego Lopez. The same Diego Lopez who was in prison with Le Grand."

Parents deceased. One sister, Rosa, residence unknown. At the age of nine, the siblings were separated. Diego was taken into state custody and placed in a foster home. From the age of ten until sixteen, Diego had apparently spent time in juvenile detention, doing community work and attending counseling as he did in public schools. From petty thievery, usually in mini-marts and grocery stores, to joy-riding in stolen cars, all of which were returned unharmed, Diego appeared directionless and unrestricted.

Her hands slid away from the keyboard, no longer needing to search, dig or uncover.

Josh's words rushed back in a torrent. *I stopped counting after twelve. But there were plenty.*

She slid her hand over her mouth and stared blankly at the screen.

I could fix just about any engine you put in front of me. Antique. Foreign. Domestic.

Violet felt an internal shift like one of those perspective-altering revelations that turned sinners to saints.

"Two boys caught in the same predicament. One, Josh, is shuffled from home to home and finds his calling in a car engine. Curiosity spurs him to tinker and repair engines. A happenstance person is put into his life, Paul Saylor, who not only likes cars but sponsors race cars and drivers. Josh Stevens's future is made."

She held her left palm in front of her. "Here we have Diego Lopez. In the process of being shuffled from home to home, Diego only wants to break out. He finds nothing to pique his curiosity or any natural talent. He turns to crime. It's easy, and the consequences are little different from foster care. Upon maturity, he discovers the monetary gains in drug dealing satisfy his need for excitement and wealth. And somehow he buys or acquires a hundred-thousand-dollar-plus Maserati."

Violet gnawed her bottom lip, hit print and walked to the printer.

As the pages of Miguel Lopez's bio spat out of the machine, Violet composed the oral report she'd give to Detective Davis in the morning, along with her research notes and conclusions.

At her desk, she stapled the pages together, turned off the computer and glanced at her cup of tea.

She hadn't taken the first sip.

"OFFICER HAWKS, I'D appreciate an explanation of what is going on here." Detective Trent Davis held a set of Violet's reports in each hand.

"This—" he shoved the single sheet in the

air "—appears to be a petition to the court by Josh Stevens's lawyer, Paul Saylor, to expunge his arrest from the records. Which, no doubt, will happen, given Mr. Saylor's tenacity. However, with it are emails from both Josh Stevens and Paul Saylor to Chief Williams and to me, asking to stop you from retracting your arrest. It seems that Mr. Stevens is concerned about your career, though his lawyer counseled him not to be."

Violet interrupted, though she knew she didn't have permission to speak. "I wanted to talk to you about that, sir."

"Feel free. But let's start with the fact that you can't do anything about the arrest. It's done."

"I know that, sir."

"Good."

"I wanted to apologize to Mr. Stevens. I got carried away."

"Like you did during the arrest?"

She kept her eyes on her superior, knowing that her impetuosity could cost her her job. "Sir, I was hasty. It won't happen again."

Trent's shoulders relaxed. "That's what I wanted to hear. Learning from our mistakes is essential. And for the record, I made plenty of missteps when I was a rookie."

"Thank you, sir."

"Now, about this report?"

She swallowed hard. Was he still upset with her? Had she crossed another line? Detective Davis had wanted to stay on top of Miguel Garcia, but they'd been short of manpower and hours so she'd done all the research herself.

"Yes, sir?"

"When did you have time to do this?"

"Last night," she answered honestly. "One thing led to another…and I…"

"It's good work, Hawks."

"Thank you, sir."

"With the intel we've had from the CPD and this new information you've dug up, I agree with your findings that Miguel Garcia is trying to round up others of the old Le Grand gang. Miguel has lived in Chicago for the past ten years. This we know. Richard has quite a dossier on him. Richard suspects Le Grand has never stepped out of the picture and that he's heading up a new operation from prison. And Miguel is his right hand."

"So, he's more dangerous than you'd thought?"

"All drug traffickers are dangerous. But my guess is that Miguel is highly motivated."

"He'd have to be. That's an expensive car he drives. No telling what other toys he wants."

"People like Miguel? They want it all, Officer Hawks. Money. Power over others. Fame."

"Fame?"

"They crave attention. Probably didn't get it as a child. Says here he grew up in foster homes. Had a rough time there. So, as an adult, he can't live without the limelight. He can't get attention legitimately, so he goes for headlines as a criminal."

"Negative attention is still attention."

"Bingo."

Violet's mind raced as she voiced her thoughts. "And to turn on megawatt lights—perhaps a grand jury investigation? A trial so controversial that it's covered by all the media... And you think if you catch him, he just might turn state's evidence? He'd be a star on a witness stand?"

Trent pointed to her with his finger. "That quick mind of yours is why I wanted you on my team."

A strong surge of gratification coursed through her. She had to fight back a smile. *Too unprofessional.* She said simply, "Thank you, sir."

"I want you to continue digging," he said. "The more we know about Miguel Garcia, the better. I want everything. Start with these foster homes. Check his juvenile record more thoroughly. Anything you can find."

"I'm on it."

VIOLET WAS ON a call to the fourth foster home where Diego Lopez had lived in Zionsville, Indiana, when her doodling hand absentmindedly wrote Josh's name.

"What…am I doing?"

The call was picked up.

"Hello," Violet said. "This is Officer Violet Hawks of the Indian Lake Police Department. I wonder if I might speak to—" she checked her notes "—Mrs. Duprce?"

"This is she. What can I help with?" an elderly sounding voice asked.

"I'm calling to inquire about a foster child you had in your care about seventeen years ago."

"That's a long time ago." She chuckled. "Lord, but I can't remember how to make lasagna from one day to the next. I've had over eighty foster children in my years. Of course, I don't have any now…since my husband passed away."

"I'm sorry for your loss, Mrs. Dupree. This would be about Diego Lopez. He would have been about twelve at the time he lived with you. According to my records, he stayed with you a little over two years."

"That one I remember. Not that I don't remember them all. But he was a pistol. Always in trouble."

"With the law?"

"I'm afraid so. He was only twelve, and he saw a fancy Harley-Davidson outside a diner where we'd taken the two boys after a baseball game."

"The Indianapolis Indians? The Triple-A team?"

"Why, yes. You know them?"

"I used to watch the games when I was at the police academy in Bloomington."

"Yes. My husband was a fan. So were Josh and Diego."

Violet stopped rolling her pen on the desk. It fell to the floor. "Josh?"

"Yes. He was our other foster son during those years. Those two were like dark and light. I'd always hoped that Josh would have been a good influence on Diego, but if you're calling about Diego, my guess is that he's in trouble again."

Like a jet that had missed takeoff, Violet's mind had yet to jettison. "Josh Stevens?"

"Yes."

"The race car driver?"

"Yes. I'm so proud of him. I always was proud."

Violet closed her eyes and opened them. She heard Josh's voice. *Then Carmel. Then Zionsville. I stopped counting after twelve.*

Her eyes popped open as reality struck like lightning. Her investigation into Miguel Garcia had unraveled a twisted path that took her straight back to Josh. "Mr. Stevens has become quite a celebrity," she said.

"He certainly has. Though to tell the truth, I never saw that for him when he was young. It was Diego who played the guitar and made up songs. Diego wanted to be a famous singer."

"He did? That's interesting. Was he any good?"

"I got him to sing for our church choir and play the guitar at some of our church dinners, but he didn't like our hymns."

"What did he like?"

"Rap," she said. "I never understood the words he made up. Always about fighting..." Mrs. Dupree paused. "Is Diego in jail?"

"No, he is not. I'm assigned to a drug task force here in Indian Lake. And I'm checking any kind of leads I can find to help us."

"Drugs. I see."

"May I ask? Did Diego do drugs or have an interest in them when he lived with you?"

"Not that I knew about. Josh didn't like the older boys Diego hung around with after school, though. Josh was always going down to Minor's Auto Service after school or playing baseball in the spring. Josh didn't see Diego much on the weekends, either. That boy couldn't get his head out from under a car hood for love, money or fireworks." She chuckled.

Clearly, Mrs. Dupree had a soft spot for Josh. But not for Diego.

"Do I understand correctly, Mrs. Dupree, that you didn't know where Diego went after school every day?"

"Oh, he would tell us he was going for a run. Or he was playing basketball with friends, but even the times when he didn't come home right at suppertime, my husband would drive to the schoolyard or gym, and he was never there. Diego kept to his room on weekends, playing that guitar. One day, he left for school and never came back."

"Interesting. How old was he then?"

"Fourteen. Almost fifteen. He was six feet by then and looked older."

"And Josh?"

"Not long after that, my husband had his first heart attack. I had to take care of him and didn't have time for parenting. The state placed Josh in a different home. It was in Bloomington."

"Bloomington. Do you know the name of the foster parents?"

"Why, yes. The Killingsworths. Josh always

sent me a Christmas card. So, I kept up with him. I still do."

"And Diego?"

"I haven't heard from him since the day he disappeared. We called the police and filed a missing person's report. But apparently, he didn't want to be found."

"It happens a lot. Mrs. Dupree, I can't thank you enough for all your help today. In the event I have more questions, do you mind if I call you again?"

"Of course, dear."

Violet replaced the receiver in the cradle. Her fingers shook. She used her left hand to steady her right. One investigative phone interview had careened Violet's perspective of the case around a hairpin curve.

Not only had Josh Stevens known Diego Lopez, but they'd bonded like brothers. A brother Josh had protected.

The bigger question was whether Josh had kept in contact with Diego, rather, Miguel. When she'd been on stakeout and seen Josh's car, had he been looking for Miguel? Did he know Miguel was a drug dealer? Was he involved with Miguel?

And if Josh was involved, how would Violet get the truth from him?

She put her hand on her shoulder where Josh

had last touched her. That moment, she'd been a tangle of apology and emotions that went past fondness. She'd wanted to touch his hand, hoping he would forgive her. It had been more than a mere touch. It had been a caress. Had he felt close to her? Attracted to her?

But in that second, when she'd reached for him, and as she'd looked into his eyes, she realized she wanted more than forgiveness. She'd wanted to hold his hand. Maybe walk with him. Get to know him better.

Then Katia and Austin had appeared. Shockingly, Violet had been jealous of their friendship and the closeness they shared. Violet had never been jealous of anyone. But something happened in those few magical and inexplicably important moments.

She swiped her palms against her slacks.

Being a part of their group isn't enough. I'm already friends with Katia and Austin. It's Josh I want.

Exhaling deeply, she slid her eyes around the station. Sal Paluzzi was typing a report. Trey darted through the hall with a clipboard. The dispatcher took a 9-1-1 call. This career was all she'd focused on for years. Graduating from the academy. Getting out on her own. Being the best of the best on the job. Her goals had been as precision-cut as diamond facets.

Since that moment with Josh, her vision had become hazy.

Violet's future had always been logged into an Excel sheet. Predictable. Precise.

Now she felt as if she were looking through a kaleidoscope. She'd never thought of her future as disseminated. Or as colorful.

CHAPTER TWELVE

AT PRECISELY 11:00 A.M. Eastern Standard Time, Violet fine-tuned the radio dial to the Speedway, Indiana, announcer explaining the "knockout qualifying" system to award the pole position for the Indianapolis race.

"The race is nearly two weeks away," Violet said to Detective Trent Davis as they sat in the Taurus cruiser on stakeout.

"Yeah, but it's the buildup that's half the fun."

"Like engines being revved."

"Yeah." He lifted binoculars to his eyes. "Turn it up a bit."

"See anything?"

"Nah. That farmhouse is vacant. So far."

"We've been surveilling it for weeks. Maybe our intel is inaccurate."

"Not likely. I got this tip from Richard Schmitz." He tried to stretch his long legs. Not an easy feat in the Taurus, Violet thought.

"He's your friend on the Chicago PD."

"Yes, and he's good." Trent cast her one of

his "and that's final" looks she'd come to know within hours of working for him.

The radio announcer stated that the cash prizes for front-row positions were increased.

Trent still had the binoculars leveled on the farmhouse as he commented, "That should be more money for Josh."

Josh? Now her mentor was on a first-name basis with Josh? "Like he needs it." She jotted down the time of day in her notebook and wrote there was no new activity. "You're a fan?"

"I am," he replied. "He mailed me an autographed poster for Danny and sent a replica of the Formula One car he drove in Dubai." He smiled behind the lenses without looking at Violet.

The radio announcer rambled on about various races, but Violet's head was filled with the report she'd yet to discuss with Trent.

"Sir, about Josh Stevens."

He lowered the binoculars. "This sounds official."

"It is. I've been doing some research, on my own." Trent's serious expression showed he'd picked up on her tone.

"Go on."

"Our intel revealed that Josh Stevens knew Diego Lopez aka Miguel Garcia."

Trent carefully placed the binoculars on the dashboard. "I know." He faced her. "Continue."

"My search led me to a Mrs. Dupree, who was a foster mother to both Josh Stevens and Diego Lopez when they were in middle school. She was quite forthcoming with information."

"Now that *is* interesting."

"She said the boys were close. Josh looked out for Diego during those years. Apparently, Josh was a pretty good kid. Diego disappeared after school every day, and neither she nor her husband knew where he went. It was Josh who usually brought him home to dinner. I got the feeling that Diego had a real chip on his shoulder."

"An unredeemable one?"

"She wouldn't go that far, but that was my conclusion."

Trent drummed his fingers on the steering wheel, considering the information. "You think Josh might know where Miguel is now?"

"I think it's worth asking him."

"Interesting. Who would have guessed?"

"Going another step further, it's my hunch that Miguel bought that Maserati of his to emulate Josh."

"Possible. Or…"

"Josh is involved with Miguel?"

"As detectives, we have to go there, Hawks.

Stevens spends his life in a very fast lane. It's not out of the question that he uses illegal drugs."

She nodded. "Always going for that adrenaline rush?"

"Exactly. And what do we know of Josh's finances? What if his extravagant lifestyle is bogus? He could be broke. Owe money to dealers."

Violet followed his lead as she offered, "Dealers like Miguel Garcia."

"What better way to cover up the truth than to buy his drugs through a childhood friend? Few in Josh's entourage would think anything of it. His own manager might not know. He could be living a double life."

The possible fallout hit Violet harder than she'd expected. She wasn't a Josh groupie, but she had to admit she liked him. More than liked him, she thought, remembering their private minutes together.

They'd only just met, and already she felt a closeness with him.

No, she didn't get the feeling that Josh was an addict or a dealer. The idea just didn't gel with her intuition. But the truth was clear.

Josh had known Miguel.

"I want you to continue this line of investigation, Hawks. I know you arrested the guy, but do you think you can get close to him?"

"What do you mean, sir?"

"Find some way to be buddy-buddy."

Her mind whirled. "You want us to be friends?"

His neck jerked forward and his eyes were stern. "Yes, Hawks. That's what an undercover cop does. Hook the perp. Reel him or her in. Wheedle information using guile, lies and persuasion. I want to know if Stevens is part of Garcia's gang."

Astonishment and ripples of guilt whirled through her. Though she held disdain for entitled people, he'd shown her that he'd worked hard to earn his success, that he was unique. Now she was being ordered to put that aside, and she didn't like the thought of deceiving him.

"You think that?"

"I'm a detective, Hawks. I have to investigate all possibilities. Think about it. Two foster kids. No parents. No money. A great many criminals come from such backgrounds. Parents, older family members, even siblings—all teaching the youngest kid 'how to navigate the real world.' Except their world is dark. All of which perpetuates criminal behavior to the next generation."

"I understand."

"So, how are you going to do it?"

"Uh…"

"Given the fact that Stevens most likely considers you anything but his friend—after the court verdict."

Immediately, Violet remembered her dinner with Mrs. Beabots, Maddie, Sarah and Liz. "Believe it or not, I have exactly the 'in' we need."

Trent clenched his jaw as if holding back surprise. "Continue."

"Mrs. Beabots is starting a fund-raiser to build a foster child care facility here in Indian Lake. She plans to endow it in the future. She's asked me to approach Josh about being the celebrity host at Austin McCreary's antique car museum."

"Have you contacted Stevens about this?"

"No, sir. Not yet."

"Do it."

"What if he refuses, er, uh, because I'm the one asking?" Violet's insecurity surfaced much too quickly.

He tapped his temple. "My intuition about you is that you're the only one for this job."

"I'll do it."

It was only a flicker of appreciation that crossed his eyes as he lifted the binoculars.

"And Hawks." He paused. "Get me everything you can on Stevens. However and whatever it takes. You must understand that he may be our fast track to nailing Miguel Garcia."

Violet was impressed that as soon as her boss realized the possible criminal connection between Josh and Miguel, he dropped his fanboy attitude and went all-cop. "I do. Copy that."

"And I want a report covering your conversation with Mrs. Dupree on my desk tomorrow."

"It's in your inbox."

Trent focused the binoculars on the farmhouse. "Good."

VIOLET FINISHED HER report about the stakeout that day, which rendered inconclusive results, and emailed it to Trent and copied Chief Williams.

She'd rehearsed what she planned to say when she phoned Josh and actually made notes in case she faltered. For positivity, she'd put his number on her speed dial, planning to receive many calls from him in the future.

She was on assignment. She had to convince him to help with the fund-raiser.

She lifted a very cold, half full Styrofoam cup of coffee to her lips as she placed the call.

She sipped the coffee. Josh answered on the first ring.

"Josh Stevens," he said.

The sound of his voice and the fact that he'd answered so quickly caused her to choke on the coffee. "Ach! Josh? Ach!" She cleared her throat.

"Who is this?"

"Off-Officer Hawks. Er, Violet."

"It doesn't sound like you."

"My coffee went down the wrong way." She turned her head and coughed hard. "Sorry."

"Are you okay? You want to call me back?"

"No! I mean, no. I'm fine now."

So much for handling the situation professionally.

"What can I do for you?" he asked.

Violet heard the sound of other voices in the background.

"Sure," he said to one of them. "I'll do it in a sec."

"Is this a bad time?"

"I'm always busy right after training. The post-position trials are a week away."

"Yeah. I know. So, you're really tied up, then?"

He paused for a long moment. "Officer Hawks…"

"Violet, remember?"

He spoke to someone in the background. "There was too much drag on the chassis. Increase the tire pressure, and then I'll run it again." There was a pause. "Sorry. Violet. So, let me take a stab here. This isn't a professional call? Not something about the verdict or my community service?"

Violet cringed. Her call and all that she was about to do with Josh was most assuredly "professional," but he couldn't know that. "I want to ask you a favor."

"A what?"

"Favor."

"Just a minute. Let me go to another room where I can hear myself think."

Violet waited and heard the background noise fall away.

"That's better," he said, his voice softening, sounding familiar and engaged. "Violet, I have to say, I find this—extraordinary, really. It's not a joke? You don't want photos of me behind bars for some PR for the Indian Lake cops?" He chuckled.

"I would never defame you, Josh," she replied honestly. "But you're not far off. My favor is charity related."

"Just so you know, Violet, I get a lot of these kinds of calls. My agent gets hundreds. A month."

"Really? I never thought of that." And she meant it. "So, I'm adding to your long list, then."

"Okay. So pitch me," he said in a clipped tone.

"Katia and Austin's friend and mine, Mrs. Beabots, is intending to build a foster child care center here in Indian Lake. She's having a fund-raiser Thursday night at Austin McCreary's car museum."

"And you want me to sign autographs?"

"I do. And could you bring your Bugatti and let us take photographs of you and the donors?"

"Is that all?"

"Uh, as far as I know, yes."

"Well..." He inhaled so deeply she could hear how long he held it before he exhaled.

His hesitancy troubled her. This was resistance. She'd been right to feel doubtful about her skills of persuasion. "I know it's a lot to ask, Josh."

"The thing is, I'm pressed for time down here in Indianapolis. The official time trials are next Saturday. After that is the race."

"The fund-raiser starts at six and only goes to eight thirty. You could drive up in the evening and come straight to the museum. I talked to Katia. She said you could spend the night with Austin and her."

"I don't know..."

"We need you, Josh. Your presence would give our efforts a massive push. We can take it from there. It's such a necessary cause."

"Violet, believe me, there are so many good causes in this country, if I had the time, I'd do this for all of them. But of all the weeks to ask..."

"I understand."

Silence.

Violet liked that he was taking time to consider the offer. She crossed her fingers and closed her eyes. Isabelle had always told her that making wishes needed concentration and action.

"Tell me something, Violet."

"Sure."

"I find it interesting that your group chose you to talk to me and not Katia. Why is that?"

She kept her fingers crossed. "I got railroaded."

He burst into laughter. "Well, that's honest."

Violet felt anything but honest. Not only had she been petitioned by Mrs. Beabots, but she'd been ordered by her boss. Failing to get Josh's cooperation would not sit well with her superiors. She resorted to begging. "Please, Josh?"

"I'll talk to my manager and crew. Thursday is doable, though I have to be here Friday and obviously on Saturday for the trials. I may not get there till six thirty, but I'll be there. I'll have my agent send you a stack of publicity photos, too."

Violet felt her heart jump, a feeling of uncontrolled joy. Was she feeling triumph over bagging his participation, or was it the anticipation of seeing him again? "Thank you, Josh. This will mean a lot to us. And to the kids who need a home."

"I'm happy to do it. See you Thursday."

CHAPTER THIRTEEN

JOSH PULLED UP to the front door of Austin's antique car museum at six fifteen, following the valet's guidance to park between the two cordoned-off brass poles. He assumed this was where the photographs of him next to his Bugatti Chiron would be taken.

Judging by the packed parking lot, there wasn't another space open anyway. He got out of the car, took out his suit coat and put it on. He smoothed his dark blue slacks and pulled the cuffs of his white dress shirt down to cover his gold watch.

"They're waiting for you inside, Mr. Stevens," the tall and very young valet said.

"Thanks," Josh replied and walked inside.

The place was packed with well-dressed men and women.

He'd texted Austin when he passed through Kokomo to give him an ETA. He'd worked with his crew from dawn till the minute he left, and had managed to conduct three podcast interviews that day, too. The PR this year was relentless, he thought, but as he walked through the crowd, all he could think about was the call from Harry. Yet all around him, heads turned his way, smiles erupted on faces and he heard his name shouted with that familiar ring of adoration.

"There he is! Josh!"

"Over here, Mr. Stevens!"

As Josh crossed the room, receiving slaps on the back and far too many flirtatious gazes, all he heard was Harry's voice.

"Stay close to these people, Josh," Harry had said. "Humor them. Treat them with respect and kindness. This fund-raiser was a godsend for your career. Hug all the old ladies and shake hands with the guys. These photos will be all over social media. This couldn't come at a better time. Who should I thank for it?"

"Officer Hawks," Josh had answered.

"Hmm. I don't like it."

"But you just said..."

"I know what I said. And this is great timing. This confirms to me that she knows about you and Diego. You watch your back. This kettle you've landed in can turn out to be a powder keg. So, keep the lady cop close."

"As in, 'Keep your friends close and your enemies closer'?"

"You got it," Harry had said.

Violet.

Josh had no more thought her name than the crowd thinned and he saw her.

And it was a shock.

She'd had her back to him so that all he saw at first were long shimmering curls over her shoulders. She turned her head and spied him. Her green eyes were made more intense by her expertly applied makeup. This very feminine, entrancing woman bore no resemblance to the cop who'd tossed him into jail. She wore a lavender dress that was cut in a V in the front and wrapped around her small waist, and fell tightly down her softly curved hips. It caused him to miss a step. He glanced behind him.

"Sorry." He touched the arm of the man he'd nearly bumped into.

She walked toward him with an engaging smile. "Josh," she said, reaching for him.

He'd expected a kiss on the cheek like most socialites and infield girls would do. Instead, she held out her hand for him to shake. He was surprised at his own disappointment. "Officer Hawks. Violet."

She grinned at him and tilted her head. "Austin is over here. I'll take you."

"Fine."

She kept fiddling with a gold and crystal bracelet she wore, as if its presence made her uncomfortable. Or was it being with him? He reached over, took her arm and put it through his. She looked up at him.

"You're not used to these events, are you?" he asked.

"You can tell?"

He felt relief ease on through his body. "Stick with me. I do this all the time. There's nothing to it."

"I wouldn't say that."

"What's the part that makes you most nervous? That clingy dress or the people?"

Her eyebrows nearly hit her hairline. "You think the dress is inappropriate? I told Isabelle it wasn't exactly me, but she insisted..."

"Because it's flattering," he finished her thought.

"Yes."

"I agree with your sister. And I suppose the makeup was her idea, too?"

"Nope." She lifted her chin haughtily. "My deep dark secret is that I adore makeup. Off duty, I comb YouTube for all the latest trends."

"Well, aren't you full of surprises?"

They came to a stop as they saw Austin with his arm around Katia's waist, talking to an elegant older couple. Austin gestured to the architect's rendering of the proposed center.

"So, that's it?" Josh whispered into Violet's ear.

"It is. Sarah Bosworth and her boss, Charmain Chalmers, worked it up so that we'd have something to show this evening."

"It's fantastic. And who is that talking to Austin?"

"That's Gina Barzonni Crenshaw. She recently married Sam Crenshaw, who owns the vineyard north of town," Violet said. "Mrs. Beabots has asked her to donate five acres of her farmland to build the center on."

"That conversation looks intense."

"I'm not sure how happy Gina was about the request. Maybe we shouldn't interrupt them," Violet offered.

"Nonsense, this is exactly when I move in." He dropped Violet's arm and moved over to Austin. Though he held his hand toward Austin, he never took his eyes off Gina.

Violet followed him.

"Josh!" Austin said, shaking his hand. "How was the trip up?"

"Smooth," Josh replied. He leaned toward Gina and held his hand to her. "I understand you're Gina, the gracious benefactor who has donated the land for the new home."

"That's right. It's a pleasure to meet you, Mr. Stevens." Gina beamed. She turned to Sam. "This is my husband, Sam Crenshaw."

"Nice to meet you, Mr. Stevens." Sam smiled.

"It's my pleasure to meet you both." He turned back to Gina. "So tell me, what do you think of the rendering?"

Gina pointed at the drawing. "It's too small."

Josh could hear Violet's gasp behind him. "Really?" He inspected the drawing. Then looked over at the table where there was a rough interior blueprint. "It's my understanding from Officer, er, uh, Violet here, that this is a fairly new enterprise for Mrs. Beabots."

"That's right," Violet took over. "Sarah hasn't had a great deal of time to work out the details."

Gina slipped her arm through Sam's. "I've raised four sons, and I admit I don't know much about raising girls or their needs, but boys need activity space. What about a basketball court?"

"Gina," Austin said, "I believe that with the budget Sarah had to go on, this was a very good design."

Gina considered Austin's comment for a long moment and said, "I want to talk to my sons about this. I know that I donated five acres, but looking to the future, say in thirty years, is that going to be enough? What if we need extra buildings on the property?"

"What are you thinking?" Violet asked.

"I have more land than the law allows. Perhaps it should be ten acres." She smiled up at Sam who beamed back.

Josh watched as Sam squeezed her hand and kissed her cheek. "I'm proud of you," he said with so much love, Josh felt something in his heart tighten. When he took his eyes off the couple, he saw that Violet was watching him.

A waiter passed by with glasses of wine. Josh snagged one off a tray for himself and one for Violet. He took a long sip, thinking to wash down the dryness from the long drive up to Indian Lake. He didn't want to admit it was emotion. Josh's experiences in foster homes weren't always positive, and his mind went back to his childhood friend. He and Diego had too much time on their hands, which Diego used to get into trouble. Josh had been lucky and found cars; tinkering with motors and pistons could be exciting. Josh had to give these people credit for wanting to improve the plight of homeless, parentless kids like he'd been.

From behind him, Josh heard several voices.

"Mr. Stevens," an older woman with an air of authority who could only be Mrs. Beabots said, as she walked up with Maddie and Nate Barzonni, Sarah and Luke Bosworth and Isabelle and Scott Abbott. "All my friends have donated generously to get a photograph of you with them."

"I'd be most happy to oblige," Josh replied, and handed his wine to Violet. He leaned close. "I'll be back. Don't go away."

"I won't."

As he walked with Scott and Isabelle, listening to their appreciation for his help, Josh glanced over his shoulder at Violet.

She was watching him. She hadn't moved a muscle. This time as she looked at him, he didn't feel like a criminal being interrogated. He felt something else. He could have sworn it was want, but he didn't trust the feeling. Harry had warned him to keep her close, but he'd be playing with fire if he allowed his heart to interfere with common sense.

Yet, she intrigued him. Her genuineness caught him by surprise. He'd pegged her for a by-the-book bureaucrat, but her offer to retract the arrest had been unexpected. Her interest in the foster care center was real. She wasn't like a lot of wealthy fund-raisers he'd known across the country who volunteered for events just to see their photograph in the media. Violet cared about the kids and the parents.

And she said she wasn't good with kids.

Josh knew it took heart to relate to a child. That much he'd learned on the race circuit talking to young fans. He'd bet Violet would be a good mother—someday.

What am I thinking?

Kids? Motherhood? Violet?

Who was this Violet Hawks and why was she getting under his skin so readily?

THE EVENING WOUND down around nine thirty, one hour later than planned. Violet stood at the door, thanking the last guests for their donations as they walked to the parking lot. The serving crew had cleaned up the glasses, bagged the linens and swept the floors.

Violet noticed there wasn't a single glossy photo of Josh remaining. They'd all been autographed and given away.

Sarah and Luke had driven Mrs. Beabots home. Austin, Katia and Josh were the last to leave.

"It was an amazing success, Josh," Austin said, holding Katia's hand as they walked outside into the spring night. Austin locked the museum door.

Katia hugged Violet and then Josh, saying, "We'll see you at the house, Josh."

"Thanks for putting me up," he said as they walked away, their arms wrapped around each other. Austin leaned down and kissed Katia as he opened the car door for her.

Violet took her keys out of her gold envelope purse. "I can't say thank-you enough, Josh."

She looked up at the museum. "You were amazing. Mrs. Beabots said they raised three times what they'd estimated. And Gina—doubling her acreage."

"I didn't do much, Violet."

"Yes, you did."

"No." He swept his arm over the expanse. "All of you are doing it. This is a lifetime kind of effort. To build a center for these kids." He looked down at the concrete and toed a stray piece of gravel. "They need it. When I think of what this can mean." He put his hand over his heart. "To kids like me—like I was, I mean."

"You did this because you were a foster kid."

"Yeah."

She nodded. "I thought so."

"Yeah? So you thought I'd be a soft touch?"

"No. But I thought you'd see its worth."

"I do." He shoved his hands in his pants pockets, considering her. "So, tell me. Was any of this part of my 'sentence'?"

A breeze wafted through the flowering crab apple trees, sending white blossoms down on them. A petal clung to her cheek.

Josh withdrew his right hand from his pocket, reached over and plucked it off. His fingers were warm as they grazed her skin. She fought the impulse to touch him. She remembered how he took her arm and put it through his, as if the gesture was natural. She had expected nothing of him. And he continued to surprise her.

"Your— Oh! The court thing. No. I was only..."

"Only what?" He stepped closer. "Still investigating me?"

Stunned that he'd brushed the edge of the truth, Violet stared at him. She lowered her eyes so he wouldn't see that he'd hit a mark. Her reaction was about as stealthy as a bomb. She'd never make undercover detective.

When she looked up, her gaze halted on his lips, which were moving closer to her own.

"Violet." He whispered her name just as his lips fell on hers. She meant to jerk away, but didn't. Regs mandated she shouldn't fraternize with him. Instead, she heard Detective Davis's order to keep Josh close. But she knew it wasn't her job that caused her arms to slip around his neck. It wasn't a police matter that made her lips seek the taste of him. Or press her body a bit closer.

His soft lips trembled slightly as if he'd never been kissed before. It was an incomprehensible observation about a man who'd had liaisons with attractive, accomplished women all his career.

Violet found it impossible to remember her

purpose in being here with Josh. She was supposed to subdue him, keep him unaware of her intentions. Instead, he had her off balance. Way off.

He slowly broke the kiss, then came back for another. Then another, short but oh, so sweet. "Violet."

"Yes?" She finally opened her eyes.

He was smiling. "Do you want me to apologize for the kisses? I mean, I'll do it, but I won't mean it."

"I think it's okay. I'm off duty."

"Oh, good."

He kissed her again. She felt a rush of emotion coming from him that pulled at her. Violet didn't know what he was doing to her; it was indescribable.

He was her quarry. There was a strong chance he was involved in criminal activity with a known drug dealer. Violet was on the verge of making a name for herself with this case.

But at what cost? The reality was he was her "person of interest," and she was supposed to report on everything he said and did. But his kiss? That was personal. If she told him the truth, that she was only investigating him, would she hurt him? Did his feeling run deep enough that she could wound him?

Violet had never betrayed anyone. She'd never walked this line, always done what she thought was right. If she hurt Josh, she would be the villain. For this instant, she wished with all her heart she'd never met Josh Stevens.

CHAPTER FOURTEEN

VIOLET WALKED OUT of the shower, wrapped her hair with a towel and grabbed another towel when her cell beeped a text.

"Josh? It's not even six thirty. Why's he up so early?"

She read the text. Austin and Katia are making breakfast. Can you join us before going to work?

She started to text back that she had to be at work in thirty minutes, then stopped. "Josh *is* work."

She texted: I'm going in late today. Love to. When?

He texted back: How soon can you get here?

She smiled. Josh was at minimum intrigued by her, just like Trent wanted. Right? Maybe she could get more information about his background. More intel on Miguel. She texted: Be there in thirty minutes.

He returned: I'll be at the front door. Coffee in hand.

Violet put the phone down and looked at

herself in the mirror. If she went in uniform, it could possibly upset him. Clearly, last night's party and those kisses had given her the advantage.

She called the station and left a message for Trent that she would be late by an hour, so that everyone at the station would know she'd phoned in. Then she sent a private text to Trent's cell explaining that she was seeing Josh Stevens.

Within seconds she read Trent's reply: Copy that.

She rushed to her closet and withdrew her black-and-silver spandex running clothes, and shoes. Trent had told her to lie. She'd just told her first one to Josh. When she was at the academy, it was easy to define situations as black and white. Place blame. Uphold the innocent. She was quickly learning there was little in her job and life that was either black or white. Ethics were varying shades of charcoal to gray. This vast new territory made her uneasy.

VIOLET STOOD ON Austin's front porch and rang the bell. The door instantly flew open.

Astonishment filled Josh's face. He looked at her hair. "Wow. Some workout, huh?"

She smoothed a hand over her still-damp

hair and chuckled. "I wash my hair before my run. I know it's backward, but I don't have much time before my shift. I change at the station," she lied—almost like a pro, she thought.

"Well, come in," he said, and handed her a small blue-and-white china mug of coffee. "As promised—coffee at the door." He grinned charmingly.

She felt her heart flutter. It was no wonder he captivated the public, she thought.

"Austin and Katia are on the terrace."

He was dressed in white summer slacks, a navy knit shirt and white-and-navy sneakers. He'd pushed the long sleeves of the shirt to his elbows, exposing taut, muscular forearms.

She guessed his arms had to be strong to handle a multimillion dollar race car going at breakneck speed around hairpin turns. And yet, those fingers that gripped his steering wheel had gently whisked an apple blossom from her cheek just last night.

She walked past him, admonishing herself for thinking intimate thoughts about a man who might be a criminal.

"I figured you'd be out of town before sunrise," Violet said, going through the French doors. "With all you have to do—for the race."

"I have time," he replied, standing close to her as they went through the doors together.

Violet nearly shivered at his closeness, but the spring sunshine filled the flowering gardens and terrace with warmth. Austin was wearing tennis shorts and a white shirt. Katia wore tangerine capris and a matching blouse with aqua flip-flops. She had placed two cups on the table.

"Hey, guys!" Katia smiled. "I'm making cappuccinos. I got a new machine." She pointed to the espresso machine on the granite-topped serving counter against the brick outer house wall, where it sat next to a bowl of freshly cut fruit and a plate of croissants, muffins and toast. "The foam is to die for. Want one?"

"I sure do," Josh replied, walking up to Katia and giving her a quick hug. Then he slapped Austin on the back. "Beautiful day, huh?"

"It is," Austin replied. "Welcome, Violet."

Josh held a white wrought-iron chair for Violet. "Come. Sit."

"Thanks," Violet said as she sat across from Austin. "It's gorgeous out here," she said. "Thank you for inviting me."

Josh plunked down in the chair next to her. "How's the coffee?"

"Loads better than the coffee at the station," she said.

"I can vouch for that!" Josh said.

Austin halted his cup mid-motion and stared

at Josh. Katia stopped serving up the fruit. Violet blinked.

"What?" Josh raised his shoulders and smiled good-naturedly. "Like I don't know about life at the police station. I was her prisoner, after all."

"Don't kid about stuff like that," Katia said. "I want to forget about it."

"Exactly," Austin concurred.

"It's a point of fact," Josh said, looking at Violet.

"That's right. It is. But since you appear to be making restitution, we should put it in the past," Violet said.

Josh's smile was faint and broke slowly, but his eyes probed her face. "You mean that?"

"Uh-huh." She picked up a sugar cube with tiny gold tongs and plopped it into her cup. "I'm more interested in why you asked me here."

"Ah, ever the investigator," Josh replied with a chuckle, and slid his hand to her shoulder. He retracted it almost immediately.

Almost.

"It's a beautiful day and Katia's cappuccino..."

Violet leveled her eyes on him. "You want witnesses for some reason."

He dropped his smile. "Actually, you're

right. And far too serious for such a glorious morning. But, the truth is, my reasons are two-fold."

"Ah," Austin said, taking a plate of croissants from Katia. "Now you've got my interest."

"Good, because they both concern you, my friend," Josh said. "First, I want to thank you, Violet, for coercing me to participate in your fund-raiser. Even Austin said he didn't think I'd do it this close to the race. This is a worthy endeavor you all have undertaken. I want to help."

"You already have," Violet assured him.

He placed his hand over hers. "I've been thinking about it all night. I'm going to talk to my accountant about a substantial donation."

Violet put her cup down with a clank. Was he serious? Would a criminal be this generous? Or was this a cover-up for something else? A way for him to keep her off track? Was he being wily or benevolent? "That's very generous," she said. *And he can afford it.*

Josh placed a linen napkin on his lap. "It's not enough. Austin and Katia. Violet. I'd like to do more, but I don't know what you need."

"What are you saying?" Violet asked.

"I'm not sure. I'm not the guy to help with the planning or engineering, but I could help raise money across the state. I could start a blog for you all and raise even more. I made notes last night." He reached in his pocket and pulled out scraps of paper.

Violet looked at his scribbles. He'd written on the backs of envelopes and a couple sheets of notepaper.

She picked up a couple notes. Her eyes widened. "You want to donate how much?"

Josh plucked the paper from her hand. "I have to talk to my accountant. I don't know how much I can handle, but I've never felt quite this affected about a project before. Because of my past, in and out of many foster homes and being shuffled from school to school, I felt I never got the education I wanted and certainly little attention or affection. It took my mentor, Paul Saylor, to change my life. This center is a good idea. A place for kids and parents to come for counseling and day care. I read over the list of activities. I had some thoughts of my own, but they're in the soft-gel stage."

His voice was croaking from emotion, Violet thought. Was he serious? Was she seeing another side of celebrity? Or did he want to make it all about him? Another way to promote his name and gain more stardom.

"I suppose, Josh, you'd like us to name the home after you?" Violet probed.

"Not at all. Though I'm sure my accountant will explore the tax advantages to something like that—now that you mention it."

Violet avoided everyone's eyes. She'd hit a mark. There was a real possibility Josh's intentions were not all that altruistic.

Katia stirred her cappuccino. "Josh, there's no question that our new foundation would appreciate your donation. I'll talk to Mrs. Beabots. Can we give you a call about it?"

"Sure. But after the race." He snapped his fingers. "Which reminds me. My second point of conversation. I'm having your tickets to the race Express Mailed to the house. Is that okay?"

"Wonderful!" Austin smiled. "We wouldn't miss it for the world."

Violet felt Josh's hand squeeze her forearm. "I'd like you to come, as well."

Without thinking her reply through, she blurted, "I have to work."

"Right. Not off duty."

Her eyes met his, which was a big mistake. His voice was soft and far too reminiscent of last night. She had to pull her eyes from his lips, otherwise Katia and Austin would know what she was thinking. She felt a jab of duplicity go straight through her. If she stayed around Josh any longer, she might not be able to resist the strong magnetism between them. She looked at Katia. "Speaking of which, I have to get to work."

"So soon?" Josh squeezed her arm again. "Stay."

"You haven't finished your coffee," Katia said pleadingly.

"I'm sure the Chief would understand," Austin agreed.

"Yeah," Josh whispered.

The pleading look in his eyes was sincere enough to strike out every doubt she had about him.

Her reason tried to remind her that Josh was under investigation. Just because he was handsome, rich and famous, she couldn't cut him slack or jeopardize her job.

She stood instantly, nearly knocking the chair over. She held the back to right it. "Thank you for the invitation today." She leaned over and hugged Katia. "I gotta run."

"Will I see you at the next committee meeting?" Katia asked.

"Absolutely."

She turned to Josh. "I'll talk to Mrs. Beabots tonight."

"Good," he said. "I'll walk you to the door."

"No need. I can find my way."

"I insist," he replied.

No man had ever treated her with such manners. He'd been raised in a foster home. Maybe Mrs. Dupree had taught him to be a gentleman. Maybe it was part of being a celebrity. She didn't know.

She did know she liked it.

He opened the front door. "Call me tomorrow?"

"Call?"

"Yeah. After you talk to Mrs. Beabots."

Violet stepped across the threshold. He didn't pull her back for a kiss or a hug. She was surprised she noticed that. "I will."

"Great," he said, and thrust his hands in his pockets. "We'll talk then."

"Sure."

"Well, goodbye."

He closed the door before she'd turned away to walk down the sidewalk.

Violet hoped Trent and the Chief would be pleased that she'd seen Josh again. She began wording her report in her head as she walked to her car. Weeks ago she'd volunteered to work all Memorial Day weekend in exchange for having Labor Day off. Nearly all the officers were expected to work Fourth of July since over twenty thousand tourists and visitors swarmed to Indian Lake for the holiday.

As she backed out of the driveway, she saw the living room drape fall over the window.

Had Josh been watching her leave? If so, why? Was he worried about her? Or was he reporting on her whereabouts to Miguel?

Her job was to find the truth about Josh Stevens. Not to create a portrait of Indian Lake's next philanthropist, which already looked like a premeditated strategy. Was Josh using her?

She was using him, though if the chaos that surrounded Miguel came close to Josh, it would be her job to protect him.

The arm of the law swung both ways, and if she wasn't careful, her betrayal of Josh would cause her to be the one who got hurt.

CHAPTER FIFTEEN

IT WAS PAST ten o'clock when Violet drove to the farmhouse. The county roads were illuminated only by a three-quarter moon. With her superiors' trust in her, Violet felt an unfamiliar confidence that bordered on imperviousness. She knew she should have waited to go through proper legal channels and obtain a search warrant, but her intuition had nudged her out of a sound sleep and urged her to action.

Her list of "what ifs" grew by the minute as she dressed, checked her gun and dashed to her squad car.

What if at this very moment Miguel Garcia chose to make his move? What if there were other gang members descending on the farmhouse?

In the meeting that morning, Trent stated that the lack of activity at the farmhouse did not substantiate a reason for further surveillance. He'd received intel from Chicago PD that a shipment of drugs was reported to arrive at a boat warehouse across from Indian Lake that evening. Trent shifted the team to surveillance at the boathouse. Violet had wanted to protest, but knew better than to object to her superior.

She couldn't help wondering if her natural instincts for detective work had finally kicked in professionally.

And at full force? She smiled as she pulled up to the house.

"Not a light on in the place."

She parked the car behind a cluster of bushes and trees where she knew she wouldn't be seen. She turned off the engine and decided to wait out the night. She wanted to be as good as Trent. She wanted the chance to test her instincts. She might have been breaking protocol, but she felt it was worth the risk. If she was right, she might be dressed down, but above all she would have proved something to herself. She needed to know she was detective material.

She made notes and recorded her time. She noticed a Beware of Dog sign.

"That wasn't there before." She took a photo on her phone, not that it would show all that well in the dim light. She knew signs like Private Property and Beware of Dog were tip-offs to drug operations. She peered through binoculars, looking for newly installed surveillance cameras or any kind of extensive security that was new.

She saw nothing else.

"Maybe I missed that sign last time… Nah. No chance." She made more notes.

Twelve minutes later she heard an owl hoot. A flock of geese flew across the moon. The night sky was cloudless.

The area was dead silent.

And every nerve in her body was on high alert.

"I can't take this!"

She leaned under the seat and took out her flashlight. She got out of the car, and without turning on the flashlight she stealthily approached the farmhouse. Just because there were no lights didn't mean the house was empty.

Without that warrant, Violet knew she couldn't go into the house, but there was nothing to stop her from looking in the windows.

For the most part, the interior of the house was shut off from view by cheap, bent mini-blinds. The front door was locked, she found when she crept up to the door and tried the knob—just to see.

The house was old and obviously hadn't been painted in decades. The front porch steps were rotted enough that she was certain a man of Trent's stature would break the boards.

She crouched under the cracked glass picture window and went to the corner of the house. She didn't hear a single sound coming from within.

She jumped off the wooden porch to the unkempt flower bed that was home only to weeds and a few withering peony bushes. The dry dirt exploded into tiny clouds under her regulation boots. She slammed her back against the garage wall, looked right and left. With the bright moonlight, she hadn't needed to turn on her flashlight yet. Moving along the garage wall, she noticed a window.

With no covering.

She slid to the window and peered inside. The interior was dark, but she could see the garage was full…of something.

She turned on her flashlight and put it up to the window.

"Whaaat?"

Squinting to make out exactly what she was seeing, she gaped at the number of boxes stacked against the walls. She moved the light beam down the pile. She saw nail polish remover. Decongestants for colds. Hydrochloric acid for swimming pools. Batteries. Toilet cleaner. Drain cleaner. Brake fluid.

She swung the beam over to the end wall where a dozen recyclable propane tanks, like the kind her brothers used for the barbecue grill, were lined up. On a long folding table she saw plastic tubing, hot plates, blowtorches, funnels, three Bunsen burners and dozens of empty plastic milk jugs. Large bags of kitty litter leaned against the wall.

Though she knew her phone's camera might not capture the interior, she risked using the flash to take half a dozen photos. She turned off the flashlight and raced back to the squad car.

She kept the headlights off as she eased the car away from the cluster of pines, forsythia and lilac bushes. Once she was on the main road, she hit the gas and peeled away.

At some point over the last ten hours as the ILPD team had concentrated its efforts on the new boat warehouse target, believing the farmhouse was a decoy, the gang had moved a great deal of equipment and supplies.

Violet knew if they showed up at the farmhouse in force and saw her, she could be captured, ransomed or worse. But the risk had been worth it. She'd heard every detail of the gamble that Trent Davis had taken when he brought down Le Grand. He'd risked his fiancée, her child and himself. Violet's ante in this game seemed small compared to what he'd done.

Still, she couldn't put enough miles between her and the methamphetamine lab.

THE NEXT MORNING, Violet met with Trent Davis and two drug task force members, Sal Paluzzi and Bob Paxton in Trent's office. Violet remained silent as Trent scanned last night's photos of the farmhouse garage.

"I don't get it," he said. "When could they have moved all this stuff in?"

"During the window of time yesterday from my last shift to when I arrived on scene at 10:43 last night."

He rubbed the side of his strong jaw. "Hmm. Right after I gave the order to withdraw surveillance—for the time being."

Sal glanced at Bob, whose expression was granite.

Violet knew that both Sal and Bob had requested to stay on stakeout—even on their personal time. She'd heard them say they thought it was important.

"And it was while I was busy with the fundraiser for the foster home," Violet added, feeling guilty and conflicted. Yes, she'd thought staying close to Josh was the priority, but she'd also felt community service was more than part of her job. It was a calling of its own. She couldn't imagine not helping Mrs. Beabots and the kids who'd wind up homeless, joining a gang or—desperate enough to be part of the methamphetamine cookers who would soon descend on the farmhouse. At the same time, *if* Violet had been on stakeout, she might have caught the gang members who'd filled the farmhouse garage with acetone, anhydrous ammonia, lithium, hydrochloric acid and lye—the lethal ingredients in methamphetamine. All thoughts that had to be going through the heads of the rest of her team members.

Trent leaned back in his chair. "It's doubtful they know of our presence on the site. Otherwise they wouldn't have stocked the place. The fact that you broke protocol is noted. However, I'm not above coloring outside the lines when we're this close to our mark."

"Yes, sir."

"With all this product, it looks to me like these guys plan to move in for quite some time," Trent said. "Did you go around back? See any trash?"

"There was a garbage can in back, but all I found were empty pizza cartons, fast-food wrappers and beer bottles."

"No red-stained coffee filters? Empty Drāno? Antifreeze?" Sal asked.

"No, there wasn't."

"What about solvent smell?" Bob asked.

"No. And no hoses hanging out of the windows."

Trent stood and clasped his hands behind his back. "So, we've got them before they've cooked the first batch." He frowned.

Violet watched as deep furrows creased his brow. "Sir? That's good, right?"

"Not exactly," Sal interjected.

"Sal's right," Trent continued. "We need to catch them in the act."

"But before they distribute," Violet concluded.

"Yep," all three men chorused.

Violet felt a rush. Her discoveries were valuable to their investigation. They looked at her as a contributor. "Sir, I'd like to move forward with that search warrant."

"Yes. Put it in motion, but we're not going to move on the farmhouse until we're certain we've got the gang leader."

"And you think that's Miguel Garcia?" Violet asked, knowing the answer but she wanted to hear it. For the record.

"I do. However, Richard Schmitz tells me that his men tailed him to Oak Street Beach yesterday where he appeared to join in a friendly family picnic."

"Garcia is still in Chicago?" Sal asked.

"He is," Trent replied.

Violet peered at Trent. Something didn't make sense to her. "But Miguel doesn't have a family."

"That we know of."

"This could be another ruse," she countered.

"Richard has a man who has been trying to infiltrate the gang since Le Grand's arrest."

"Was Richard's man at the picnic?" Violet asked.

"No. But he was at the beach and recorded a great deal. He took these..." Trent picked up a manila folder and opened it, looking at the pages.

Violet, Sal and Bob huddled over the photos of three men, dressed in shorts and casual shirts holding beers and paper plates of food, talking to each other. The expressions on their faces were intense. Trent continued. "The taller one in the middle is Garcia. The other two are his lieutenants. Now, look at the next photo." He showed Violet another shot and then another. "These two guys leave, and in minutes we see this other guy talking to Miguel. He's only there a few seconds." Trent pointed to the time line printed out on the bottom of the picture. "He walks away and another guy comes up. Miguel talks to him for one minute and fourteen seconds. In this next photo, he hands this unnamed guy a set of keys. We cropped it and enlarged the keys."

Sal took the photo and inspected it. "That's a Ford truck key."

"I want all three of you working on this one. There's a truckload of drugs coming in from Detroit tonight. Intel informs me that we're looking for a brand-new Ford 450. Silver or gray."

Sal whistled. "Nice ride."

Trent scowled. "Payload on this one is close to five thousand pounds of heroin. So the truck will be riding low."

He held the photo up. "The driver is going to be this guy here."

Violet memorized the man's features—thirties, dark hair, on the short side. Overweight. Although it had to have been hot at Oak Street Beach yesterday, when temperatures in Indian Lake were grazing close to ninety, the man wore heavy work boots and jeans along with his muscle T-shirt. She could only imagine the brawn it would take to unload five thousand pounds of heroin.

"I'll venture a guess that one of these other guys, if not a couple of them, will be helpers," Trent added.

"Sir, do you have a lock on the exchange point?"

"Indian Lake Marina boat warehouse."

"This is why you pulled the team off the farmhouse?" Violet asked.

"Yes," Trent replied firmly. "Hawks, I want you to be lookout. I've commandeered a ten-year-old Chevy truck, rusted and in need of a new back fender for you to drive. Park at Red-beard's Mini-Mart across the street from the warehouse. I want photos. Video. Everything."

Trent turned to Sal and Bob. "Both of you will be on the inside. Stay close to the doors. I'll be in the warehouse yard, out of sight. It's going to be a quick exchange. This truck will pull in, possibly followed by the next driver." Trent sat on the edge of his desk. "One of two scenarios will transpire. There will be an ex-change of drivers and the loaded Ford 450 will continue on. Or, what I'm hoping for, they transfer the drugs to the next truck."

"But either way, we've got them," Violet of-fered.

"Correct, Hawks," Trent confirmed. "Trans-ferring the drugs would take time and gives us the chance to arrest them. I want to avoid a highway chase. That's all."

"Got it." Indian Lake with its web of country roads, interstates, farm roads and state highways was exactly why drug dealers chose the area for these drop-offs, transfers and deals. Escaping cops in cars was their norm.

Fast cars reminded her of Josh.

As they walked out of Trent's office and Sal and Bob went to their desks, Violet took out her phone and texted Josh.

Hi. I hope you're good. I was thinking about you and wanted to wish you well in the time trials.

CHAPTER SIXTEEN

JOSH CLIMBED OUT of his Indy race car, took off his helmet and smiled at his engineer, Stubby Kits. Stubby exemplified his nickname. Five feet five inches tall, he'd worked with drag cars, NASCAR and Formula One all of his seventy-one years. Stubby claimed he would never die as every internal organ in his body was permanently ossified by gas fumes and engine oil.

"Josh! My man!" Stubby slapped Josh on the back of his red-and-blue driving jumpsuit. "You did it."

Josh's smile faded. "I didn't make the pole position. Crash Crain did."

"Only by two seconds," Stubby informed him.

Josh whistled. "Closer than I thought."

"You're number two position. And how many times have you won top position? Three, four? Heck, even six?"

"I should have taken this," Josh said as they walked out of the pit, his crew fast at work.

"Harry's here," Stubby told him.

"Yeah. I saw him before the trials."

"He said he wants to talk."

Josh grinned down at Stubby and put his arm around the older man. "Stubbs, one thing you gotta know about Harry—he always wants to talk."

JOSH LIFTED AN enormous pork tenderloin sandwich, the traditional food of choice of the Indianapolis racetrack and peered at Harry just as he was about to take a bite. "What?" he asked. "You look, uh, not happy."

Harry clasped a can of beer. "How're you feeling?"

"I'm fine."

"No worries? No superstitious tingles about the fact that you just lost to your nemesis?"

Josh wiped his mouth with a napkin, glanced around the diner, which wasn't far from the garage area where a lot of drivers and pit crew guys hung out. "Crash Crain is not my nemesis. He's just another driver. In case you haven't noticed, there are thirty other guys on the track this year."

"Cute." Harry leaned closer and whispered, "There's two point four million dollars and change riding on this purse for you this year if you win."

Josh took another bite of his sandwich. "I know."

"You do know your pit crew guys have bet on you fairly heavily. More than usual."

"That's because the stakes are higher. And I told them not to do that. They have families they need to be concerned about. What if I don't win? What if they lose too much money? Their wives will be mad. And the kids. How do you tell a kid they can't go on vacation because there's no money?"

"Josh?" Harry's eyes narrowed. "Since when have you been worried about their finances? You pay them well."

"I do. But they should be careful. Plan for the future. If I died out there, where is their next job? I mean, think about it. College is expensive. And what about their pensions? Maybe we should increase their 401(k) percentages."

"You're thinking about this on the day before the race?"

"Family is important." He glanced down at the wrapped straw on the table. "Maybe it's all important."

"What's gotten into you?"

"Nothing."

"You're nervous."

"Harry, after all this time as my manager,

you should know that very little makes me nervous."

Josh's cell phone alerted him to an incoming text. "Excuse me."

"Who is it?"

"Violet."

"Ah. I shoulda known. A woman."

"Officer Hawks." Josh raised his eyes to Harry's concerned eyes. "She wished me good luck."

"Yeah?"

Josh smiled. "She's thinking about me."

Harry leaned back and tapped the table with his forefinger. "It's a ploy. She's a cop. She's up to something."

"You think?" Josh couldn't help smiling broadly now. If he was honest with his longstanding manager and friend, he'd tell Harry the truth, which was that he should have placed first in the trials. He was the best on the track and he knew it. Crash had gotten lucky because Josh had made that last quarter turn, and in that second, he'd thought about Violet.

In all his years of racing, Josh had never lost his concentration. His focus was the track, his speed, the smell of rubber against hot asphalt, exhaust fumes and the rush of adrenaline through his body so strong he thought he and the car could levitate.

But he'd been thinking about Violet. Not his mother. Not his father. This time, he'd seen Violet and how she'd looked with her eyes slowly opening right after he'd kissed her. Almost exactly the same time she'd sent this text. He started tapping out a reply.

"What are you doing?" Harry stuck his hand over Josh's hand to stop him.

"What does it look like? Texting her back. You're the one who told me to be friendly. Show my community spirit to Indian Lake."

Harry pursed his lips, glanced around the room in what Josh often referred to as his "reconnaissance scan" to make sure they weren't being recorded, before proceeding. "You have that seldom seen, but undeniable sappy look on your face. The last time I saw it was four years ago and her name was Andrea."

"Andy."

"Yeah. And what did she cost us? A couple hundred thousand to go away?"

Josh frowned. "Okay, so she was a nutcase. And after my money, not me."

Harry folded his arms over his chest. "Come clean. What's with this cop?"

Josh exhaled and put the phone down. His sandwich had no appeal. "There's something about her..."

Harry swiped his face. "I've heard this before."

"I mean, something different. She's smart, dedicated, intense, but in a good way. Soft..."

"Uh-oh." Harry dropped his forehead to his palm. "This isn't good."

"How can it not be good? So, I like her. Okay? That's all. She's a friend of Austin and Katia."

"Josh, when have you ever had time for friends?"

Josh's reply died in his mouth. He stared at Harry.

It's true.

He didn't have friends. He didn't have family. He had responsibilities. He had a manager. An attorney. An engineer. A pit crew. Sponsors. But other than Austin and Katia, he didn't have any real friends. Josh had been riding the fast track so long, he couldn't remember what it was like to spend a holiday sitting around a barbecue or dinner table and talking about something other than racing, the next commercial or travel plans to yet another race.

"So you like the cop who caused me to buy acid reflux medication in bulk?"

"Don't exaggerate."

"I wouldn't dream of it," Harry retorted,

then pushed aside his beer and signaled the waitress.

"Yes, sir?" she asked.

"Bring me a large milk," Harry said, casting Josh a hard look. "Whole milk."

"Yes, sir." She left.

Josh finished his text to Violet. *I was thinking about you, too.* So, thinking about her caused him to lose a few seconds in the time trials. When it came to race time, he wanted to know she was in the stands. Close. And he would see her after the race. After the win.

While the waitress went to get Harry's large milk, Josh ate half his sandwich. His phone rang as she reappeared. He checked the ID and answered, "That was fast. How are you, Violet?"

"Fine. Working. I saw you posted in the second position," she said.

"Keeping tabs on me, huh? Is this friendly surveillance?" he joked.

"The guys in the station are listening to the radio."

Josh's disappointment surprised him. Why would he care how she came to have information about him? "So, I got your text."

"Actually, I shouldn't have sent that. It was a whim. Silly, really."

"Yeah? Well, that goes both ways. I thought it was sweet."

He heard Harry groan.

"So, Violet, how's everything going for you there?"

"The usual. Lots of bad guys. Not enough cops."

"And you're being careful?" He halted. Harry was concerned with Josh's welfare, but suddenly, Josh cared only about Violet. If Violet was going after drug dealers and she thought Diego was one now…

Josh had not hung around Diego's "drug friends" when they were in school, but he'd seen enough in his years to know drug lords were ruthless. Josh also believed that if Diego was vying for a kingpin position in the drug world, Violet's ambition could bring her close to real danger, even death.

"So when can we start in on our charity plans? After this race, obviously," she said. "And if you win…"

"When I win, I'll be jammed for weeks with appearances and interviews. Harry has me booked for most of June until Le Castellet."

"What's that?"

"French Grand Prix."

"You'll be in Europe?"

"Yes. I'm booked there through the bulk of the summer. The British Grand Prix in July."

He looked up. "Harry, did we get the Belgium Grand Prix for August?"

Harry nodded.

"That's confirmed."

"I... I had no idea," she said.

Josh clearly detected a note of disappointment in her tone. He didn't want to joke around. "I asked you to come to the race. Do you think you could talk to your boss? Or superior or whatever you call the chief?"

"I could try."

"The race is Sunday, two days from now. Austin and Katia are driving down. I'm sure they'd be happy to bring you."

"Let me see if I can wrangle the time off."

"Text me when you know, okay?"

"Okay. Will I see you before the race?"

"No. But after. I've already talked to Austin about what we want to do after I tie Al Unser's record."

"That's ambitious. Four wins. Just like A. J. Foyt."

Josh smiled. "You heard that on the radio."

"You will find, Mr. Stevens, that I know a few things about racing. And race drivers."

Josh said goodbye and put the phone in his pocket. Still thinking about Violet's challenging last statement, he realized that Harry was staring at him. "What?"

Harry's face was implacable. "You listen to me, Josh. Officer Hawks is not some model or soap-opera actress you can make a headline or two with and forget about. She wants something."

"Jeez. I hope so."

"Wipe that grin off your face. She wants your head on a platter, I'm betting. I wanted you to make nice with the folks in Indian Lake until that arrest charge was forgotten. Hopefully, it's behind us. Once you win, grab that celebratory bottle of milk and wear the wreath of flowers, we move on. You got that?"

"Yeah."

"It's what we always do."

"Right." Josh looked down at his half-eaten sandwich. Another race. Another trophy. A plane ticket to Dubai. London. Paris. Brazil. He'd race around the world. Again. It was what he always did.

For once, he wondered what his life would look like if he didn't do what was expected of him.

CHAPTER SEVENTEEN

VIOLET SAT HIGH up in the stands at the finish line. The best seats in the house, Austin told her, next to the Hulman Terrace Club tickets, which Josh had also provided. Austin liked being outside in the hot sun, but the air conditioning, VIP drinks and food in the Terrace Club had beckoned Katia once already.

Violet had worn a wide billed baseball cap that shielded her face, and a gauzy long-sleeved top with navy capris and navy beaded sandals. There was a light breeze that they all welcomed.

She was still amazed that she'd been given the nod from Trent to come to the race. But then, the 2:00 a.m. drug trafficking bust had been executed perfectly by the Indian Lake team. Every cop had followed orders. Set in their positions, it had been Violet's call from across the street at the marina mini-mart parking lot that the silver Ford 450 had approached the boat warehouse. She had further noticed a second blue pickup truck.

Due to her diligence and alertness, Trent, Sal and Bob had been able to apprehend the drug dealers, arrest them and take them in. The entire shipment of heroin had been confirmed and confiscated.

The driver of the blue truck broke down after only two hours of interrogation and confirmed to Trent that he was an old member of the Le Grand gang. His new gang leader—Miguel Garcia.

Once again, Trent had congratulated Violet on her work.

He told her she'd earned the trip to the race.

Trent had also told her she was still "on duty," and she was to report back to him via phone on Monday, Memorial Day.

The warehouse bust had emphasized to her how important it was that she do everything she could to bring down Miguel. These drugs were moving into Indian Lake like fast-flowing lava, and someone had to stop it. If it meant that Violet would lose her heart in the process, then so be it. Her duty was to the citizens of her town.

OF THE QUARTER of a million spectators watching from seats and another one hundred thousand in the infield, Violet guessed she was most likely the only person on duty.

Due to their prime seats, she rubbed shoulders with recognizable people from movies and television to sports stars.

After the national anthem was played by the Purdue All-American Marching Band, "Taps" was played. A US military aircraft performed a flyby. The announcer commemorated all those who had perished in combat and those who had perished in automobile racing.

Listening to the traditional words, Violet felt a chill sweep across her heart.

Not once since she'd met Josh had she thought he might die on the track.

Violet's strong and ever-present intuition shot up her spine. Was it a warning?

She leaned forward and watched as the announcement was made.

"Drivers…to your cars!"

The drivers in their colorful jumpsuits dashed across the track to where their expensive race cars sat in their positions.

"There he is!" Austin pointed to Josh in a red-and-blue jumpsuit, covered with a jigsaw puzzle of corporate logos.

He waved to the crowd, his charismatic smile on his face, before getting into his car.

"Drivers! Start your engines!"

The roar of the cars revving caused Violet to slam her palms over her ears. She felt a rush of euphoric anticipation shoot through her body. Along with the crowd, she bolted to her feet. Austin cupped his hands over his mouth, shouting Josh's name. Katia waved a red-and-blue flag that read: JOSH #1.

Violet didn't know what to do. She felt odd cheering for him, knowing she was Josh's guest while he was her mark.

Katia was still yelling Josh's name. Austin was whistling.

Violet clapped and smiled, certain she was blending with the crowd. She couldn't help wondering what was going on in Josh's mind as he waited for the green flag to fall. Surely, he was exhilarated. Revved more than the engines. This race was unique. It took place on his home turf.

"They're off!" Katia screamed as the flag dropped and the cars shot down the asphalt straightaway.

The first laps came at Violet fast. The race wouldn't be over until the cars had executed two hundred laps. The winner would be that one car that would complete the five hundred mile distance in the shortest period of time. Even if Josh crossed the finish line first, he might not necessarily be the winner. All the finishers had to clock in with their hours, minutes and seconds.

From their vantage point under the covered seats high above the straightaway between the first and fourth turns, Violet felt as if she could fall straight into the car with Josh. After the first hour, it was clear to her that Josh could win. He hung back only a few seconds behind the front-runner, Chuck "Crash" Crain, so nicknamed because he'd been accused of causing two major crashes to insure his win, though the judges and race commission never filed a grievance against him.

"Take my binoculars," Austin said, handing her a pair of Bushnells that she guessed were thirty years old.

"Thanks," she said. "Family heirloom?"

"My dad's." He smiled and took Katia's hand and kissed it.

"Here he comes again," Katia said, pointing to the track.

Violet turned the glasses on Josh's car. He was inching toward Crash. If she hadn't had the binoculars, she would have missed the slight, though aggressive, swerve Crash made to the right, nearly missing Josh's back right tire.

"Did you see that?" she gasped, lowering the binoculars.

"No, what?" Austin squinted as he looked at the cars.

"It looked like Crain was trying to run Josh off the track."

"Again?" Austin reached for the binoculars. "He's done this before?"

Katia nodded. "Last year. But Josh won anyway."

Violet swung her eyes back to Josh as the cars came back up the straightaway. "Somebody could get hurt!"

"Not Josh," Austin said. "He's too good."

"The car might take a beating," Katia said. "His car this year cost three million."

The crowd cheered as the cars made the fourth turn. Austin leaned across Katia. "That's nothing compared to the Formula One cars he races in Europe and South America."

"What do they cost?"

Austin shrugged his shoulders. "Nobody really knows. It's a well-kept secret, but I've heard that two hundred million is not out of the question."

Violet's jaw dropped. "Two…"

"Uh-huh. Formula One racing is all about the cars, not the driver. That's why Josh likes this race. It's a driver's game."

Katia shot to her feet. "Oh, good Lord! Austin!" She pointed at the track.

Violet was so caught up in her scenarios

about Josh that she hadn't paid attention to the race.

Then she saw it.

Pillars of smoke swirled from the back of Josh's car. In a flash it looked as if the smoke had cocooned the entire vehicle.

"What's going on?" Violet asked, realizing her mouth had gone dry with fear.

"His tire!" Austin shouted.

The people around them were on their feet, screaming, cursing, yelling.

Josh was in trouble.

The car came around the fourth turn, snapped loose and in the blink of an eye, hit the wall. The back right tire shot away from the car. More smoke filled the air. The car spun once then spun again.

Violet screamed, "Josh!"

Her hands covered her open mouth as she watched with terrified eyes while Josh struggled to steer the car across and down the track to the infield side of the track. The oncoming cars threatened to smash his vehicle and send it spinning again. Or worse, smash his car—and him—to pieces.

The other cars raced around the broken, smoking vehicle.

Then Violet saw flames.

"Oh no!"

Austin grabbed Katia's hand. Katia took Violet's hand.

"C'mon!"

They made their way out of the stands and down the aisle, almost running. Violet paid little attention to the chills that shot down her arms and across her skull. Her legs felt numb as she pumped them and raced down the steps to the concrete landing.

"Where will they take him?" Violet asked Austin.

"To the care center. I'll show you."

"I hope we're not too late," Katia said.

Violet's heart raced faster than any Indy car. *Too late?*

Her intuition had sent her warnings just hours ago. This was one time she hoped she was wrong.

CHAPTER EIGHTEEN

THE CROWD GATHERED outside the medical center was deep, but Austin saw Josh's manager, Harry Wilcox, on the other side of the paned glass window. Harry waved back.

Violet was just about to pull out her police badge from her purse, thinking they'd gain a quicker entrance, when Austin said, "Let's go. Harry'll get us in."

Austin stood aside, holding out his arm to keep the onlookers at bay so that Violet and Katia could enter the care center.

Harry rushed up to them. "Austin. Good to see you again. And Katia." Harry kissed her cheek. "Josh will be glad to see you."

"Harry," Austin began, "this is Violet Hawks. Josh's other guest."

Surprise scribbled across Harry's face as he smiled slowly and then held out his hand. "Officer Hawks. Nice to meet you. I didn't expect…er…"

"It was last minute," Violet said.

"I meant, I didn't expect you to be so pretty,"

he continued, holding her hand. "He's down in bay 4. This way."

Violet observed there were numerous gurney-beds. Each of the bays was separated by curtains on ceiling tracks, and every bay was sufficiently equipped to handle emergency patients. It was her guess that during the race, which was always held on the Sunday before Memorial Day when temperatures as a norm were over eighty degrees, there would be heat-related cases.

"Is he all right?" Violet asked as they approached bay 4.

Harry stopped just before pulling the curtain back. "He's gonna be okay. He has too many responsibilities not to be."

Violet clamped her mouth shut and swallowed her gasp before she blurted something inappropriate. Harry was his manager of many years. She'd assumed they were closer than friends. But in this moment, she realized that Josh was primarily a meal ticket for Harry.

Empathy shot through her. If she'd been in a terrible accident, all her family and friends would have descended on the hospital with everything from hugs and kisses, to flowers and offers to pick up her laundry.

Harry pulled back the drape.

Josh sat on the gurney, bare chested, as

a doctor in a white lab coat wrapped gauze around Josh's six-pack abs.

Surrounding Josh were people wearing matching jumpsuits with Josh's name embroidered on the backs and sleeves—members of his pit crew. Two astonishingly beautiful women stood in the far left corner. Violet wondered if they were his girlfriends, until she saw one of them hold a portable microphone to her mouth with her news station's call letters on a square disk attached to the mike. The other woman handed her a page of notes.

The one thing that most captured her attention was the smile Josh gave her as she walked up.

"Violet! You're here." He held out his right hand. "I was hoping..."

She glanced back at Austin and Katia, who both smiled at her. Austin torqued his head toward Josh giving her the signal to go to the man.

She glanced from Josh to the doctor. "What happened? Are you okay?"

"He will be," the doctor said.

"Violet, this is Dr. Herman. He takes good care of all of us."

"Nice to meet you, Doctor," she said.

Josh took Violet's hand, turned it over and kissed her palm. "I'm so glad to see you."

"But are you okay?" she asked.

"A gash on my side and a busted rib."

"Two broken ribs," the doctor corrected. "And his biceps has separated from the bone. Tore his rotator cuff. Other than that," Dr. Herman said, "he'll be fine after surgery."

"Surgery?" Harry gasped. "When?"

"As soon as possible," Dr. Herman replied. "I'll check with the med center and press for Wednesday."

"Sounds good to me," Josh replied. "What's the recovery time?"

"The usual. Six weeks to two months. Then rehab for three months," Dr. Herman said as a nurse brought in a dark blue sling for Josh.

"That's impossible! No. No!" Harry protested. "He's racing in Europe. Brazil. All summer."

"Not anymore. If he gets on a track before these injuries heal, he could cause more damage than he's got now."

"You don't get it, Doc. This could ruin his career. He might never get back on top." Harry thrust his hands in the air.

"I'm his doctor. I'm telling you straight. The wear and tear on his shoulders could debilitate him if he doesn't take it easy after surgery."

Violet listened to the exchange between

Harry and Dr. Herman, yet all the while she noticed that Josh's eyes hadn't left her face.

"You don't look all that concerned about your injuries," she whispered.

"I'll heal." He leaned closer and grinned. "I'm made of tough stuff."

"Josh, how can you joke at a time like this? Harry is..."

Josh squeezed her hand. "What did you think of your first Indy race? Was it all you thought it would be?"

"No. Yes. What do you want me to say? That you were amazing?"

"Not really." He pulled on her hand and she stepped closer. "I was hoping you had a good time."

"I was having a great time until you crashed and I thought..."

"Thought what?"

"That you might be dead."

"Oh, that." His grin turned impish. "I wouldn't let that happen. Not now."

"Now?"

"Josh!" Harry bellowed. "How do you feel? Really? Tip-top, right?"

Exasperation deflated Josh's banter. He turned toward his manager. "I'm in pain, Harry. I'm putting on a good show for these correspondents you wanted here." Josh looked over Violet's head. "Stubby, will you and the guys go check out the car and give me an assessment?"

"Sure, boss."

Austin whispered something to Katia, then walked up to Josh. "I don't think you should be alone."

"I'll get him a nurse," Harry snapped as his cell phone beeped. "Great. Just great. It's ESPN. They want a statement." Harry turned his head away.

Josh did not relinquish Violet's hand as he asked Austin, "What did you have in mind?"

"Katia and I are taking you back to Indian Lake with us. You can have the surgery here or up there. We have an excellent orthopedic surgeon—a friend—and the staff at the hospital is incredible. You can recuperate at our house."

"We won't take 'no' for an answer, Josh," Katia agreed. "This is not the time to go this alone. Your injuries are serious. And we're just as serious."

Violet felt Josh's fingers tighten around hers. He started to reply, cleared his throat and when she looked at him, she saw tears well.

Josh considered Austin and Katia nearly family. He probably hadn't needed help with any facet of his life since childhood. But he did now.

Their gesture moved him.

And his response struck Violet to her core. As much as she tried to put Josh Stevens in categories, slap him with legal definitions and nail him with possible criminal involvement, when she witnessed Josh, the man, the human being, all of that faded.

His entourage walked away from him, already knowing their jobs were on hold for the rest of the summer. Harry banged out a text with frustrated fingers, revealing to her that his connection to the media was priority number one.

Not Josh.

Josh turned to her. “What do you think, Violet?”

“Me?”

“Yeah.”

His eyes were the most sincere she’d seen outside her family. She knew he wasn’t asking a simple question. The way he looked at her was compelling and eager.

He glanced at her lips.

And she knew he was remembering their kisses. He was waiting for her to give him an invitation. In his head right now, she was Violet. Not an officer of the law.

"Come home with us," she said aloud, though the words had been in her head from the moment she'd walked into the bay. The room had been filled with people she should have observed and who should have been the subjects of her notes to Trent.

But she'd been worried about Josh. Her emotions had pitched from fear to terror and now to relief. The idea that he would consider recuperating in Indian Lake sent a thrill through her.

"You really want me to come?"

"Yes," she said, and smiled slowly. "Just remember, I'm a cop. Not a nurse. I don't have much experience in that line of work."

"Like Harry said, we can hire a nurse."

He peeled his eyes off Violet and said to Austin, "You guys are too generous. But I'll try to be on my best behavior. I accept your invitation."

Austin chuckled. "Buddy, I promise you, the minute you get to be a pain, Katia will set you straight."

"Yeah?"

Violet laughed. "And if she doesn't, I will."

"Oh, you will?" Josh leaned over and kissed Violet's cheek.

His lips were soft and lingered a fraction longer than was just friendly. His nearness was a heady experience. Though he smelled of rubbing alcohol, there was an undercurrent of spice and citrus. His cheek was smooth, having been prepared for paparazzi photos.

She didn't want to step away. "I will, Josh Stevens."

After Dr. Herman gave him care instructions and follow-up info for surgery in Indian Lake, they got ready to go.

"And now we have to get your sling on," Violet said, looking at the nurse. "How?"

"It hurts to move my arm," Josh said. "I'll put the sling over the jumpsuit and we can tuck the jumpsuit sleeve inside."

Harry chortled. "Good thing you kept up all those sit-ups. Every camera is gonna be zeroed in on those bandages."

"And then some," Violet whispered, and quickly glanced away.

Josh laughed and put his good arm around Violet's shoulders. "C'mon. Let's give them something to talk about."

"What?"

Josh's arm was strong as he herded her out of bay 4 and into the corridor. Several camera crews filmed their exit out of the hospital.

The world wanted to know that Josh Stevens had lived.

Violet couldn't help but think that he wanted the world to know that she was by his side.

But why? She wasn't his girlfriend, but the press could easily manipulate a story about their closeness. Was this Harry's idea?

They walked down the hall, and the reporters parted to allow them through. She saw how little they cared for him. He was a story. It had surprised her how deeply she'd felt for him at the moment of the crash. It startled her that her emotions created a combustion of their own. She'd come here on police orders. But her duty receded the moment of the crash.

The media cared only about his fame or if he'd finally fallen from it. And what if he did? Was that an even better story?

She should zero in on her duty, but right now she cared only about Josh.

CHAPTER NINETEEN

ON THE DRIVE back to Indian Lake, Josh had held out his hand and said, "Gimme your cell phone."

"Why?"

He'd wiggled his fingers. "I'm not going to bug it, Violet. C'mon."

She'd handed him her phone and watched as he added his name and number. Fiddling with the settings for a moment, he'd grinned and handed it back to her. "Just a sec."

Taking out his cell phone, Josh opened up his "favorites," where he'd stored her number and called her.

Her phone began to play "On the Banks of the Wabash, Far Away."

"Why'd you do that?" she asked.

"So you always know it's me calling and not some other guy."

"Most of my calls are official. Except for my family. I may be the youngest, but I've always come up with solutions and fast. My friends tell me the same thing."

"I can see that."

"Yeah?"

"Uh-huh. You didn't flinch when I came at you when you arrested me." His smile was faint but sincere. "You followed me out of the diner to apologize that day after the trial. And you were ready with an idea to 'fix' my arrest that I'd never thought of. You have a lot of heart, Violet. You're the first person, ever, really, who saw me for myself. Not my fame or career. I'm just another guy to you."

"Well, I wouldn't say that..."

"No?"

"No."

She stared at him and saw him catch his breath intake as if he'd forgotten to exhale.

"So now you'll take my calls?"

In the split second she hesitated, wondering which category she should place him, "official business" or "friend," Josh leaned over and kissed her cheek.

"I'm going to be in Indian Lake for quite some time this summer, and I was hoping I could be your friend."

EVEN NOW, AS she watched dawn pierce across the cloudless sky and across greening rows of soybeans and corn, her head was filled with Josh thoughts, images. Feelings.

Friends.

What did he mean by that? Exactly?

She'd never had a "friend" who kissed her like Josh had. It was possible he was looking for a summer romance to occupy him while he recuperated. Someone to take his mind off the pain. The boredom.

How could a guy like Josh—a celebrity—be into a small town cop?

She pinched the bridge of her nose.

"This guy gives me a headache already, and I'm not even involved with him!"

Violet reminded herself she was a rookie—in her career and in relationships. She had friends in high school and at the police academy, but she'd never had a real romance. She was too focused on studying and earning money to pay for tuition.

She rubbed her temples. Josh was as different from her as night was from day. Looking back on her life, she realized there had been no romances because there'd never been anyone like Josh. He was the first guy to come along who was not intimidated by her ambition. He valued her career and her goals. He was ambitious, too, and he understood what that meant.

But he'd said he wanted to be her friend. No commitments. No promises of romance or a relationship. Just friendship.

And then he kissed me.

Not a real kiss, but he'd lingered, and she'd felt the warmth of his lips against her skin. Lifting her fingers to the place where he placed that kiss, she smiled. It still felt tingly.

Violet rolled her eyes.

"I'm only twenty-four years old. I have all the time in the world for love. Later. I shouldn't be thinking about Josh. My mind should be on work." She groaned and poured out the last bit of tepid coffee from the thermos she'd drained over her all-night stakeout.

Amazingly, she'd remained awake since she'd taken over from Sal Paluzzi just before midnight. It was now five fifteen.

She glanced up. "What?"

She saw a 1998 beige Chrysler pull into the drive of the farmhouse. While she'd been at the race, Bob Paxton had reported seeing a beige or light gold old Chrysler drive slowly past the farmhouse, but did not drive in.

Violet feared she'd blundered due to the fact she'd been watching for an expensive foreign car. She grabbed her phone and took a photo. She emailed the shot to the ILPD station. She scribbled notes on her ever-present log sheet.

Following Trent's orders, she immediately phoned him.

"Davis," he said groggily.

"Officer Hawks, sir. I have movement at the farmhouse. The 1998 Chrysler that Detective Paxton reported is back. It's parked in the drive close to the garage."

"How many in the car?"

Violet could hear rumbling on Trent's end of the phone as if he were rising from bed and getting dressed. She picked up her binoculars. "Two men. No, wait. There's a third in the backseat."

"Stay out of sight. I'm sending Paluzzi and Paxton. I'm on my way."

"Sir…"

"Remain in your vehicle, Officer. That's an order!"

"Yes, sir." She hung up.

Peering through the binoculars, she watched as two of the men went into the house through the back door. The third remained by the driver's side of the car, lit a cigarette and watched the sun rise.

As dawn came, Violet zoomed in and snapped the license plate. She emailed the photo to the station and left instructions to have a trace run on it.

In addition to photos of the sentry, now smoking his second cigarette, Violet jotted down his mannerisms, his apparent nervous habit of shaking his right leg every few seconds. The man did not inspect the garage, the surrounding area, look for cameras or a cop lurking behind a blind of trees and bushes.

He was awfully comfortable.

Ten minutes later, the passenger door of Violet's car opened and Trent crawled in.

"Good morning," she said as he closed the door.

"I parked—"

"Across the soybean field," she finished for him. She tapped the rearview mirror. "I saw. And—" she pointed out her window to the left "—Detective Paluzzi is going in the back?"

"Correct."

"Am I to follow you?" she asked.

"Officer Hawks, you've been out here all night. No sleep makes your slow reflexes a danger to the operation."

"Sir, I feel fine. I'd like to participate."

"Duly noted. You were an asset on the warehouse bust. Judging from your somewhat bloodshot eyes, I'm quite sure you didn't nod off for a minute all night."

"No, sir. I was on duty."

He pursed his lips to stifle a satisfied smile. "I'll take over from here." He pointed at the farmhouse. "We're staying put until we see them move something in or out. Until then—"

"Ten four." She nodded.

Trent took out his car keys. "Take my car back to the station. I'll bring yours back later."

Violet handed him the binoculars. She grabbed her notes and got out of the car. Crouching low, she made her way across the soybean field.

If those gang members made the slightest move into the meth lab garage, Trent and the team would make their bust.

She'd be left out.

The glory of the arrest would not appear on her record. Which could lead to her being passed over. Trent had won accolades and even a commendation for his work. So had Sal and Bob when they took down Le Grand.

As her booted feet scraped past the soybeans, she thought of Josh and wondered what it would be like to see him at the end of the day, tell him of her defeat. She was off base to think of them as a couple, sharing joys and trials. They were only beginning to be "friends." But she couldn't help thinking that perhaps he might hold her hand, his warmth and concern giving her that fraction of hope that she needed to keep going when everything looked so gray.

AT THE POLICE STATION, Violet filed her report, put Trent's car keys on his desk then walked across the street to her apartment.

She had just pulled a bright pink T-shirt over her head, when her cell phone pinged with a text from Katia.

I'm at the hospital. Josh just went in to surgery. A day early.

Violet texted back: I'm on my way.

Without her car, Violet didn't have a vehicle. Fortunately, the Indian Lake hospital was only six blocks from her apartment. She put on her running shoes, shoved her phone, cash, ID, badge and apartment key into a fanny pack, strapped it around her waist and raced out the door.

At the landing, she saw Mrs. Beabots in the kitchen. She tapped on the door.

"Come in, sweetie," Mrs. Beabots said as she poured boiling water into a French press. "I thought you'd be asleep by now. Honestly, I don't know how you stay awake all night long..."

"Josh is in surgery."

Mrs. Beabots put down the kettle. "I thought it was tomorrow."

"So did I. Katia just texted me. I can't help thinking something happened. I'm on my way there now."

Mrs. Beabots held up her palm. "Wait." She

went to the sink where an armful of peonies and roses were resting in water. She took half a dozen flowers, put a wet paper towel around the bottom and then wrapped it in aluminum foil. “Give these to Josh when he wakes up. The fragrance will help him heal.”

Violet hugged Mrs. Beabots. “You are the best.”

“It’s what friends do.” She smiled. “Oh!” She opened the dishwasher and took out a clean jar. It still had the peanut butter label on it. “A vase.”

“Perfect,” Violet replied. “I’ll call you from the hospital once I know what’s going on.”

“Thank you, dear.”

Violet found Katia in the surgery waiting room. The television blared the news as an elderly couple strained to hear the announcer’s voice.

Katia stood by the window looking down on the street, a fashion magazine in her hand. It was eight twenty in the morning, and Katia looked more put-together than the supermodel on the magazine cover.

“Katia, is Josh in trouble?” Violet clutched the flowers to her chest.

“No. Nothing like that. The surgeon had a cancellation, that’s all.”

Katia looked at the flowers. “Those are pretty.”

“Oh. They’re from Mrs. Beabots’s garden.” She lifted the jar. “And she provided the vase.” She chuckled. “I’ll get some water from the drinking fountain.”

“Take your time. The doctor said the surgery could last four hours barring complications.”

Violet’s heart skipped a beat. “Complications? What could happen? I mean, Josh is young and fit and...”

“Apparently the tears in his shoulder are more extensive than originally thought. They did another MRI and found some old ruptures. At some point, Josh had broken his clavicle. This is the second break he’s had.”

Dread washed over Violet. Until this moment, she’d downplayed the seriousness of Josh’s injuries. He’d created an impervious, almost immortal persona, dodging death on the race track month after month, so she’d dismissed the reality that his injuries could incapacitate him. Or kill him. They both danced with the devil in that way, though. Still, she couldn’t help think her choice was more noble than his.

“Did you talk to Josh? Was he worried?”

“You know Josh. He downplays every hurdle in his life.”

"No. I didn't know that," Violet replied, wishing she'd had time to know that about him.

Katia put the magazine on a chair. "I don't know him as well as Austin does, but he's told me quite a bit about Josh. On my own I've discovered that he's honest and loyal. Thoughtful and kind and so giving. What he wants to do for Mrs. Beabots's children center alone..."

"I know. That's amazing." Violet glanced down at the flowers and realized the petals were quivering because her hand was shaking. Guilt had rattled her but good. When she wasn't remembering Josh's kiss and promising herself it would never happen again, she was stealthily probing for a flaw, a rip in his story that would connect him to a dangerous drug lord. She was the one wearing the mask in this scenario. It wasn't Josh's practiced performance for the crowd that gave her caution. It was her own diametrically opposed motivations.

Was she the good guy doing bad or the bad guy doing good?

"Do hospitals make you nervous?" Katia asked.

"Yeah."

"Me, too. Austin and I had dinner with Nate and Maddie last week, and Nate told us about a couple of his surgeries when he was a resident and the patient died. I can't imagine how terrifying that has to be for a family, sitting out here, waiting for the doctor to come to them and he has to announce that their loved one died."

Violet felt the tear on her cheek before she realized her eyes had welled. "Poor Nate. I don't know how doctors do all they do." She wiped her cheek. "But Katia, Josh isn't having heart surgery."

"The anesthetic alone can cause complications. Blood clots to the brain. The lungs." Katia's hands flew to her cheeks. "If that was Austin in there..."

"But it's not. It's Josh."

Her knees weakened. Violet lowered slowly into the chair. She looked at the flowers. "I hope he likes roses. They have the highest vibration of any flower on earth. Both Isabelle and Mrs. Beabots say they can heal a person."

The flowers swam in front of Violet's eyes. She lifted them and inhaled their sweetness, then put the makeshift vase on the table in front of her.

Katia sat next to her and placed her hand over Violet's. "I'm sorry for blubbering on like I did. I didn't know."

Violet pursed her lips to keep from sobbing. "Know what?"

"That you're in love with Josh."

"Don't be ridiculous." Violet's hand flew to her heart, then to her throat as if she needed to stop the next words of admission. She couldn't be in love with him. She looked at the flowers. It hit her that if Mrs. Beabots hadn't given her the flowers, she would have asked to pick some for him.

Because I care.

Fortunately, her landlady's kindness gave her an excuse.

Katia's eyes narrowed. "You can't fool me. I've seen that same look in my own reflection when I worry about Austin. I've always been in love with him, even when I was a kid and my mother became his parents' housekeeper. When I lived in Chicago and we were separated, I never saw that open and deep emotion in my eyes. But I see it in you. If you're not in love with Josh, I'll swear off discount designer stores."

"Don't do that." Violet tried to joke. She wanted to tell Katia the truth, that she was investigating Josh, but her assignment was top security. At the same time, Katia would press her until she beat her down. She had to dodge and weave. "I don't know what I feel. The truth is, Katia, we're from two different worlds. Maybe all I am is a fan."

"You don't like racing all that much."

"I really don't like it now that he crashed. Still, his skill is amazing. He's very talented." She gnawed at her bottom lip. "I keep asking the same question. How long till his number's up?"

"Violet, don't take this to the extreme. Most drivers quit or retire. They do other things."

Violet shook her head. "Other things?" Josh's lifestyle was out of her hometown league. He was a global phenomenon. The roar of the crowd was in his blood. Meanwhile, she'd come to the hospital to see him with garden-picked peonies and roses in a peanut butter jar.

She'd be a fool to let herself fall in love with Josh.

Mirror reflections or not, Violet had never been labeled a fool.

CHAPTER TWENTY

NO STAKEOUT, NO heart-pounding drug bust, no all-night, on-duty stint at the police station had dragged on for Violet like Josh's four hour and twenty minute surgery. When Josh had signed into the hospital, he'd listed Austin and Katia as "family." Interestingly, he had named Violet Hawks as "close friend," so Dr. Evans, the surgeon, reported to all three of them.

He had told them, "Once we got in there, I found several old injuries that Josh had sustained. I repaired them all. He's in recovery now. It should be about an hour before he's awake and they take him up to his room."

Josh would be asleep for at least an hour, so Violet said goodbye to Katia and Austin and walked to the station. She saw her squad car in the parking lot. "They're back."

Racing inside, she was at her desk before she realized she was out of uniform. She didn't care. She went straight to Trent's office and rapped on the door.

"Yes?" Trent answered from inside.

She opened the door. Trent, Sal and Bob were huddled around Trent's desk looking at photos.

"May I ask what happened?" She was surprised at the anticipation that filled her.

"No arrests," Trent replied.

She walked in and looked at the photos. Half the printouts were shots she'd taken and emailed to the station. The others were new. "Who took these?"

"We did. After the perps left," Sal said, tilting his head toward Bob. "He followed them."

"Yeah. For the past three hours. Then I lost them up in Michigan."

"We're guessing they're headed for Detroit."

Violet narrowed her eyes as her mind shunted into detective mode. "You sure? Not west toward Chicago?"

"Not sure." Trent pushed a photo aside. "The license plate is Michigan."

"But it could be a flipper," Bob suggested.

"You mean one of those rotating plates that has Illinois on one side and Michigan on the other?" Violet posed.

"Yep," Bob replied.

"And the trace?"

"Nada."

"Figures," Violet said with a deflated sigh. She'd been the one to get a bead on the plate.

Then it turned out to be bogus. And why wouldn't it be? These were highly organized and professional gangsters.

Trent peered at her, straightened and put his hand on his hip. "I told you to get some rest."

"Oh. That."

"Officer..."

"Sir, I was at the hospital where Josh Stevens underwent surgery this morning."

"And how did it go?" Trent queried.

"Long. Thorough. Successful."

"Excellent. This time I order you to get some rest. Then continue surveillance of Stevens."

"Yes, sir." Violet started to leave. "Should I put my activity this morning in my report?"

Trent didn't look up. "Yes."

"Thank you, sir."

She went to her desk, typed her report quickly and sent it to her boss. She didn't include Katia's observation that she'd fallen in love with Josh.

VIOLET HAD FOLLOWED ORDERS. At home, she'd slept till 8:00 p.m. She washed her face, put on white slacks, a thin aqua turtleneck and white slip-on canvas shoes, and a bit of makeup.

She drove her squad car to the fast food drive-through, then to the hospital.

Visiting hours were over, but family and "close friends" were allowed to visit patients anytime. There were few people in the halls, and one of the night nurses knew Violet from high school.

"Lila, how are you?" Violet asked.

"Great. How's Indian Lake's newest rookie?"

"Oh, thanks," Violet laughed. "But I'm off duty now." Liar. Liar. The words from the Castaways song filled her head.

"Who're you here to see? I didn't see anyone from your family on the patient list."

"Oh. I'm a friend. Josh Stevens."

"Aw, c'mon. You know him?"

"Lila, your 'groupie' vibes are shooting off the top of your head."

"Sorry. I haven't been this way since Boyz II Men were on the scene," she laughed. "I gotta run. See you around, Vi."

"Later."

Violet walked to Josh's room and slowly pushed the door open.

He was asleep, propped up in bed, three pillows behind his head. His chest was bare, but most of his torso was covered in gauze, swabbed with an orangey-red Betadine solution, and his left arm was stabilized in a sling. Huge bandages crossed over his shoulder. She guessed this was where the incision was made. Though the surgery was arthroscopic, Dr. Evans obviously had worked on several areas. Violet couldn't help the flash of anger she felt against Harry who was all too ready to hand-wave all Josh's medical concerns, when he needed even more care than any of them had imagined.

A light above his bed had been dimmed, casting eerie shadows about the room. On the wheeled tray to the side of his bed was the peanut butter jar with the roses and peonies from Mrs. Beabots's garden.

She placed the bag of food and the drink carrier on the tray.

"Josh?"

He didn't move.

With the lightest touch, she smoothed a lock of hair off his forehead. She hadn't noticed how long his eyelashes were before. Looking down on him from this angle, he looked very young and peaceful.

She couldn't help wondering if he'd ever had any peace when he was growing up in the foster homes. Did he have peace now with all the demands from his career and his entourage? Or was this moment of medicated surgical anesthesia the only respite he'd had?

His stomach growled. Her stomach growled in answer.

"Josh, I'm here." She leaned down, placed

her hand over his right hand and gently kissed his forehead.

Without opening his eyes, he whispered, “You missed.”

Josh encircled his fingers around her wrist. “C’mere.”

He kissed her.

His lips were tender and soft. As they lingered, she couldn’t pull away. For a moment, she wondered if he even knew who he was kissing. After all, he could be in the middle of some anesthesia-induced dream.

“Violet…” he said as his kiss grew with eagerness. He dropped her wrist and lifted his hand to her nape, pulling her in for a deeper kiss.

He moaned.

“Josh, I’m hurting you.”

“No, honey. You’re healing this pain.” He captured her mouth again. This time his lips trembled with emotion.

Violet wasn’t sure if the moisture she felt against his cheek were his tears or perspiration. The room was warm.

Or was she warm?

Reluctantly, she pulled away. “How are you, really? Does it hurt?”

“Only when I breathe and move.”

“I’m sorry.”

He stared at her. "Did they tell you how long the surgery was?"

"Nearly four and a half hours."

"Really? Why?"

"Dr. Evans said there were more injuries, Josh. Things that were torn and ruptured from previous accidents."

"Oh. Those."

"You knew about them?"

"Yeah. Kinda."

"And you still raced? Josh, why do you take so many chances with your health? With your life?"

He pressed the back of his head into the pillow as if to put distance between them. He looked at her dubiously. "Look who's asking that question. Turn that finger around. You're the one who puts her life on the line every morning. You're in far more danger on a daily basis than I am."

"You got me there. But the thing is, I've known since I was a kid that I was going to be a detective someday. It's in me. I feel it. I sense things that other people don't. And if I can be part of the force that brings down this, this—" she flipped her hands in the air "—wave of illegal gangs in Indian Lake, I'll be..."

"Happy?" Josh interjected.

"Fulfilled." She smiled.

"And then?"

"Then I could get that detective position in Chicago or even New York, like I told you."

"Oh, my." He grinned broadly with merriment dancing in his eyes.

"What?"

"Admit it. In your way, you need a portion of fame to get you to where you want to go. I admire that in you, Violet. You have ambition. Just like me. So, you see? We're not so different, after all."

"You think?"

"Uh-huh." He reached up, clasped her chin between his forefinger and thumb and gently pulled her toward him. "I especially like how we like kissing each other."

Violet's lips grazed his. "Who said I like it?"

"Please don't argue."

He kissed her sweetly. Then his stomach growled again.

"Josh."

"What?"

She lifted her head away. "I brought you something to eat."

"I'll say." He grinned impishly, then immediately winced. "Sorry. Bad joke. But I do like the way you taste."

"I meant dinner. I haven't eaten, either."

"Yeah? What is it?" He looked past her at the drive-through bag.

"Your choice. Healthy or unhealthy?"

"Unhealthy."

"Why am I not surprised." She chuckled. "Burger. Fries. Milk? Water?"

"I better leave the hard stuff till later. I'll have the water." He traced his finger along her jawline. "Vi, thanks for coming."

"I wouldn't be anywhere else," she replied, surprised at her own admission.

"You mean that?"

Her hesitation lasted a nanosecond. "I do."

"Good. Then will you promise me something?"

"Uh." She eyed him.

"Always the untrusting cop."

"Josh…"

His face was serious. His eyes pleading. "Stay with me tonight. I don't want to be alone."

She inhaled. This was the first time any man had asked her to sleep over. Granted it was in his hospital room.

"I'll stay," she answered, then turned and opened the food bag. "Oh, good. They gave me plastic utensils. I'll cut up the cheeseburger for you. It'll be easier to eat."

"You're not going to feed me?"

She jerked her head around and glared at him. "Don't push it."

"Kidding. I was kidding." Then he asked, "Where did the flowers come from?"

"The flowers are from Mrs. Beabots."

"No one's ever given me flowers in a peanut butter jar before. I kinda like it."

"Stop kidding."

"I'm not. It's homey. And you brought them."

"Yeah. I was in a hurry."

"A hurry." He paused as his eyes locked on hers. "To see me?"

She stopped cutting the cheeseburger. "Uh-huh."

"Well, well." He smiled faintly and laid his head back on the pillow. "Suddenly, I'm really tired."

"My fault. All this chatter."

"I like your chatter."

He closed his eyes. "Maybe a nap before I eat." He shivered. "Cold."

Violet put the burger back and pulled the extra sheet and thin cotton blanket up to his chest, carefully placing the covers over his sling and bandages.

Violet pulled the large faux leather chair closer to Josh's bed. She took out the black plastic container of salad, opened the packet of raspberry vinaigrette and drizzled it over the field greens. She ate, watching Josh sleep. She also noted that he didn't move his arm, legs or head. She didn't know much, but in an academy-recommended six week course in emergency medical treatment she'd taken her first year, she'd learned that injured victims who remained very still were in a great deal of pain.

Though Josh was asleep and the anesthetic was still doing its magic, his body was in discomfort.

And how long have you been in pain, Josh? What pushes you to race when you know you shouldn't or that you're putting your health at risk? Fear of failure? A need for success? Or is it something deeper? Something darker?

She finished her salad and put the empty plastic container in the trash. She had just finished the milk when Josh roused once again.

His eyes opened slowly. He looked surprised.

"Hi," she said, as she rose from the chair and stood by the bed. She touched his cheek. He was cooler than she'd expected. "Can I get you another blanket?"

He laid his hand over his stomach. "I'm really hungry."

"The burger and fries are cold. Sorry," she said.

"I'll brave it." When he tried to sit up, he groaned.

"Here," she said, grabbing the pillows. "I'll put these behind the small of your back. That'll help."

Violet plumped the pillows and helped him sit up straighter. Then she raised the back of the bed.

"Better," he said.

Violet took out the burger and fries and placed them on the inside top cover of the second salad. "In case you change your mind, I got a second salad and three different kinds of dressing."

Josh dipped a French fry in the ketchup. His stomach growled loudly. He took several bites of the burger. "Mmm," he said with his mouth full.

She handed him a paper napkin. "I told them to hold the onion."

"But I love onion."

"I figured that, too. But I didn't want to be kissing you with onion breath."

His hand halted as he was about to bite into another fry. "You were planning to kiss me?"

"Uh-huh."

"When you were at the drive-through?"

"Uh-huh." She took the paper off the straw and put it through the opening in the plastic cover on the container of water. "Is that bad?"

"No." He shrugged his shoulder slightly and winced. He rolled his eyes at himself.

"Are you okay?" she asked, putting the water back on the tray. "You look really pale."

Josh slid his hand over his stomach. "I feel cold again."

"I'll cover you..."

"No!" His hand flew to his mouth. "I'm gonna be sick."

Violet whirled around, grabbed a blue plastic vomit bag from the top of the night stand and held it up to Josh's mouth just as he threw up into it. He gagged. Spat. Gagged again.

He nodded. "Okay."

Violet handed him the water. "Here, take a sip and spit. I'll find a toothbrush and call the nurse."

Violet hit the call button and went to the bathroom to find a toothbrush and toothpaste. Just as Josh had put the toothbrush into his mouth and made the first swipe, Lila came in.

"Mr. Stevens, are you all right?"

"I threw up," he said with the toothbrush dangling from his mouth.

"Was there bile?" Lila asked.

"No." Violet shook her head. "Cheeseburger."

Lila looked from Josh, who took the toothbrush out of his mouth, to Violet. "That's what was in the bag you brought in?"

"Yeah," Violet replied sheepishly. "Not good, huh?"

"Uh, no. I'll bring some gelatin and lemon-lime soda. Tomorrow morning he can move to the hard stuff like toast and tea." Lila took the barf bag, frowned at them both and left.

Violet moved back to Josh's side. She couldn't help smiling. "I'm so sorry."

"Well, there's one thing about all this, Violet."

"And that is what?"

"You've certainly seen me at my worst." He held up his index finger. "First, you arrest me and put me in jail. Then you witness the worst crash of my life. Now, you've seen me cut up, stitched up and throwing up."

"It's been—different."

"Not disastrous?"

"No."

"That's good." He held her gaze with so much sincerity that Violet found her doubts being erased.

He tried to reach behind his head and move the pillow, but she was faster than he was. "Don't do that. Let me help," she scolded.

He leaned his head back again. "I'm still

more tired than hungry, I guess." He closed his eyes.

"I can imagine. You get some rest. Uh, maybe I should go. I'll see you tomorrow."

She started to gather her things.

"You said you'd stay."

"You really want me to?"

"Yes."

"Okay. I'll be here when you wake up."

"Promise?"

"I promise."

Violet sat down in the chair and laid her head on the side of Josh's bed so that he could touch her each time he awoke. Violet didn't have much experience with caregiving, but she did know that if she'd just had surgery in a strange town, she would like to know someone cared enough to quell her fears and spend the night with her.

Violet had never thought about being a special someone before, but now she was filled with an unfamiliar warmth. She felt at peace, which was just as unfamiliar as the warmth. She had no idea if this was love, but if it was, she suddenly realized that if it was taken from her, the loss would be painful.

CHAPTER TWENTY-ONE

JOSH OPENED HIS eyes and saw Violet's sleeping head on the gurney. He touched her hair, amazed at its silky feel. "Hey, you."

She lifted her head and opened her eyes. Amazing. Clear and bright upon first awakening.

"You stayed with me."

"I did." She leaned back and stared at him. Her smile was faint, but it felt like sunshine resting on his face. "Oh!" She looked at her watch.

"What?"

"I'm late for work. I have a meeting in fifteen minutes."

"Good thing we're only six blocks from the station."

"Good thing." She grinned.

Just then an orderly brought a breakfast tray and placed it on the swivel tray table.

Violet stood. "The nurses will be back in a few minutes."

"Yeah. Go. Will I see you later?"

"Sure. I'll text you."

"Okay."

She stood and moved toward the door, still looking at him. She wasn't out of the room and he missed her. How was that possible?

"Bye."

Josh lifted his hand to wave, then dropped it. "Don't go," he whispered, but there was no one to hear him.

FOR A GUY who prided himself on remaining calm in a crisis, Josh's frustration level was volcanic. "I can tie my own shoes," he grumbled as Lila tied his running shoe.

"Not today you don't."

"I'm sorry. Truly. It's just that I've never been this helpless before."

"According to your history, you've never had surgery before. Not even a tonsillectomy," Lila said as she stood. She stared at him stone-faced. "Now, you gonna remember all the pointers I gave you about showering?"

Josh blushed and kept his eyes down. "The rope! You mean the rope."

"Put the rope on before you take the sling off. Make sure there's a safety bar in the shower to catch you if you start to slip."

"Check. Austin had a guy put one in yesterday."

The hospital room door opened and Austin walked in. "Hey, buddy. They tell me you're ready to go."

Josh picked up his release papers from the nightstand. "I'm free!"

Austin looked at the sling. "Not quite."

Lila smiled at Austin. "Hello, Mr. McCreary. I'll get his wheelchair and be right back."

Josh held up his hand. "That's not necessary. I can make it on my own."

"Hospital rules," Lila replied, and left.

Josh looked at Austin. "Rules. You think there's any place where there aren't rules?"

"Outer space?"

"Nah," they chorused, then laughed.

JOSH WAS AMAZED he'd slept the entire afternoon. When he awoke, he opened his laptop and found dozens of emails from Harry, Paul, his crew members, his sponsor, the heads of his two fan clubs and a couple old girlfriends. He turned on his cell phone.

Harry had left seven voice mails. Paul had left two.

Blessedly, Katia and Austin had telephoned them both with the news that he was out of surgery and doing well. Harry wanted media dates booked during his recuperation. Paul wished him well and asked if he'd received the flowers.

Still dressed from the morning, Josh left the guest room and walked into the main hall of Austin's family mansion. He smelled cooking garlic, olive oil and tomatoes.

"Italian?"

He glanced in the dining room and saw the table set for four. In the center was an enormous arrangement of roses in red, yellow, pink, orange and white.

"Spectacular," he said as he walked into the kitchen where Austin's housekeeper, Daisy, was taking a pie out of the oven.

"Hello, Daisy."

Gingerly, she placed the pie, double crusted with fluted edges, on a rack. Then spun around and shook her oven mitts at him. "Don't ever do that again! Guest or no guest. Injured or not, I'll tan your fanny. You scared the bejesus out of me. I could have dropped the pie."

"I'm sorry," he replied, looking at the delicious treat. He looked back at Daisy. "I hear the blueberries around here are spectacular."

"They are. But it's too early for them. By the end of June, Katia and I will spend hours picking them. Austin loves anything with blueberries."

"So, she picks them for him."

"Yes."

"That's sweet." He smiled and felt the warmth of it all the way to his toes. He wondered if Violet ever went blueberry picking. It seemed like a thing Violet would do. Like staying all night by his side in the hospital with him. She wasn't family. But she acted like she was. Or wanted to be.

Had he become someone important to her? She had lots of friends—and he understood why. She had a way of gathering everyone in, not just to protect them, but to help and care. Even save them?

Save him?

"I'd like to try picking blueberries sometime," he said.

Daisy looked at his sling. "Then we will." She put the mitt down on the counter.

Josh watched her face soften with a smile. Daisy was in her mid-sixties, but she had the energy of a child. She wore her blond hair short, and there was no lack of glittering costume jewelry hanging around her neck or dangling at her ears. Her blue eyes literally twinkled.

"Why, thank you, Daisy." He glanced back to the dining room. "I saw there were four for dinner. Will you be sharing that pie with us?"

"Nope. Mr. Austin invited a guest." She winked at him. "Everyone is on the terrace.

Cocktails are out there. Though you might want to take it easy, you bein' all shot up with ether and all."

"I don't think they use ether anymore."

"Well, it was something strong, judging by all the work they did on you."

"Yeah. It was somethin'."

Josh walked through the French doors to the terrace, wondering who Austin and Katia had invited for dinner, and pulled to a dead stop.

"Violet?"

She had her back to him. Her thick dark hair swirled around her shoulders as she turned in the chair. She wore a white flowered sundress with skinny pink straps, and there were pink jeweled sandals on her feet. He hadn't noticed before that she was tan, but he could see that she'd obviously been out in the sun. Or was that from her day at the race?

Her makeup made her eyes smolder, and she'd added pink lipstick and pink hoop earrings.

He was tongue-tied. Astounded. All he could do was stare.

She rose from the chair, a look of concern on her face, and walked toward him. A gentle warm breeze carried the scent of jasmine and rose across the terrace.

Or was that her?

Josh had heard that there were moments in a man's life that caused the senses to overtake reason. One of his pit crew had told him that on the day he'd met his future wife, it was as if lightning had struck him. He knew.

She's the one, Josh thought. But how could she be? To truly love someone, you had to trust them. He wished he knew where her job ended and where "they" began. Because there was a "they." He felt it as strongly as the triumph on the last lap of a race when he knew he'd win. His heart nearly spun out of his chest at those moments. That was how it was now with Violet.

"Are you okay? Dizzy? Gonna throw up again?" Violet asked, putting her hand on his good arm.

"Huh? No. I'm fine."

"You don't look fine."

"Okay. You're right," he replied, not taking his eyes from her face. "I'm a little out of it. Must be the meds."

"And you haven't eaten a thing from what Katia tells me."

"Hey, buddy," Austin said from his chair, holding up a tall glass of what looked like lemonade. "You're probably dehydrated. C'mon over and get some iced tea. Or an Arnold Palmer."

"Sounds good," Josh replied, still looking at Violet.

She took his arm. "I'll put lots of ice in it for you," she said as they walked together.

He sat down in a wrought-iron chair next to Katia. Violet sat to his right. His uninjured arm. He hoped she wanted to hold his hand.

And why was that important to him now?

Katia lifted a platter with bruschetta. "I made these very light for you, Josh. Mango, pineapple, avocado. Hint of basil. They shouldn't upset your stomach. And the fruit has sugar. It should help you get back in the pink."

"In the pink." He looked at Violet. "You're beautiful. Er, tonight."

"Thanks. It's Katia's dress. And the shoes. I had a good time playing in her closet."

Katia smiled. "I had a blast. We should do it more often."

Violet looked down at the dress. "I love pretty clothes, but haven't had much time for them." She looked up at Josh. "Katia's going to take me to some designer outlets."

Violet poured a tall glass of iced tea, adding a sprig of mint. She handed it to him. "The mint is from Mrs. Beabots's garden. I brought some basil for Katia, too."

"Are the roses in the dining room from you, too?"

Austin laughed. "Oh, no. Those are from your attorney, Paul. Harry sent a fruit and cheese basket. Did you see the flowers in the living room?"

"No."

"Seventeen arrangements," Katia said, sipping her iced tea. "I haven't seen that many flowers in this house since our wedding day."

"That's right! You got married here. Sorry to have missed it."

He turned to Violet. "I was racing in Dubai."

Then he said, "That must have been—wonderful. Married in your family home." Josh gazed at Violet, wondering what she'd think of a wedding at home.

"It was," Austin replied, taking Katia's hand and kissing her palm. "A day to remember. Including the near tornado that ruined the garden reception."

"Austin!" Katia retorted. "It was marvelous. We moved everything inside and had dinner in the house. The lights went out. We lit a lot of candles." She laughed.

Josh watched a bead of sweat run down the side of his glass. "I don't have a family home. Just condos where I crash for a couple weeks before flying out to another city."

Violet reached over and touched his hand.

"I'm sure they're marvelous. All those exotic locations."

"Yeah."

Daisy walked out the door and smacked two huge knives together. "Dinner's ready!"

Everyone laughed at the show.

Katia rose. "We better get in there and eat before she feeds it to the neighbor's dogs."

Josh looked at Katia, horrified. "Would she do that?"

Austin nodded. "She's been known to."

DAISY'S ITALIAN DINNER, which consisted of vegetable lasagna, grilled salmon, plain angel-hair pasta with olive oil for Josh's "delicate" stomach, salad, bread and balsamic dipping sauce, was more than filling.

However, after dinner, Austin declared that he positively had to have Louise Railton's salted caramel ice cream with his blueberry pie. While Daisy cleaned the kitchen and Austin and Katia drove to the Louise House Ice Cream Shop, Josh took Violet back out to the terrace.

He lit a citronella candle, and they sat at the table sipping decaffeinated coffee.

"I do feel better after eating."

"I'm glad."

He chuckled. “Luckily, no queasiness. You won’t have to run for a barf bag.”

“Darn.” She snapped her fingers. “And I had an extra one in my purse.”

He swiped his forehead. “That was so embarrassing. I apologize.”

“I’m the one who fed you the cheeseburger. You couldn’t help it.”

He rested his eyes on her. Not a hard thing to do. “You know, you are so different when you’re out of uniform.”

She stiffened. “How so?”

“You know. Rules. Regs. Laws. Arresting people.”

She tilted her head back on her shoulders and gripped the chair arms. “You’re going to hold that against me forever, aren’t you.”

“No. I’m not.”

“Look, Josh. There’s truth to what you say. I’m a cop. I’m sworn to uphold the law. I like going after bad guys. I want to make the world safe, or at least my little world here in Indian Lake. I want to be the best detective this town has ever seen.”

“I still wish your job wasn’t so dangerous.”

Violet stared at her coffee cup, gnawing on her bottom lip. “We both live with danger sewn to our heels. I think you race for thrills and fame. I’m trying to save lives.”

Josh tapped his forefinger on the table as he considered her point of view. She wasn't all wrong, but she wasn't all right, either. "You only know the tip-sheet facts about me, Violet."

She folded her arms over her chest. "Then why don't you tell me?"

Moving his eyes from her stern expression to the flickering candle he said, "You know my parents died and that I lived in a series of foster homes. In a way, I had it easier than some of the other kids. In other ways, it was worse."

"How was it worse?"

"I knew my parents. Knew they were good people and that we loved each other. We did lots of things together. Went to the state fair every year. My dad taught me to ride my bike, and Mom showed me how to measure the ingredients to make chocolate chip cookies. Not just slice them from a pre-made roll. She was warm and always had a hug for me."

He smiled at her. "I don't race for the thrills or fame. I feel like I've been racing against death all my life. When I'm out there on a track or coming around to the straightaway and I hit it one more time, trying to find that speed that will lift me off, deep inside me, I feel this 'closeness' to my parents. There's been times when I actually see my mother again. I can

feel her arms around me. I hear my dad sometimes. I know he's right there. Just a few feet away. I have things to say to them. And I go faster. It's like I'm in an altered reality." He didn't have a death wish, he just wanted to be closer to them.

"Josh..."

"When I drive close to death, I feel I'm with my parents."

"So, if you keep racing against the devil, you feel you will heal your grief?"

"Yeah. I do."

She dropped her arms to her sides and leaned forward. "There's something you're still not telling me, Josh. I can feel it."

He turned his coffee cup in the saucer, but he didn't drink it. He barely nodded as he felt his eyes sting and his head pound. How could she know him this well? Was she the friend he'd been looking for, the kind of person he could count on? The cops knew about him and Diego or now Miguel, his alias. Josh'd be a fool if he trusted her completely. Like his car revving at the starting line, Josh was caught between his heart, which wanted to open up more to her, and his head, which slammed on the brakes.

Violet put her hand on his good shoulder. It was the lightest touch, but he could feel her caring seeping through his skin, consoling him.

"I've never told anyone," he said as a burn moved up from his throat and cut off his words.

And I probably shouldn't now.

"You don't have to tell me if you don't want to, Josh. But I'm not going to run to the media and expose you. And if it's illegal…"

"Illegal? Why would you think that?" He'd been right to play it cool with her.

"My training, I guess. I don't know where you're going. Did someone hurt you? Is that it?"

"No. Not directly." He could barely swallow. But for the first time in his life the words had to come out. He'd kept them entombed for too many years. "Sometimes, my parents would get into nasty fights and when they did, I hid in the basement or my closet. I had earphones I stuck on my ears and pretended to sing along with Motley Crüe. I didn't have any other family I could talk to. I didn't know what to do."

"What did they argue about?"

"Me."

"You? Why?"

He sucked in a deep breath as much for courage as to still the rapid beating of his heart. "They were kids when I was born. Sometimes my dad would get drunk. I heard him say he didn't want me. That I was a mistake."

"Oh, my God, Josh."

He didn't look at Violet, but he sensed that she was crying. Empathy for him. That was a new feeling. He almost didn't know how to process it. "My mother wanted me. I heard her say that whenever they fought. The night they died, they left the house fighting. My dad went out to the car and backed out of the drive. My mother clung to the door. She finally got it open and got in. He peeled away. Fast. I was the last thing on their minds. I was at the living room window watching them, and I saw another car swerving toward them, only a half mile away. No one else was hurt, thank the Lord."

"And you've felt responsible for their deaths ever since?" she asked.

He put his hand over his face. He felt his own tears. He hadn't known he was crying.

"Josh." Violet pulled his head to her shoulder.

He nestled his face in the crook of her throat. He put his good arm around her. "Thank you, Violet."

She rubbed his back, soothing him. Giving him comfort.

He kissed her neck and wiped his cheek in her satiny hair. He kissed her ear. "Violet..."

She kissed him then with lips that told him he was good and clean, and that he should let go of the guilt he'd carried in his soul all these years. Her hands pressed against his cheeks as she held his face. She kissed him over and over. His eyelids, his forehead. His lips.

She told him wordlessly that he was not to blame.

That he was wanted.

There was so much about her that mesmerized him. He knew Harry and Paul didn't trust her, that the Diego issue hung over them. And she had an uncanny ability to wrest personal information from him, details he'd never shared with anyone. It was her compassion that drew him in. He knew it was impossible to have a connection like this so soon, but though Violet was a cop, she listened with her heart like a confidante.

He liked that she was an enigma. She fascinated him.

Can't let that happen.

I have to focus.

As she slipped her fingers across his cheek, he felt his resolve melting. He wanted to believe she might trust him enough to confide in him. And if she did, would that mean that she loved him? Or was she using him for her job?

DAY THREE OF Josh's recovery, Violet texted him and asked him to share lunch with her.

She was operating on Trent's orders to stay close to him.

"You don't mind riding in my squad car, do you? It's the only vehicle I have access to."

"It does feel kinda weird being in the front seat."

"Sorry." She smiled widely.

He gazed at her. "No, you're not. I think you're glad you arrested me."

"I am now." It was true.

"Where are we going?" Josh asked as they passed the courthouse with its red sandstone clock tower.

"My secret place," Violet said. "I figured since you didn't know your way around Indian Lake all that well, you might enjoy taking a break from Austin's house and Daisy's marvelous cooking."

He chuckled. "So, you're telling me your cooking isn't great?"

"I'm more of a grab and run kinda gal," she replied. "But I went all out for us today."

"Wow. Thanks."

She snickered as she turned off Indian Lake Boulevard on the road that circled the lake. "I love this drive. And the trails are the best."

"That's right, you run."

"Sure do."

"When is best for you? Morning or evening?"

"My favorite is sunset. But because of my job, I have to hit it in the predawn hours."

"Once the doc says I'm healed enough, I'd love to run with you."

"You're on."

Violet drove past the parking area for the beach, past the boat launch and toward the north, which at one time had been a dense orchard with apple and cherry trees. The area was ringed with blue spruce and dotted with naturally grown hundred-year-old oak, maple and black walnut trees, which created a shadowed cool woods.

English ivy, springy moss and tiny wildflowers carpeted the ground.

"This is amazing," Josh said as she parked the car under a blooming low-limbed Japanese magnolia tree.

"Are you up to walking? There's a stone bridge I want to show you."

"Sure." He unbuckled his seat belt and opened the door.

Violet went to the trunk and pulled out a red department store Christmas bag with green ribbon handles.

Josh laughed. "Aren't we rushing the season?"

"I don't have a picnic basket. And since this was a last-minute idea—" she lifted the bag and grinned "—I improvised."

They walked through dappled sunlight as robins and blue jays swooped overhead. A yellow butterfly lit on an apple tree branch and waited for them to pass before flying away.

"Can you hear the water? The brook is over here. Follow me, it's not far, but I don't want to tire you out," she said, skirting around a tangle of low-growing vines.

"I hear it," he mumbled.

A few steps more and they came to the bridge. The sun threaded through the tree limbs, illuminating the water as it slid over moss-covered rocks in the stream.

"There's a natural spring not far from here. The water is cold and crystal clear. I adore this place."

"How did you find it?"

"Isabelle. She paints water sprites and fairies. She claims she sees them. Or did, when she was young."

Josh walked to the middle of the bridge and looked down at the iridescent water. The sun glinted off the surface, refracting light. Coming down the stream and cascading over the rocks was a lily pad. A dragonfly skittered off the surface of the water.

Violet stood next to Josh and watched the water. "What do you think?"

"It's magical."

"It is, isn't it?"

"Do you come here often?"

"Not so much anymore. I'm too busy."

He turned to her, adjusting his sling at his neck. He looked past her and then to either side. "There's no one here."

"Few people trek back here anymore." She leaned forward teasingly. "Very private."

He touched her arm and slid his hand to her shoulder. "And you wanted to be alone with me?"

Violet's ulterior motives pricked at her. She did want to be alone with him—even more than she wanted information. She felt her heart opening to him, but her mind quelled it with caution. "I've always felt this place was healing. That's a kind of magic, isn't it?"

"It is."

"I thought it would help you."

Josh pulled her closer, their noses nearly touching. "Thank you for showing it to me. I can only think of one other thing that will help me as much."

"And that is?" She lowered her eyes as his lips sought hers. His kiss was tender. Violet was surprised again by him. When he kissed her, she felt as if she were the only person in the world to him. Nothing about him was boastful or egotistical.

When he pulled away, he rested his forehead against hers and touched her cheek. “Just so you know, you don’t need any magic to bewitch me, Violet.”

His admission stunned her so much she lost her footing and fell toward him, the red bag hitting his thigh. “I’m so sorry. Did I hurt you?”

“No, but what’s in the bag? Rocks?”

“Oh,” she answered, looking into the bag. “I brought the fixin’s for lunch.”

“Let me guess. Peanut butter and jelly?”

“How did you know?”

“When you arrested me, I thought I smelled peanut butter on your breath.”

“That was…observant.”

“I’m a racer. I pay attention to very tiny details,” he replied, kissing the tip of her nose. “Got anything else in there? In case I’m not a PB and J fan?”

“Uh, yeah. As a matter of fact. Turkey and guac. On pumpernickel.”

“Now you’re talkin’.” He spied two large boulders at the end of the bridge. “Let’s sit there where we can still see the water.”

"You don't want to go back to the picnic area? There's tables..."

He took the bag from her, gesturing toward the boulders. "I don't want to break the spell."

Violet didn't want to admit it to herself but she was a spellbound by Josh. Try as she might to focus on her duty as a detective, to probe Josh for any intel, she liked being with him.

But the truth was that she felt ripped through the middle using Josh to advance her career.

Her heart wouldn't let her walk away from her job...or from Josh.

Inevitably, Josh would discover that she'd been investigating him. Would he think that she'd been using him to get ahead? That was what nearly every person in Josh's world did to him. She was no better.

Whoever said that falling in love was like a dream had no idea of the nightmare she was living.

CHAPTER TWENTY-TWO

DAY FOUR OF Josh's recovery, the ILPD amped the tension. Violet sat in Trent Davis's office and listened while the rest of the team discussed her progress as if she was invisible.

"As a person of interest, Stevens should be followed 24/7," Sal Paluzzi said.

"That's what I'm doing," Violet said, but Bob Paxton started talking over her.

"That farmhouse is the key, not Stevens," he argued. "I'd give anything to get in there..."

"Stop!" Trent snapped. "There's no law against storing cleaning products in one's garage. If there was, I'd be up on charges."

"That's because you're never home long enough to help your wife use them." Sal chuckled.

"Officer Hawks—" Trent turned to her "—when do you see Stevens next?"

"This afternoon. We're going out to the Barzonni farm to look at the land Gina is donating to the new Foster Child Foundation."

"You and who else?"

"Katia and Austin McCreary. Sarah and Luke Bosworth. Luke is putting in a bid for the construction."

Trent folded his hands on the desk and peered at her. "How close are you with Stevens? Has he confided anything about Miguel Garcia yet?"

"In addition to the facts that I've uncovered and given you, yes, sir. I know that he felt responsible for Miguel. He hasn't told me in so many words, but I believe he's bailed him out of scrapes before. If that's true, and Garcia is in the area, and we all believe that he's near, I have a plan to smoke him out."

Bob Paxton started to take a sip of coffee and slowly lowered the Styrofoam cup. "And that is?"

"Today when we go out to view the land that Gina is donating, I've invited my brother-in-law, Scott Abbott, to accompany us to the farm. I've asked him to bring his camera and write an article about Josh recuperating here in Indian Lake. Since this article is not about my blunder and Josh's arrest, Josh will easily navigate any misgivings from his manager."

"The manager is a problem?" Trent asked.

"From what I've observed—always. But Josh does keep him in line. Scott will publish the article in the newspaper. I also know he sends his articles to the *Chicago Tribune*, the *South Bend Tribune*, *Indianapolis Star* and other local newspapers. If Miguel is anywhere between Chicago and Kalamazoo and sees the article, he'll see Josh's photograph. I'm working on having ESPN pick it up, too."

"Josh's manager should hire you," Bob said.

Trent's expression was granite, but Violet detected appreciation in his eyes.

Violet continued. "I know that Austin has security cameras around his house. If Miguel tries to contact Josh, we'll have it on video."

"Can you bug his phone?" Bob asked.

"I can try to get a warrant," she replied, though the thought caused her to squirm. She hated this, spying on Josh, orchestrating a newspaper article about him to smoke out a criminal, bugging his phone. And not just because Josh sent her texts that bordered on romantic. The invasion of privacy felt wrong.

"But sir," Violet said, "we have no evidence to prove that Stevens is involved with Garcia's criminal activity. I'd rather not bug his phone."

"Excellent work, Officer Hawks. And I admire your integrity."

Violet expelled relief.

Trent dismissed the team.

VIOLET WORE CROPPED skinny jeans, a lavender sleeveless knit top and white sneakers as she walked with Josh, Katia and Austin up the grassy hill on the south end of the Barzonni farm. Mrs. Beabots rode in a golf cart with Gina and Sam. Sarah carried two rolls of blueprints, while Luke stopped to take photos of the geography. Scott followed at the back of the group, snapping action shots of Josh.

It was a breathtakingly beautiful June day. The grass was green and velvety. Along the east side of the tract marched a line of Bradford Pear trees, their blossoms almost gone. Beneath them were naturalized irises and late blooming narcissi.

Gina Barzonni parked the golf cart, while Mrs. Beabots got out.

"Here at the top," Gina began, "is where the building should be. As you can see—" she pointed to the north "—and Sarah will confirm this, I think there's enough flat land here for the building. I was thinking we could have gardens and playground equipment there to the west."

"What about parking?" Josh asked.

"At the bottom of the hill?"

"That's a lot of plowing in winter," Josh observed.

"Anytime there's a parking lot, it's a lot of snowplowing," Violet added. "At least the hill has a long slope and it's not steep."

"Not at all," Gina said. "Which is why we couldn't plant anything here. The drainage is fast. The land here won't hold water."

"Which is perfect for a structure," Sarah commented. "No water in the basement."

"Sarah, Mrs. Beabots, come with me over here. I want to show you this particular hundred-and-fifty-year-old oak. It's one of my son, Rafe's, favorites. I was thinking that in the shade of this tree, we could build a separate library or a movie house for the kids. Nothing big."

"You have been thinking, haven't you, Gina?" Mrs. Beabots said.

"It was Sam's idea."

Josh reached for Violet's hand. "Thank you for suggesting I come along today."

"I think it's important you hear all the plans. And feel free to jump in when you want."

"I like the idea of a movie house. What if we had other separate activity houses? Like little casitas? I can see a series of little tile-roofed houses and in each one, the kids learn a skill. Botany. Cooking. Baking. Carpentry."

"And car mechanics?" She'd meant it as a tease, but his face was serious.

"Yes. Exactly. I could teach them."

"You? Would come here to teach the kids?" Violet couldn't help but gush. Her heart swelled in her chest. She imagined Isabelle's kids, Bella and Michael. They were always eager to learn. And Bella loved art and painting just like Isabelle. It was all Violet could do to keep her eyes from welling. "We should have a little art studio. Kids love to paint."

"They do." He smiled. "And what about music? They should have instruments and a teacher."

"There's a girl who was in my high school class, Tara. She teaches. Sarah has taught piano, too."

Josh put his arm around her shoulder. "I can see so much potential here, Violet—for the kids and the parents."

She hadn't expected this much enthusiasm from him. She could tell from the light in his eyes and the way he surveyed the property, he was seeing the future for these kids. Maybe he was reliving a bit of his past, as well. Each time she was with him, a new facet of him was revealed.

Yet, even this outing was underscored by the fact that the police believed they could use Josh to get to Miguel. She had to stay on target. "You've always been like this, haven't you? Helping others. Like your friend Miguel."

He kept his eyes on the horizon. "I tried. Often I've thought he was a lost cause."

"Lost? You don't hear from him?"

"No." He turned, his eyes no longer open and trusting. "Why would I?"

She shrugged. "I was just curious."

"You sure?"

"Yeah." She tore her eyes from him. Deflecting his thoughts. "I was thinking about Scott and Isabelle's children," she said truthfully. "How lucky they are to have loving parents. The kids here, they'll need more than art and music and cars. They'll need people who care." She looked back. "People like you, Josh."

Josh started to reply when Scott jogged up. "Hey, guys! Can I get a shot of you both?" He held up his wide-angle-lens camera.

"No," Josh said.

He whispered to Violet, "Harry wants me to keep my activities, all of them, dialed down."

Scott lowered the camera and shook his head. "This isn't for the paper. It's for me and Isabelle and the kids. Kind of a family portrait thing."

"Family..." Josh's voice trailed off. "Okay."

Violet said, "Try to cut Josh's sling in the pictures. I doubt he wants a reminder of the accident."

"No." Josh smiled. "It's like a badge of courage. You can shoot the sling."

"Cool." Scott took photos. "So, Josh. What do you think of these visionary plans of Mrs. Beabots and her committee?"

"On the record? I think they're what every community across the country should consider. Today, our need is greater than it's ever been. We can't all be foster parents, like Violet tells me you are, but we all can care for kids who don't have a family. I should know. I was one of these kids. I was moved from one home to another, and most times, I was simply the means to another government check the foster parents could cash. I would have given anything to have a place like this to come to."

Scott walked up and shook Josh's hand. "You really are amazing."

"No, Scott. You are. I wonder how different my life would have been if a man like you had stepped in to be my dad."

Scott cleared his throat. "Thanks."

Their raw emotions scraped at Violet's suspicion and distrust.

She wanted to believe in Josh Stevens.

Scott shook Josh's hand one more time. "I promised your manager, Harry, I'd send him my copy before it goes to press. I'd better get to it."

CHAPTER TWENTY-THREE

"So, HOW AM I doin', Doc?" Josh asked Dr. Evans as he got his blue button-down shirt back on under his sling. He stuck his right arm into the sleeve, pulled it up and started buttoning the shirt one-handed.

Dr. Evans typed his findings into a laptop. "Better than I'd expected given the amount of repair we had to do. And don't you dare ask when you can start driving."

"I wasn't going to."

"Like heck you weren't. It's all over your face."

"Well," Josh demurred, "I wasn't thinking about racing. Just driving my car. I feel pretty good after ten of the most relaxing days of my life."

"Yeah?" Dr. Evans stopped typing. "Maybe it's our small-town lifestyle."

"It's not that. In fact, I can't believe how busy I've been. I barely get a nap."

"Don't tell your doctor that."

"Oops."

Dr. Evans spun around on his stool. "Six weeks from the day of surgery, Josh, and no sooner. Twelve weeks before you think about racing. And I mean *think* about it. I'd like to see you lay off till next year."

"If I tell that to my manager, you'll have me as an inpatient, not an outpatient. And I'm not kidding."

"Neither am I." Dr. Evans stood. "I'm hoping you take your rehab seriously and spend a good three or four months with a therapist. Yes, you are healing faster than most. You're very strong and surprisingly healthy."

"Why surprisingly?"

Dr. Evans shrugged his shoulders. "I figured you for late nights, partying..."

Josh held up his palm. "Stop right there. I've never done drugs. Ever. I despise them. Never smoked. The only thing I drink is a light beer or glass of wine, and not often. My duty to my crew and sponsors is to keep healthy. That's why this accident has upset them so much. Sure, they get their regular salaries while I recuperate, but if I don't race, there are no bonuses. And there's the fear that I may not be one hundred percent afterward. We're a team. I can't let them down." He banged the fist of his uninjured arm on the exam table.

"Will you listen to what you're saying? You

just told me you're busy here, but you're relaxed. Not stressed. The second you talk about your racing life, your gestures are erratic and forceful. Words fly from your mouth."

"What are you sayin'?"

"If I didn't know better, I'd say you're at a crossroads, Josh. Maybe this wasn't so much an accident as a life warning to you. Think about where you're going." He started for the door. "In the meantime, hire a driver. Walk. No driving or even jogging till the sling comes off."

"Got it."

"See you in two weeks," Dr. Evans said, and left.

Josh hopped down from the examination table and finished buttoning his shirt. He tried to adjust the sling.

"Darn. It's not sitting right."

But then, little "sat right" for Josh at the moment.

Not since he'd gotten the phone call from Diego.

Josh leaned against the exam table, remembering Diego's words.

"*Hermano*," Diego began, but Josh cut him off.

"Fancy hearing from you after all this time. I

guess you heard about my accident. Seriously, I'm touched you'd call to check on me."

"You crashed?"

Josh felt a pang of disappointment.

"At the race," he explained.

"Oh. Sorry. But you've got a beautiful new girlfriend. I saw the photo in the newspaper."

The twist in Josh's heart dug deeper. Clearly, all Diego wanted was information. He didn't care about Josh, and whatever brotherly love there once might have been between them had vanished.

"Don't give me that, Diego. I haven't heard from you in forever and now suddenly you call me? What do you want? Money?"

"The name's Miguel now. And I have plenty of money," Miguel boasted.

"I'll bet you do. Trafficking drugs."

"You know this because your new *hermosa novia* is a cop."

Josh had swallowed hard. Miguel was digging for information. "I don't have a girlfriend."

That was the truth. And Josh already knew he would hide the fact that he'd been in contact with Miguel from his not-girlfriend. He couldn't tell Violet and put her at risk.

Every time he was with her, he felt sad when their meeting was over and began counting the hours till he saw her again—even though he still didn't entirely trust her motives. Violet's boundless compassion for people was something new to him. Sure, he provided for his employees and team, but Violet had a way of assuring total strangers that no matter the problem, everything would turn out all right. Those were the words his mother used to say to him when he trembled during thunderstorms. Violet's reassurances flowed from her like a melody.

His mother had once said that when you felt love from another human being, it was an angel's song.

"Miguel, the cops are on to you. Leave town. Leave the state. Get your freakin' act together."

"This place is sweet. I like Indian Lake. You leave. I need it. It's what I need to expand my network to the south."

"How far south?"

"Kentucky. If I'm lucky, my cartel will give me Tennessee."

"Your what?"

Miguel made funny crackling noises into his phone. "Sorry. Bad connection."

"There is not. Miguel, don't do this. Get out now. You're not in so deep…"

"You are *estúpido* if you think I'll stop. I'm almost to the top. You like walking over me…"

"That's not true," Josh retorted. "I've always tried to help you. Even now."

"Screw you, gringo."

"Get off it. Why did you call me?"

"I saw Indian Lake first. With you around the media is everywhere. Your presence is not good for my business."

"Thank goodness I'm good for something."

"You're a pain in my backside. Always have been."

"Dieg… Miguel. I'm not leaving. If anyone should split it's you."

"Adios, bro." Miguel hung up.

Josh rationalized that since he hadn't uncovered any information about Miguel's location, there was no point in telling Violet about the call. He could have been calling from Chicago or down the street. But Josh had warned Miguel the cops were out for him. If Miguel hadn't known that, Josh had given him a chance to run.

And if he told Violet, by-the-rules Violet would accuse Josh of aiding a felon. He might confirm his niggling fear that she was just using him. And that bothered him a lot.

Josh didn't know if Miguel would ever go straight, but he kept hoping. If only Josh had influence on Miguel, to help his old friend and to rid Indian Lake of the last of the Le Grand gang, Josh would feel exonerated. He would have helped this little town he'd come to love.

And the woman he was falling for.

VIOLET BALANCED TWO tall frosted glasses of lemonade, complete with paper-thin rings of lemon and mint sprigs, along with a pink-flowered Havilland china plate mounded with cookies she and Mrs. Beabots had spent the afternoon baking, on a silver tray. She pushed the front door open with her hip. "Here we are," Violet announced.

"Thank you, Violet," Mrs. Beabots said, setting aside the newspaper.

Violet set the tray on a white wicker table between two large antique wicker chairs with thick bright floral covered cushions.

"I just love it out here in the summer," Mrs. Beabots crooned. "The moonlight melds with the lamplight through the maples, and the shadows across the boulevard are so…romantic." She sipped her lemonade and eyed Violet. "Don't you think?"

"Romantic? Or good cover for thieves and criminals."

"Oh, Vi! You're such a killjoy!"

"I'm teasing." Violet laughed and picked up her glass. She eyed the newspaper. "What are you reading?"

"Look." She leaned over and picked up the article. "We're in the paper again. Josh has no idea how he's helping us with the fund-raising. My phone rang incessantly all day. Sarah said it's the same with her whether she's home or at work. Everyone wants to help."

"Josh told me he was happy with it."

"He was eloquent. He said what needed to be said about the center. And you have to admit, Violet, those words coming from him have a lot of impact."

"According to my sister, Scott is over the moon. The wires picked up the story. Scott put together a YouTube video showing Gina's land, Sarah's blueprints and the model for the main building. It's gone viral with stock photos of Josh since he didn't want the photos of the day used."

"That's good, right?"

"Oh, yes. That's why your phone keeps ringing."

They clinked their glasses. "To success!" Violet said, and Mrs. Beabots smiled.

JOSH SLID HIS hand over the highly polished chrome grille on a 1914 Duesenberg. "Was this here the night of the fund-raiser?"

"No. I just brought it in from Scottsdale. I

loaned it to a friend out there to help sell tickets for the Fine Arts Commission."

"Did it help?"

"To the tune of one hundred and six grand. Yeah." Austin smiled proudly.

"I gotta say, Austin. I have some nice toys, but this..."

"Have you ever seen Jay Leno's garage?"

"No. I was invited once, but I was in—Paris."

"Oh, bad luck. It's not to be believed. But then, you had to have seen all kinds of antique cars in the Middle East. The Sultan of Brunei has the most cars."

Josh whistled and pointed his finger at Austin. "You're spot on. But it's Dmitry Lomakov's antiques I love. I met him at his home in Monte Carlo."

"I thought he was in Moscow, being the director of the Moscow Car Museum and a member of the Vintage Racing League. Mrs. Beabots was going to give me an introduction."

Josh's eyes widened. "She knows him? How?"

"Seriously, that woman has more secrets than the Dead Sea Scrolls. Some of my antique cars were ones that she gave my father."

"Gave? Not sold?"

"Nope. This museum was his dream. She donated them for the people of Indian Lake."

Josh raked his hair. "The more I learn about this place, the more amazed I am."

"Good. Because I need your help," Austin said.

"Sure, pal. Anything you want."

"Well, hear me out before you commit. This is the deal. I'm snowed under with this new tech project I'm working on. One invention leads to another. I need to spend more time in Scottsdale with my partner out there. I can't run the manufacturing here, meet with my inventors there and run the museum, too. I don't have time to go to the auctions. I should be trading up and grabbing some of these vintage cars that are on the block in Europe and Russia."

"What do you want me to do?"

"Help me with the museum. Once you're healed, you'll be going back to your places in Monte Carlo and Dubai, right?"

Josh's breath halted in his lungs. Since the day of the accident, he hadn't thought about leaving. Sure, he'd talked to Harry and signed on for an ad campaign or two, but he was doing those in Chicago or Indy. Because his rehab and recuperation was going to take many months, Josh had focused on the here and now.

He liked being around Katia and Austin. Sparring with Daisy over what he should and should not eat for breakfast. He looked forward to his daily text messages from Violet. Sharing a bag lunch with her when she wasn't out on some stakeout or in meetings. He especially liked brainstorming ideas with Violet for Mrs. Beabots's foster care center. When he was with her, he had to remind himself that she was undoubtedly still investigating him and Miguel. And he'd still kept the call from Miguel secret from her, fearing that she'd use it against him. The fact that they kept secrets from each other gnawed the edges of his integrity and caused doubts about her true feelings for him.

Yet when she so much as touched his cheek, he felt a depth of emotion from her that was overwhelming.

He hated that they were on opposing sides of the Miguel issue, especially since Josh was just as much against drug dealers as Violet was.

Miguel's choices were wrong on every level, and Josh didn't fault her for doing her job. If only he weren't part of the job to her.

Admittedly, he'd plunged into those big green eyes of hers, and opened his heart and told her about his past. Violet hadn't judged him. She listened with an attention he'd never experienced. Because of her, he realized that he'd harbored pointless fears about his past.

Violet had helped him see they were just

that—useless. He'd allowed his fears to control his life. For the first time, he asked himself just exactly what he would do with his life if he didn't race.

Did he want to continue racing?

Was the thrill still there?

Or was it all merely habit?

Surprising as it was, the day Violet had tossed him into jail, everything about Josh Stevens's life changed.

Thinking about her brought a smile to his face. Sometimes, she would kiss him for no reason at all. Every day he saw Mrs. Beabots working in her garden as he took a morning walk past her house. They chatted and hugged.

He felt accepted. Like a member of a family. It had been a long time since he'd felt quite this kind of closeness and true caring. Though he'd always been loyal to Miguel, he was seeing that was a one-way street. Josh remembered those early years when he and Miguel were boys and genuinely close. He was stunned over how deeply Miguel's lack of caring now hurt him. No, there was no way he could tell Violet about that phone call. And there was that faint, but ever-present hope that Josh could still bring Miguel around.

He wondered if Austin would still be his friend if he found out Josh had hidden his communication with Miguel, a dangerous drug dealer, from the community.

What of Katia? Mrs. Beabots?

And Violet?

Was the foundation of this new world he'd found in Indian Lake totally at risk? If it was, he had no one to blame but himself.

"You and Katia have been more than just kind to me, Austin. You took me in when I was at my lowest. I hadn't known how to repay you. Now I do. I'd be honored to help you out."

"Josh, you're the best!" Austin grabbed him and hugged him a little too hard.

"Ow!"

"Sorry." Austin backed away.

"C'mon. I'm betting Katia and Daisy have something great cooked up for dinner. We can work out the details on the way home."

They walked past a 1956 Mercedes Convertible 190SL.

"Oh, now that's sweet." Josh admired the car, leaning to look at the Moroccan leather interior and the refurbished dashboard.

"Want to drive home in that?"

"Would I!"

"Done," Austin said. "I have a gas pump outside. There's just enough gas in the tank to get it down the elevator and out the back. Insurance rules, you know."

"Sure."

"We'll bring it back in the morning."

Josh sighed and looked at his sling. "It feels like forever before I can drive again."

"I'm sure it does. But hey, we can still travel in style." Austin grinned and took the keys from under the tire.

VIOLET HAD JUST finished her lemonade when she heard an unusual horn honking. She looked out to the street and saw Austin driving something vintage and beautiful. She didn't know much about antique cars, but the convertible was beautiful as it gleamed in a puddle of golden lamplight.

"Hey, beautiful ladies!" Josh called from the passenger seat.

She stood slowly. "Josh?"

"We're on our way home for dinner. I'll call you later," he said.

"Okay! Have fun!" She waved.

"I am!"

Violet sat back down. "He looks happy."

"He does," Mrs. Beabots mused. "I was always happy in that car."

Violet swung around and faced her. "That car? That particular car?"

"It's a 1956 Mercedes."

"Is it?"

"Austin let you drive it?"

Mrs. Beabots rose. "I let him drive it. I'll get us more lemonade. The pizza should be ready by now."

Violet looked back to the street, processing what she'd just heard. She was a detective. She should know how to wrangle information from just about anyone. Prying secrets from Mrs. Beabots, however, was impossible.

Josh had looked particularly gleeful, she thought. Why was that? She would have guessed that by now, being away from his entourage, fans and life on the track would have caused anxiety attacks and an overall sense of displacement. But it didn't.

He didn't appear to be in pain from his surgery, either.

Maybe the surgeon had prescribed a strong pain medication.

Drugs. The ultimate euphoria.

Violet lowered her glass with a thud. She hated the possibility that Josh could be a user.

She was foolish to think that small-town life would entice him. She'd be unwise to think that his attraction to her was anything more than a fling while he was stuck in Indian Lake. It didn't matter how many kisses he gave her or how many romantic strolls they took to the stone bridge. The hard fact remained that he was her person of interest.

They were a mismatched pair.

She stood and went to the screen door, looking down Maple Boulevard where she saw the Mercedes' taillights as it braked at a stop sign.

Wisdom belongs to the wary, Violet.

CHAPTER TWENTY-FOUR

VIOLET SAT ON the porch after cleaning up the dinner dishes, her cell phone at her side. The scent of roses and peonies filled the air as a night breeze fluttered through the screens. Mrs. Beabots had gone to bed, claiming she had to finish an engrossing novel.

Violet stood and stretched. She still wore the black jogging clothes from her run down Maple Boulevard over to Lily Avenue and back up to Main. She hadn't felt like driving out to the lake and running the trails. Besides, she liked the shade of the massive maple trees. Tomorrow, she'd be back on stakeout. Cramped up in her car and twiddling her thumbs.

Her hands over her head, she watched as an expensive looking blue car drove down Maple Boulevard clearly going ten miles over the speed limit. "Where's a cop when you need one?" she joked aloud, then paused.

She shot to the screen door and then raced down the steps. She peered down the street.

"No way in..."

She bolted across to the boulevard's median for a better look.

"Maserati. It has to be," she mumbled as she ran from shadow to shadow down the boulevard. There was no mistaking that car. She'd memorized photos of it. It was the Maserati reported in the intel. She kept running.

She couldn't see the license plate, but it probably didn't matter. Miguel undoubtedly had a "flipper" plate like the beige Chrysler in his employ.

Interesting that Miguel drove an expensive car and his minions made do with a twenty-year-old Chrysler. She'd have to look into that.

The car drove down to the end of Maple Boulevard and then made a U-Turn at the end of the street. Before it could come back up the other side, she ran across the street and hid behind a maple tree with a very large trunk. She was four blocks away from Mrs. Beabots's house. The Maserati's lights went off.

The car came to a stop.

"That's Austin's house!"

She slammed her back against the maple and peered at the scene. From her vantage point, she clearly saw the front door. She held her breath as someone came outside.

There was no mistaking Josh's sling as he

walked toward the Maserati. He got in, and the car drove back up Maple Boulevard.

Violet pounded up the sidewalk to Mrs. Beabots's drive and nearly flew into the house to grab her keys, her fanny pack with badge and ID, and her gun.

She pounded down the stairs.

At the landing Mrs. Beabots was in the doorway to the kitchen.

"What in the world is going on?"

"Stay in the house! Lock the front porch and turn on the security motion lights. I'll be back."

"Violet?"

"Do it!"

Violet raced to her car, started the engine and backed out the drive.

She had no idea where Josh and Miguel would go in a Maserati and not be seen by someone in Indian Lake.

If she had to drive around all night, she would.

She called Bob Paxton, who was on stakeout at the farmhouse and alerted him to Miguel's presence. Then she called Trent.

"Davis."

"Sir, I have reason to believe I've spotted Miguel Garcia."

"Continue."

"He went to Austin McCreary's house nine minutes ago. Josh Stevens joined him, and the two drove north up Maple Boulevard. I'm in pursuit."

"Have you seen him since?"

"No, but I doubt he'd stay in town driving that car. Too easy to spot."

"Roger that."

Josh didn't know his way around Indian Lake, having spent his real time in town either in jail, the hospital or at Austin's house.

Except...

"Sir, I'm going out to the lake."

"The lake?" Trent asked.

"Yes, sir. It's dark and heavily forested. There are plenty of places to hide a car around there." *And I have a hunch I know just where Josh would go to avoid being seen.*

"I'll check with Paxton," Trent stated.

"I did that, sir. He's on alert."

"Good. I'm on my way to my car. I'll check the abandoned drive-in theater and call in Paluzzi to go to the train depot lot and church lots. Hawks, I'm ordering no sirens or lights if you pursue. I don't want Garcia to know we're on to him."

"Yes, sir."

"It's like looking for a needle in a haystack," Trent groaned.

"Yes, sir. A quarter-of-a-million-dollar needle," Violet quipped. "Ten four."

VIOLET DROVE OUT to the lake, circled around to the north and parked her squad car over a block from the densely forested area where she'd parked when she brought Josh out here.

She knew that if she found the Maserati, she should check in with Trent immediately. Yet, already, she ran scenarios in her head of what she would say to Josh if she found them together. Was Josh buying drugs? Was he part of Miguel's cover? Was he a partner in this gang?

Her head pounded with the possibilities.

She'd jogged to the parking area, and just as she slid through a blind of blue spruce trees, the Maserati drove past her onto the lake road and headed back toward town.

Violet hurried back to the car, careful to stay out of their view behind the massive trunks of maple trees and full foliage bushes. In her dark clothes and by staying in the shadows, she knew they couldn't see her. She took out her cell phone, then hit Trent's number on "favorites."

"Davis."

"Sir. I found the Maserati. It *was* at the lake."

"Where's Garcia?"

"Driving back toward town. Josh Stevens is with him."

"Oh, this just gets better."

"Sir—" she opened the car door, got in and started the engine "—I'm in pursuit."

"Ten four."

Violet sped down the lake road, but was stopped by the light at Indian Lake Boulevard. Since she was under orders not to use the siren, she drummed her fingers anxiously on the steering wheel until the light turned green.

She made her way to the overpass over the railroad tracks. From this height she checked west and then east on Main Street.

She saw the Maserati.

"There you are!"

The light was green, and she turned to follow her quarry.

Miguel drove cautiously until they were out on the state highway. The Pentecostal Church evening service had just let out, and a stream of cars pulled onto the highway. The majority of cars headed east. Violet wove through them, but within five or six minutes she realized she was pursuing no one. The Maserati had dropped out of sight.

At the next U-turn in the median, she doubled back toward town, knowing that Miguel had pulled one of the oldest tricks in the book.

He had to have turned off his headlights, taken a turn and driven down a country road or one of the farmer's outlet drives. It was nearly ten o'clock. With no streetlights out this far from town and miles of unlit farmland, she knew she could spend all night combing the fields and country roads trying to find the Maserati.

Her best bet was to go back to Austin's house and wait for Josh to show up.

Twenty minutes later, Violet cut the squad car's engine and turned off the headlights as she parked around the corner and a block away from Austin's house. She felt strange staking out a house where she'd always been welcomed as a friend.

But the tables had turned just hours ago.

Josh was with Miguel Garcia. It was weird that all this time she'd assumed this connection between Josh and Miguel, but seeing it with her own eyes, it hurt that he'd lied to her.

Josh was in deep. He'd been followed by an officer of the law. Already a person of interest, the ILPD most likely would look at Josh differently from tonight forward.

Feeling squeezed between a very large rock and the hard place she'd created by allowing her romance with Josh, Violet could only imagine the betrayal Josh would feel once she arrested him—again.

Suddenly, she saw Katia's Bentley coming down the street. Violet got out of her car. Crouching low, she hid behind a row of boxwoods at the southern end of Austin's property.

Katia pulled into the drive, turned off the car and got out.

The front door opened and both Austin and Josh came out as Katia opened the trunk and began unloading groceries.

Josh took several bags in his good hand as Austin kissed Katia and helped with the rest.

Violet gasped. "Josh is here? He's home?"

She stood and walked closer, though still careful not to be seen by the trio.

She watched as Josh made a joke about four containers of Louise Railton's ice cream. They all went inside.

Violet immediately went back to her car and drove to the police station, calling Trent to report in. He explained that he'd sent both Bob Paxton and Sal Paluzzi out to the farmhouse in the event that Miguel doubled back to the meth lab.

Violet was sitting at her desk when Trent walked in.

"I don't understand," Violet said, shaking her head. "I saw Josh get in Miguel's Maserati. I saw them come out of that parking area near the stone bridge."

Trent interrupted, "How would Josh know about that old stone bridge area? No one goes there. He had to be in on something with Garcia. Maybe Josh has been coming to Indian Lake for months. Maybe he's the front man for Garcia."

"Sir." She folded her hands in her lap, the pangs of her betrayal to Josh biting the edges of her heart. If she wasn't in love with Josh, would she be this riddled with guilt? Would her eyes sting this much? "I took Josh out to the bridge."

"Why?"

"Intel work. I was hoping to get more information." Which was true, but she also wanted to be with him. There had always been this chance that Josh could be involved with Miguel, but all this time, she hadn't really believed it.

Yet, she'd been taught to follow facts, intel, discovery and forensic reports to hone her talents of detection. As a rookie, she would be judged harshly on every mistake. She had no history of solid arrests yet.

"I see."

Violet's head was tangled with her missteps and decisions she'd made based on emotions. Those feelings had caused blindness when it was her job to see. Caused her to lose her prey. She asked Trent, "But how did Josh get back to Austin's house without me seeing him? I clearly saw him in the passenger's seat of that Maserati when they left the lake area."

"Did you see him in the car when Garcia was driving through town?"

"I… I…"

“Or when you were in pursuit east out of town?”

“Come to think of it, I did not. The windows were tinted and it was dark. I only saw a shadow of the driver as I tried to watch his moves.”

“My bet is that he dropped Stevens off at Main and Maple Boulevard. Then he drove east. All Stevens had to do was walk…”

“Eight blocks to Austin’s house.”

“It wouldn’t take fifteen minutes,” Trent said, raking his hair.

“So where does this put us?”

“Closer, Hawks. Not there, but closer.” He tapped the top of her computer screen. “Email me your report. I’ll call the chief. It’s going to be a long night.”

Violet put her fingers on the keyboard, but they remained frozen.

Her report was accurate. It stated facts. There could be a dozen reasons why Josh was with Miguel, none of them nefarious. On the record, Josh was still only “a person of interest.”

As an officer, she knew they were moving close to arresting Miguel. Her duty would be satisfied. But in the process, she feared she’d lose the one thing that mattered. Josh.

CHAPTER TWENTY-FIVE

INTEL GATHERING AT the ILPD hadn't been this intense in all Violet's time here. Chief Williams had ordered every scrap of information about Josh Stevens and Diego Lopez/Miguel Garcia sent to his desk. Since the night Josh and Miguel drove to the stone bridge by Indian Lake, both Detective Davis and Chief Williams had raked through her reports, questioning her on every point. Josh had gone from a person of interest to a serious suspect.

Photographs of the farmhouse, the stacks of methamphetamine ingredients, Violet's snapshots of the Chrysler and even aerial photos that the chief requisitioned, maps with colored pins stuck in them and a blizzard of notes were taped to a large white wallboard.

"Thanks to this past week's surveillance by Detectives Paxton and Paluzzi—" Trent pressed his forefinger to the county map "—we've been able to figure out the routes the gang uses most often." He pointed to the farm road that ran by Violet's mother's house. "Because this road continues up into Michigan, we've staked more ILPD unmarked cars along here. This week alone, the Chrysler and a black Buick have been seen leaving the area of the farmhouse and driving up into Michigan."

"Sir," Violet said. "No sign of the Maserati?"

"None yet."

"Have we seen this gang member before? The one driving the Buick?"

"We believe so."

"And yet they have shown no signs of cooking meth," Violet said, peering at the photos. "These boxes are untouched and in the same order as the night I first went there." She leaned back in her chair and folded her arms over her chest. "There can be only one reason for that."

"Which is?" Bob Paxton turned toward her.

"They never intended to make meth," she said. "The farmhouse is a decoy."

Trent stood and went to the board. "If it's a decoy, Officer Hawks, then where in the blazes are they nesting?"

"I don't know, sir."

Trent frowned. "All these weeks and we've got nothing."

"Maybe not," Violet replied, pointing to the board. "What if they are doing business here in Indian Lake like we thought? What if the meth is a decoy, but they're actually running heroin? That would explain the need for the Chrysler and now the Buick and those trips to Michigan."

"Possible," Trent said.

"Highly probable," Sal added. "Go on, Hawks. You're on to something."

"We've hung back from an arrest because we wanted to nail these guys in the act. What if we got the warrant to search? Go out there when we know they're on-site?"

Trent turned to Sal. "Didn't you question those neighbors again?"

"The Hardestys. Yeah. But they said they haven't seen a thing."

Violet's eyes widened. "I talked to them just this morning on the phone. Mrs. Hardesty was aloof at first. I reminded her of the jar of honey I brought her."

"Nice." Bob nodded.

"And?" Trent waved his hand at her to continue.

"She said she couldn't sleep last night because of the ruckus at our farmhouse."

"What time was this?"

"Just before midnight."

Trent looked at Sal. "Did you see anything?"

"The lights were on inside. I saw three guys. The two from the Chrysler and a fat guy in the Buick."

Violet gave Sal a steady look. "No Maserati?"

"I kept watch for it all night. No headlights. No taillights."

Violet snapped her fingers. "Miguel drives with the lights off!"

"He does." Trent gave her all his attention.

"That's how he eluded me going out of town. I bet he can go for miles without headlights. He knows those roads."

"True, but Sal spotted the car at the farmhouse."

Trent stood with his hands on his hips. "I'll talk to the chief. Get the warrant. Tonight we move. Hawks, you're in on this one."

"Yes, sir!" Adrenaline shot through her as Trent breezed out of his office and went straight to Chief Williams's office.

She looked at Bob and Sal. Their wary expressions said it all. "I can do this," she said.

"You're good at intel, Hawks. And we all think you show a natural talent for detective work, but this is different. If it goes down badly, your skills will be tested," Sal said.

"I have to start somewhere."

Bob stood and patted her shoulder. "You'll be fine. This first time, though—just be careful."

Bob and Sal left, muttering their misgivings to each other.

Violet's earlier thrill of victory evaporated. *They're afraid I'll screw up. That my errors could cause us to blow the sting. Or worse, that someone could get hurt.*

Maybe Trent had spoken too soon. Maybe she should back up.

She wiped her palms over her face and said to herself, "Stop it, Violet!"

This was what she'd been working toward. This was what she wanted. What she'd trained for.

"Hawks!" Trent's deep voice reverberated across the hall.

She darted into the hall. "Sir?"

He motioned to her to join him in the Chief's office. "Chief Williams wants the latest on Stevens."

She nearly sprinted to the large office.

Chief Williams said, "I want to know if Stevens is part of this gang. Where is he today?"

"I don't know, sir. I saw him last night..."

"I know that. I read the report. Get him on the phone." He looked at his watch. "Take him to a late lunch or go bowling. I don't care. But stay close. If there is something going down, it's going to happen soon. I want to know where his head's at."

"Yes, sir."

"If Stevens is involved, we'll nail him." He propped his elbow on the desk and pointed at Violet. "And if he's not, I don't want the first disparaging word said about him or his activities. We don't need the national media coming down on us again. You got that?"

"I do."

"Good. Dismissed."

Violet didn't look at Trent as she rushed to her desk. She took out her cell phone and punched in Josh's number.

He picked up on the second ring.

"Violet! I can't believe you're calling me," Josh said excitedly.

"Really? Why?"

"Because I was just going to call you. That's so weird. We thought about each other at the same time."

"Yeah." She paused as a warm flutter crossed her heart. She lowered into her desk chair. "So, what's up?"

"Can you drive me out to Austin's car museum? I'm due out there in about forty-five minutes."

"Due?"

"Yeah. I have a gig," he said happily.

She felt herself smile. She was always surprised that the sound of his voice lifted her spirits. "It can't be a fund-raiser. I would have known about that."

"It'll be a surprise. I know you're working, but I thought if you pleaded with your boss—"

"Superior officer," she corrected him.

"Right. What do you think?"

She needed to hedge a bit. If it looked easy for her to leave her post on a whim, he might get suspicious. "I'll ask, but it's probably not going to happen. Rookies don't get many favors and I have very little vacation time my first year."

"Oh, yeah. Vacation time. I didn't think of that." His voice trailed off. Then, brightly he said, "Tell the Chief I'll donate to whatever police fund he chooses if he'll give you a couple hours with me."

"Josh..."

"That's not bribery, is it? I don't want to break the law." He started to chuckle.

Not only did Violet's orders include gathering intel on Josh, but she was curious about this "surprise." "Let me handle it. I'll call you back."

"Great. I'll be waiting by the phone. Thanks."

Josh hung up.

Violet rose and went to Trent's office. The door was open, so she knocked on the doorjamb.

"Hawks?" Trent looked up from the papers he was reading.

"I just got a call from Josh Stevens. He's asked me to drive him out to the car museum. He says he has a 'gig' out there he wants me to see."

The phone rang. Trent picked up the receiver and held his palm over the mouthpiece. "Go. But finish that report before you leave and call me if you learn anything." He waved her away. "Davis," he said into the phone.

Returning to her desk, she texted Josh back and told him she was nearly on her way. Quickly, she went to work, finished the report and emailed it to Trent and Chief Williams. She had exactly six minutes to drive down Maple Boulevard to meet someone who was deeply connected to the investigation.

CHAPTER TWENTY-SIX

HIS SLING NOTWITHSTANDING, Josh looked every bit the handsome celebrity driver he was, dressed in white summer slacks, a midnight blue knit shirt and navy leather loafers as he greeted her at the door.

Violet couldn't help the appreciative smile she gave him. "You look—good. Healthy."

"I've been in the sun. Helping Katia in the garden, cleaning the pool. Stuff to keep busy. My tennis game is a bit off, considering—" he lifted his sling "—the circumstances."

Without another word he leaned over and kissed her cheek.

Violet felt warmth down her spine and her rigid, official stance softened. No matter how much she tried to convince herself that she was a fool to allow emotions to block her duty, she couldn't help it. Her heart told her he was a good man. She wanted to think only the very best about Josh, but in the end, her eyes told her another story. Josh had met with Miguel. There was a story there. Was it conspiracy? She wondered…

"I got here as soon as I finished my report. Miguel Garcia was spotted in town last night." She said it casually, almost not wanting to hear his answer.

"Is that so?" Josh put his good arm around her shoulders. "We need to go. I don't want to be late."

His smile didn't falter as they walked to her squad car.

She took out the car keys and went around to the driver's side, leaning on the roof as Josh opened the passenger door. "So he didn't contact you?"

"On the advice of my attorney, I wouldn't tell you if he did. Besides, I don't want to even think about Miguel. I'd rather think about us."

"Us?" Violet felt a warm glow start in her heart and spread throughout her chest. She didn't want to think about Miguel, either.

"Uh-huh." He flashed her a charming smile. "Now, can we go?"

"Yeah."

As Josh got in and buckled his seat belt, Violet berated herself for how easily she shoved aside her duty and responsibilities whenever she was with Josh.

One kiss on the cheek and I'm toast.

"CHILDREN? THIS IS the surprise?" Violet asked as they entered the car museum and were met with twenty-three smiling kids. Then she saw her sister, Isabelle, along with Bella and little Michael.

"Aunt Violet!" Bella exclaimed and rushed up to hug Violet. Michael clung to Isabelle's leg.

"Honey, Aunt Violet won't hurt you. She's just in uniform is all," Isabelle explained.

Michael tilted his head to the left, observing Violet as if he didn't recognize her. Slowly, his blue eyes widened. "Auntie Vi!" He trundled over and joined Bella in hugging Violet.

"I didn't know you'd be here," Violet said, glancing up at Josh who beamed down at her.

"So, good surprise?" he asked with a wink.

"Very good surprise," she replied.

Beatrice Wilcox Nelson, the owner of the Indian Lake Youth Camp, waved at Violet. "Hi, Violet." She beamed as she held the hand of her two adopted foster boys, Eli and Chris. Beatrice had recently married Rand Nelson, a firefighter in Indian Lake. Beatrice walked the boys over to Violet and Josh.

Eli, the younger of the two, couldn't take his eyes off Josh.

Chris's stare was glued to Violet's gun and holster.

"I saw your crash on TV," Eli said to Josh. "Does it hurt?"

Josh looked at his arm. "Not anymore. The doctor said I'm healing fast."

"But it'll take a long time. Mom hurt her foot last summer during a fire when she rescued me. She had to use crutches for a while. Right, Mom?"

Beatrice smiled and ruffled Eli's thick hair. "I did. But the rehab and therapy exercises are vital."

"Oh, I plan to follow the doctor's instructions to the letter," Josh replied. He shook Beatrice's hand. "I'm so glad you brought all these kids. When we set this up, you weren't sure about the number."

"To be honest, we have quite a few more kids than planned. Some are from Chris's vacation bible school group. Almost none of the kids have been out here to the museum. Thanks for thinking of us."

"Thank Mrs. Beabots. While we were discussing plans for the new foster child care center, she told me about your camp and the work you do with the foster kids. I've been looking forward to meeting you in person. And, hey, Rand is a great guy. I met him at Mrs. Beabots's house."

"Yes! He told me. She's a love, always making pies and treats not only for the firefighters but for my camp kids."

Violet listened to the exchange as if it was music to her ears. Clearly, Josh was already making plans to do more for the center than writing a check.

And walking away.

"You were talking to Mrs. Beabots?" she asked. "When was this?"

"That particular conversation? A few days ago. We talk every day, actually."

"Oh." Violet had been careful not to tell her landlady any aspect of her ongoing investigation of Josh. The night she'd rushed out of the house and told Mrs. Beabots to lock the doors and check the security cameras and lights, and she returned, she'd told Mrs. Beabots only that she'd followed a suspect.

"Beatrice, would you mind giving me your input for the center?" Josh asked.

"I'd love to help," Beatrice offered. "Just name it."

"I'd like to come out to the camp and spend a day with you. I think your take on the kids' learning basic skills is important."

"Yeah." Eli frowned. "She taught us how to knit during the winter."

Violet smiled. "You don't like knitting?"

Eli looked up at Violet. "It's hard! First you

have to count all those knots. And the needles are big."

"I didn't mind it," Chris said, and looked at Violet's gun again. "I like to learn new things. I bet you're really good with your gun, huh?"

Violet didn't know much about Chris's background, except for what Scott had told her. Both Chris and Eli had been abandoned by their drug dealer parents. Child Protective Services took over, and they'd spent the bulk of last summer at the youth camp. Violet wondered if Chris's father or mother had guns. Did he have firsthand knowledge? "Have you ever handled a gun, Chris?"

"Nah."

"But you want to?" she asked.

"I want to protect people when I grow up. Like my new dad. He's a firefighter. Police protect people, too. Like little kids who can't take care of themselves."

Violet's heart swelled. She hadn't met him before, but in less than five minutes, she knew she wanted to get to know him better. Be a friend to him. "Chris, protecting people is more than just having a gun. And remember, I was trained to use it safely. It took a lot of lessons. But anytime you want to know about my career, I'm here to talk to. Okay?"

"Okay. Thanks," he said with an intake of breath that puffed out his chest.

Josh turned to the group. "Okay, kids! I want to take you through the museum and show you the cars and tell you a bit about their history. I've started to rearrange some of the cars so that you can follow the progression of technology from the early years."

ONCE INSIDE THE MUSEUM, Josh began the tour. He was full of fun and interesting facts about all the cars.

Violet had been to the museum several times, both for fund-raisers and due to the fact that she'd always been intrigued by antique cars. Growing up in Indian Lake, the Cruise Night party on the first Friday night in June had always been her favorite. For the past thirty years, every owner of an antique car in the surrounding area paraded up and down Main Street from dusk till nightfall. It was almost impossible not to know something about antique cars.

And in the Hawks family, with three brothers who tinkered with anything mechanical, she learned about cars by osmosis.

The 1919 Daimler that Josh was talking about now, however, was a very recent acquisition. It wasn't here the night of the fundraiser in May.

As the kids listened to him, gone was the "celebrity worship" she'd seen in them when they first arrived. He took them on a journey back in time. He told of the hardworking inventors whose passion for the future drove them.

"Auntie Vi." Little Michael tugged on her hand. "Hold me up."

Violet looked at Isabelle, who smiled and urged her to pick Michael up. The toddler had always clung to Isabelle, but something was different today.

Violet leaned down and hoisted him up. He flung his little arms around the back of her neck. He smiled. "Thanks."

Then he looked at Josh and the car. He pointed. "I like that one."

Michael pressed his soft cheek next to hers. He smelled like baby powder and herbal shampoo. Isabelle had dressed him in a sky blue summer T-shirt and matching shorts. He had sneakers, and white socks with a Cubs logo on them. Violet inhaled and felt his velvety skin. Scott had been right about kids. All they wanted were hugs and kisses. It didn't matter how tired and cranky they got; if you paid attention to them and treated them like people and not nuisances, they were precious.

"It's a very pretty car," she said.

"No. I like him. He's nice to me."

She inclined her head back and looked at him. "Josh is nice to you?"

"He hugs me."

"When was this?"

"At Daddy's store."

"Josh went to the Java Stop? You saw him there?"

"Uh-huh. He read a book about cars to me." Michael kissed her cheek. "I like hugging."

"I like it, too, Michael. I especially like your hugs."

As Josh took the group to the next car and the next, Violet continued to hold Michael, who had no urge to leave her arms.

Violet didn't hear a lot of his presentation. Her mind was occupied with filling in a spreadsheet of unknown facts about Josh's daily activities.

She'd been remiss in thinking that recuperation for Josh meant he would spend idle days resting. Apparently, the guy was up earlier than she, walking uptown for early-morning coffee with Scott. He played with her niece and nephew, sometimes reading to them. He talked to Mrs. Beabots on nearly a daily basis while Violet was on the job or at the station. He worked with Gina Barzonni and Sarah Bosworth on the plans for the new foster child care center. He knew Beatrice and Rand Nelson. And from her own conversations with him, she knew that he conducted business with his manager, held phone interviews with newspapers and race magazines. He cut a couple podcasts.

And he'd met with Miguel Garcia.

"That's the end of our tour, kids. I hope you liked it." Josh's loud announcement broke through Violet's thoughts.

Applause rang through the museum.

Beatrice went up to Josh. "I can't thank you enough for this, Josh. It was a pleasure."

Josh hugged her. "You've been great to bring the kids here. What do you say we do it again in a month when you have new campers come in?"

"You mean it?"

Violet's sister held Bella's hand as she joined them. "Josh, you're the greatest," Isabelle said. "Believe him, Beatrice. He's helped out at the bookstore and giving Scott those interviews..."

Violet detected a sudden darkening of Josh's expression.

Isabelle rushed on. "I'm thinking your accident has been a blessing to all of us in Indian Lake."

"Well, my counselors, Maisie and Cindy, are back with the SUVs to take the kids back to camp and to the church. I gotta go." Beatrice hugged Violet, kissed Michael's cheek and hugged Bella, then hugged Isabelle, saying her goodbyes.

"Yeah," Isabelle added. "I'm off to the grocery and the art supply store."

"A new painting?" Violet asked.

"Yeah, I'm inspired." Isabelle winked at Josh, who smiled back at her. She took Michael from Violet's arms. "See you soon, sis. Bye."

"Bye," Violet said, noticing the quiet after the children were gone. She turned to Josh. "So, where do you want me to drop you off? The Java Stop? Mrs. Beabots's house? Austin's house?"

He took her hand. "You were great with the kids. I was afraid your uniform might intimidate them."

"They barely knew I was here. You're a megastar to them. You were all they could see."

He shook his head. "I don't think that's it."

Josh tugged on her hand. "Come on." He started walking.

"Where are we going?"

"Over here," he said.

Josh unhooked a burgundy velvet rope from

a brass stand. He held out his right arm. “After you.”

She looked at the priceless Daimler. “What are we doing?”

“Get in.”

“What?”

“Trust me, I’m not going to crank it up and go for a spin.” He opened the door. The interior was luxurious, the seats in tufted dove-gray velvet. The handles and bud vases on the walls were sterling silver.

“Sit next to me.”

“Are you sure about this?” she asked. “This feels like trespassing.”

“It’s not. I paid for this rental.”

“You rented this car? Why?”

“Well—” he held her hand, lacing his fingers with hers “—while I’m here, I’ve agreed to help Austin at the museum. This Daimler is one of my new ideas. Austin will continue to buy cars and keep them, but I suggested he increase the museum’s exposure and media presence by touring rare cars through here. The cars come in for three months and then move on to another museum. This one is from the Los Angeles Museum.”

“It’s a brilliant idea.”

“And fun. But that’s not the only reason I wanted this car,” he said earnestly. “I wanted a special place that you would always remember."

"Remember what?"

"I love you, Violet," he said, raising her hand to his lips and kissing her palm, though his eyes never left hers. "I've never said that to a woman. You should know that. I've never said it because this hasn't happened—not to me. I have a sense of belonging that I didn't think I'd ever find."

"Josh..."

He put his arm around her and pulled her close. "Don't say anything. Don't say something you don't feel. I had to say it, though. I've gone crazy trying to deny it."

He kissed her with so much passion, Violet felt consumed. The love he had for her enveloped them both. She wrapped her arms around his neck and pulled him closer. She slid her fingers up the back of his strong neck and into his hair.

Her heart opened and filled with love.

Though he pulled away, his reluctance caused him to kiss her eyelids, cheeks and throat. He nuzzled her ear. "I've spent my life racing around the world trying to find my life, and then you came along..." He held her face with his right hand and traced the edge of her jaw. "I want to be truthful with you, Violet."

She sucked in a breath. "I want that, too." And she meant it. Her prayer was that the investigation would end soon and when it was over, she could finally be honest and open with him. Nothing would hold her back.

"I feel like I'm going three hundred miles an hour, about to take off with you, but I hold myself back."

"Why?"

"Because you're not here—" he pointed to his heart "—with me. I think deep down you want to be. I know you're investigating me. My connection to Diego. I mean Miguel. It's your job and that's serious to you. But this is real and I don't want any suspicions or false motives between us, Violet."

"Josh—"

"You want to know about Miguel. The thing is, there's nothing. And if you don't believe that..."

"I do believe that."

"But the ILPD doesn't."

"No, they don't. And that begs me to ask, why don't you go in to talk to them? Tell them everything you know about Miguel?"

"On the advice of my attorney and agent, it would look not just a little bad, but big-time bad for me in the media if it got out that the cops and I were talking. Not to mention that, honestly, I believe Miguel is a loose cannon. I don't know what he'd do."

"He'd come after you?"

"Or you."

"You're worried about me?"

"I am."

She was overwhelmed. She hadn't expected his declaration this morning of all mornings.

If Josh was lying about his relationship with Miguel to protect him, the flip side would be a very black ending. It would be proven that Josh had been and was a part of Diego Lopez/Miguel Garcia's criminal gang. Josh would be arrested, tried and convicted. He would go to prison.

And she would never forget him.

"Josh, you know I have feelings for you…"

"But do you think you could ever love me?"

She lifted her eyes to his and felt as if she were falling into an abyss. It was terrifying. It was the step that all fools took. "I do."

He kissed her again, and Violet knew she could never turn back.

CHAPTER TWENTY-SEVEN

THE QUARTER MOON hung low in the summer night sky, with vivid Mercury above it. A slight breeze rustled through the silver maple trees and overgrown bushes around the farmhouse. Violet wore a Kevlar vest over her long-sleeved uniform shirt with the ILPD letters emblazoned in gold on the back.

"Hawks, you and Paluzzi take the back. Paxton and I will come in through the front and initiate." Trent moved away from the squad car.

Trent signaled for Violet to take the left side of the house while Sal took the right.

She quickly ran around the perimeter of the yard, keeping close to the forsythia and pines for cover. The house was dark. The Chrysler was parked in the drive, very close to the garage. The Buick was behind it.

Trent had the warrant with him, but none of the officers expected a clean search. The Chicago PD detectives on Richard Schmitz's team had followed a shipment to Indian Lake. Richard had alerted Trent, and once the dealers' car was spotted heading into Indian Lake County, Trent's team took over. Trent told Violet and the team that he expected the heroin to be stashed in the farmhouse basement.

Violet was the first to the rear of the house and pressed her back against the wall. She noted the garage was dark. Though there was a shipment that had come in, Violet did not see any gang members inside. They had yet to start cooking meth.

Sal came around the right, his gun drawn and held up in the air.

"Police!" came Trent's voice from the front of the house.

She held her breath, poised for action.

"Police!" Trent banged on the door. The sound could probably be heard a hundred yards away, Violet thought.

Immediately, she heard voices speaking in Spanish. She peered under the back door steps, where she saw a light coming from the basement window.

She signaled Sal and pointed to the basement window.

"Open up! Police!" Sal shouted.

Sal nodded back to Violet. He moved closer to the back steps.

She heard curses in both Spanish and English. Feet pounded on stairs.

"I'm coming in!" Trent's voice was nearly drowned out by the sound of the front door crashing open.

A shot was fired, but Violet didn't know from whom. She saw a flash of light from the interior as another shot rang through the house.

"Stop where you are!" Trent shouted.

Wham! The back door blasted open and slammed against the back wall. Two men rushed out.

"Police! Stop!" Violet yelled.

The first man through the door was young, fit and no taller than she. He wore a black hooded sweatshirt, jeans and sneakers. He held a gun.

Sal rushed forward, flung himself at the guy and pushed him to the ground.

The second man was rotund, not over thirty and wore a sleeveless white undershirt and baggy jeans that impeded his run. Violet took off after him. "Police! Stop!" she yelled.

He cursed at her and kept running.

Indignation stirred her into action as she poured on the heat and leaped onto the guy's massive, hairy back. She encircled his thick neck with her arm and yanked. He stumbled and fell, taking Violet with him.

He cursed her again.

"Shut up!" She bolted to her feet, which she kept shoulder width apart for stability as she leaned down. With the flat side of her right palm, she knifed him on the side of the temple, then on the throat, incapacitating him. He gurgled and was just about to grab her ankle, when she pulled her gun and leaned down and held the barrel under his nose.

"You were saying?"

Trent rushed up with his gun un-holstered. "I got this, Hawks."

"Sir. Yes, sir," she replied dutifully.

Trent hauled the guy to his feet. "Cuff him, Hawks."

As Violet pulled the obese man's hands behind his back, she began, "You have the right to remain silent..."

He spat on the ground and cursed her again.

Trent growled through clenched teeth, "Keep it up and I'll lock her in the cell with you. Obviously, you're no match for her."

WHILE BOB PAXTON CUFFED a skinny gang member who looked more like a user than a dealer to Violet, and whom Bob said he'd found huddled in the bathtub, Violet led the obese guy to the squad car. Sal followed with the man he'd cuffed. With all three criminals in custody, Violet then accompanied Trent to the farmhouse basement where they found hundreds of pounds of heroin and cocaine.

She should have felt proud of her involvement with the task force, but she didn't. Just this morning, she'd declared her love to Josh and she really did believe they had feelings for each other. But she'd still put her job first, all the while knowing that if Josh had lied to her about his participation with Miguel, she'd choose her job and justice over her love for him. She'd betray the first real love she'd ever had. Violet was committed to her career. First, last, always.

"All this," Trent said, and flung the pack of heroin down onto the dirt floor. "And we still don't have Garcia."

He pounded up the stairs. Violet followed. She might have been able to bring down one of the gang members, but no one was as good as Trent Davis at interrogation.

AT TWELVE PAST THREE in the morning, Violet was convinced that no bullet would kill her faster than the continued diet of vending machine snacks, drive-through breakfast burritos and day-old doughnuts, which seemed to be the only fare her fellow task force members preferred.

She tossed a cheese and salsa saturated burrito paper into the trash. "I'm taking Mrs. Beabots up on her offer to teach me how to make sugar pies."

"Great," Sal said, handing her a cup of coffee.

"Is this fresh?"

"No. Why?" he asked, lifting his own Styrofoam cup to his mouth and drinking deeply. He grimaced. "I see your point."

"How long can this go on?" Violet asked, pointing down the hall to the interrogation room.

"All night. That's the point. By dawn, the perp will be frustrated, tired, hungry and willing to spill. Even for a cup of this—" he put the cup down and folded his hands "—very bad excuse for coffee."

"Makes sense," she replied, then stood and took Sal's cup. "I'll go make fresh coffee. It will help."

"Dream on," Sal joked.

Just then Trent walked out of the interrogation room and slammed the door.

Violet could tell her boss wasn't happy.

Sal asked, "You want me to take over?"

"I don't think it will do any good. None of them are talking. They've called an attorney, some Chicago hotshot. But we've got them. The heroin and cocaine have been moved here to the evidence room, the farmhouse has been taped off and forensics is out there now. They may turn up something. Meanwhile, these guys will be arraigned in the morning."

"What are you going to do?" Violet asked.

"Get some sleep. All of us are. We'll hit it hard tomorrow." He turned to Violet. "One more thing. I've delayed bringing Stevens in for questioning, hoping you'd find a link between him and Miguel. Frankly, I thought Stevens might be involved with Miguel's gang. Even the ringleader—with all his money, I was suspicious. The lack of evidence he's given you isn't enough to absolve him of suspicion, though. It's time to bring Josh Stevens in for questioning."

Violet kept her expression cold as stone. That was how she felt. Bloodless. She put the coffee cup down so she wouldn't spill it now that her hands felt numb.

This was it.

The moment of truth. Josh was either guilty or innocent.

And yet…

Approximately sixteen hours ago he'd declared his love for her. She'd told him she loved him back, and she did. That had been her moment of truth. It had just rushed out of her heart like his race car, speeding to victory. She hadn't once thought of slowing things down, because he was the one she wanted. She wanted to give her heart to him.

He'd arranged for the antique Daimler to be at the museum for her. It was the most romantic throwback moment for a man whose passion was cars. He'd told her that he'd never loved anyone.

Until her.

Violet was riding the razor's edge. If Josh was guilty and she let justice take its course, she would lose him forever. But if she let him walk when she shouldn't, she would be busted back to traffic cop or dismissed from the force. Either way—she'd lose.

She swept her palm across her forehead and over her slicked-back hair.

Josh can't be involved with Miguel.

There's gotta be an explanation as to why he'd go off with Miguel.

"Hawks? You okay?" Trent asked.

"Yes, sir. Fine."

"You look beat."

Sal laughed. "She should be. You shoulda seen the way she took that guy down. He was twice her size."

"I saw enough to know you're an asset to this team, Officer Hawks," Trent said.

"Thank you, sir."

"Because you've been on top of this investigation, I'm assigning you and Paluzzi here to bring Stevens in. The gang activity is heating up, and we can't afford to let them slip by us. With this bust, Garcia might blow out of town. Clock's ticking."

Violet's mouth went dry. "You're issuing a warrant, sir?"

"No. Just bring him in for questioning. If he refuses, we'll get the warrant. See you both in the morning."

"Good night, sir," Violet said. Her stomach lurched.

Sal stepped away. "Guess we don't need that coffee anymore, huh?"

"No. We don't," she replied.

Sal went to his desk, grabbed his cell phone and waved as he passed.

Violet didn't feel like going home where she'd be alone with her guilty thoughts. She glanced around the nearly empty office, quiet now except for the hum of an oscillating fan.

I guess it doesn't matter where I am, I can't escape my feelings.

If Josh still felt about Miguel the way he had when they were young in the foster home, would he want to protect his "brother" at all costs? *Even at the cost of losing me?*

Was she a fool to give her love to Josh who had no ironclad ties to Indian Lake or to her?

In the end, if Violet could bring Miguel to justice and put him in prison for the rest of his lifetime, she'd do it.

She ground her jaw at the thought. She despised criminals. Anyone who would mistreat, hurt, kill, maim or dupe another person deserved punishment. Those who could be rehabilitated should be, but from what she'd learned about Miguel, he liked working the dark shadows. He liked turning up his nose at law and order.

Violet saw that she was guilty of using Josh to bring intel about Miguel to the surface. She'd had to. Maybe it was seeing the faces of Isabelle's kids and knowing a dealer lurked on the next street corner somewhere in their future, if she didn't *do* something. Maybe it was the fact that drugs in her lovely town were twisting it and making it less safe. And all that was more important than her own needs and wants.

And loves.

The greatest loss she'd ever encounter was the loss of Josh's love for her. But if it meant bringing Miguel to justice, she'd roll those dice.

She turned off the computer and headed toward the door. He had admitted that he knew she was investigating him. But she'd also told him she loved him. Would he think she'd lied?

No question. When she returned in the morning, Josh would have a new name for duplicity. He'd call it "Violet."

CHAPTER TWENTY-EIGHT

JOSH HAD NEVER understood what a "giddy teenager in love" meant when he'd heard about it in songs, but he was walking on air now.

Despite the fact that he'd only seen Violet once more, since he'd told her he loved her and, miraculously, she'd told him she loved him back, Josh couldn't ebb the nonstop flow of visions his head was spinning.

Yet each time he thought about their romance, his logic blasted him with the fact that he'd held back plenty from Violet. Josh had been in contact with Miguel, but not for the reasons he was all too sure the cops suspected. Josh was desperate to persuade Miguel to leave Indian Lake. He'd tried and failed to talk his former friend into going straight—since they were kids. If Miguel was determined to stay part of the drug world, Josh told him, in no uncertain terms, to take his business elsewhere.

What Josh also knew was that Miguel was seriously considering expanding his gang to Tennessee. There was a small town called

Cookeville, not far from Nashville, that suited their purposes just fine. Rural areas. Lots of places to hide and still traffic their goods.

Josh had held back going to the cops with his information, hoping that he might discover even more.

His feelings for Violet and his relationship with Miguel twisted his insides at times. He would have given anything to pursue a romance with Violet like a normal person, but he was under no illusions. He'd created his own time bomb by falling for Violet, and yet, he couldn't and wouldn't let her go. He was determined to find a way to draw her closer.

As committed as she was to her career, which was one of the things he loved about her, he believed she was a closet romantic. He'd seen that in the feminine clothes she wore whenever she was out of uniform. He'd taken a chance on his observation when he'd called the Los Angeles Museum and arranged for the Daimler rental.

The Daimler represented another era, when life was like a slow-moving river. People took time to discover nuances of each other. He wanted Violet to know that he'd put his whole heart on the line for her.

Because it was the first time he'd ever told

a woman that he loved her, the moment was important for him, too.

He hadn't figured that her job would yank her away from him so quickly. That night he'd wanted to see her for dinner, but she was called to duty. Apparently, that same order kept her from him the following day and evening.

Finally, on the second night, Josh couldn't stand not seeing her. He texted her and asked what time her shift was ending. She'd texted back that she was hoping to be home by ten and go right to sleep.

Josh asked if she could see him for fifteen minutes, and Violet had agreed.

Josh then arranged with Mrs. Beabots to "borrow" her gazebo in the backyard for that evening.

Since it was the middle of summer, the sun didn't go down till after nine o'clock. Fireflies glittered in the rosebushes and spruce trees. Josh bought a bouquet of sunflowers and lit two citronella candles in the gazebo to ward off mosquitoes.

When Violet's car came up the drive and parked in back, Josh stood up instantly. Then sat back down. He was nervous and didn't know why.

Violet had taken the clip out of her hair and let it fall in loose curls to her shoulders. She wasn't "packing" and she'd taken off her tie and unbuttoned the collar of her uniform.

"Violet." He almost skipped down the steps toward her. He rushed up to her and she ran to him. He scooped her up in his good arm. "You're finally here!"

When he kissed her, he knew it had been worth the wait. She was warm and soft and clung to him, making him think she'd never let him go.

He couldn't take his arm from her as they walked up to the gazebo. Even his sling didn't seem in the way.

"Flowers? For me?"

"They're for Mrs. Beabots—for allowing us to use her gazebo," he joked, and started to correct himself when Violet interrupted him.

"So sweet, Josh. Thinking of her like that. She'll love them. She has just about every flower but not sunflowers. She always buys them from Sophie's mother."

It was so like Violet to think of others and not herself. His heart swelled in his chest, soaking in more of Violet's essence, yearning for more.

Josh kissed her again. "Be quiet." Then he kissed her once more. "I love you, Violet. That's what I came here to say."

"I love you, too," she'd answered. The light

in her eyes was soft. He was losing his mind all together. And he didn't care. She closed her eyes, sank her fingers into his hair and kissed him with more love than he thought he deserved.

When she pulled away, she rested her head on his chest. "I've missed you," she said.

"I missed you more."

She yawned. Then she looked at the candles. "You went to all this trouble for me, and I'm dead on my feet."

He chuckled and lifted her chin between his forefinger and thumb. "I'd love to sleep out here in the gazebo with you all night, but I have little faith in citronella. Next time I'll bring mosquito netting. I'll drape the whole gazebo."

"You know, I believe you would."

"Anything for you, Violet."

"Really?" She looked at him with piercing eyes. "Anything?"

"To the moon and back. Always."

She traced the side of his throat and held her fingers gingerly at the base where he knew she could feel his pulse. "Josh, promise me that you'll always believe in my love for you."

He'd paused. The back of his neck prickled. "I promise."

"That's all I wanted to hear." She clutched

his hand. “Because I have a confession. I haven’t been entirely honest with you these days and weeks.”

“You mean because you’ve been investigating me and thought I didn’t know.”

“Yeah.”

He dropped her hand. “So, this is truth time. Tell me, Vi. Was it me you really wanted or information about Miguel?”

“In the beginning, I wanted to nail a criminal. I was using you. I have to tell you that. We can’t go on with this thing between us. It’s killing me.”

He swiped his forehead. “I know.” Then he looked at her. “And now?”

“I do love you. More than anything. That includes my job. If I lose my position on the force over this, then so be it.” She swallowed hard. “Yesterday—hours ago, I wouldn’t have said that.”

“You wouldn’t?”

“I want Miguel behind bars.”

“Me, too.”

“You do? That surprises me.”

He stared at her. His eyes unwavering. “Why? Because all along you thought I was holding something back? Like I was part of his gang or something?”

She held her breath.

"I thought as much."

"Trent suspected that. It crossed my mind, but I couldn't go there. It's not you."

"No. You're right, Violet. It's not me. I'd hoped you knew enough about me to realize that much."

"But there *is* something you know. I feel it," she said. "I kept hoping you'd tell me."

"I have told you just about everything."

"'Just about' doesn't count when it comes to the law, Josh. And if you're holding something back to protect your image and your celebrity status..."

"Stop! It's not about that, I swear." He held up his hands. He had his reasons, and they weren't about fame. As much as he loved Violet and cared about his friends in Indian Lake, he believed he was the only one who could ultimately get through to Miguel. Turn him. Halt him. But Violet wouldn't understand that. She was still seeing life in black and white. He turned. "I better go."

"Josh, please—"

"What?"

"I've made a decision. I'm going to present your information on your behalf to the Chief and Trent. I'll try to get them to drop their suspicions. That way you won't have to worry about bad publicity or go in for questioning."

"That's what they want? To bring me in for questioning?"

"Yes."

"I figured that. In fact, I've anticipated it. Why didn't Trent bring me in before now?"

"Because he was convinced Miguel would take you to another hideout. Another meth lab or drop-off point. He wanted more evidence against Miguel."

"So I was bait?"

"Yes, but once I intervene, it'll be fine."

"I trust you, Violet," he said and pulled her close, his chin resting on the top of her head.

DAISY HANDED JOSH a mug of morning coffee. "You want sugar to lighten up that sour face of yours?"

He took the mug. "Thanks. Where is everybody today?"

"Katia's at the lake for a run with her friends Sophie and Jack Carter. Austin left at dawn for the plant."

Josh whistled. "He really is overworked these days, isn't he?"

"And quite happy you're takin' over the museum business."

"Well, I wouldn't say 'taking over.' I'm helping out for a short time while I'm in town. Which won't be much longer."

Daisy rested her hand on her hip. "Yesterday you didn't look like you were plannin' to move anytime soon. But something happened, and I think I know her name."

He lifted the blue-and-white china mug. "Well, you'd be wrong."

She took an English muffin from the toaster and slid a crystal honey pot toward him. She placed the plate on the yellow-and-white-daisy-print place mat on the island. "Sit yourself down and eat. Nourishment helps heal broken hearts."

"I never heard that before. And who said my heart is broken?"

"Two days ago you were moonin' around here worse than Austin when Katia came back to town."

"Is that right?" He took a bite of scrambled eggs and mango salsa.

The front doorbell rang, interrupting their conversation.

"I'll get it," Daisy said, placing the mug on the counter. "You eat. I have strawberries—"

"No, this is fine," he replied as she left the kitchen.

Josh heard voices at the front door. At first he paid no attention to the conversation. He sipped his coffee and just as he placed the mug on the counter, he heard what he thought was Violet's voice.

He threw down his napkin and shouted down the main hallway, "Violet? Is that you? This is a surprise..."

He halted.

Daisy's face was filled with dread as her eyes tracked from Violet to the taller man standing next to her. Violet wore her perfectly pressed uniform with its straight blue tie and gleaming badge. The man behind her was in plain clothes. Khaki pants, pale blue shirt and a tan summer sports jacket. He was holding a badge toward Daisy.

"Violet?" Tingles of dread shot up his spine. He didn't have to ask what was going on.

Her face was implacable, but the morning sun through the open front door struck her eyes, and he saw what looked like a shimmer of tears. "We're here to ask you some questions, Mr. Stevens."

"Mr...." At this moment Josh wasn't so sure they weren't prepared to arrest him.

"In regard to one Diego Lopez aka Miguel Garcia," the man next to Violet said.

"I would assume that's why you're here." Josh stared at the woman he loved even now.

"If you'll come to the station willingly..." Violet began but she hesitated.

Josh detected a croak in her voice as if the words were difficult for her to say. Or maybe it was simply that she was a rookie and hadn't rehearsed her lines well enough. He ground his jaws, hoping to bite back the acidic taste. Last night she'd told him he was more important than her job. But now… "So, you chose your career after all, huh?"

She stared at him.

"And if I don't come with you?"

"We can get a warrant," the taller man said.

"And you are…?" Josh asked, stalling for time. His feet had surely melted into the floor.

"Detective Sal Paluzzi," the man said. "I'm on the Indian Lake Drug Task Force with Officer Hawks."

"I want to call my attorney."

"Absolutely," Violet rushed to say.

For the better part of his career, he'd had plenty of moments of feeling used. Corporate sponsors needed his name to sell everything from tires to potato chips. Harry needed his winning record to garner more clients who thought Harry could create for them a "Josh Stevens" level of fame. Women had wanted him to fulfill their needs ever since his first race. No one had ever wanted the real Josh. Not until Violet.

Or so I thought. Guess I was wrong.

He felt his heart close up. With Violet, he

thought he'd found the family he'd been chasing since his parents died. He'd felt accepted by her, especially after they'd opened up to each other in the Daimler and again in the gazebo. She was the first woman he'd considered spending a lifetime with. In Josh Stevens's book, that was a miracle. He respected her dedication to her job. He'd suspected she was investigating him, but he'd ignored those thoughts until she blurted out the truth last night in the gazebo. He'd hoped she would have sway with her boss and this questioning would not come to pass.

The reality was sobering.

Violet thought he was choosing Miguel over her. He knew in the end, they'd question him, even if she went to bat for him. He just hadn't thought she'd be the one to bring him in.

He turned to Daisy. "Would you be so kind as to get my wallet and cell phone from the nightstand in the guest room, Daisy? I need to call my attorney."

"Yes, sir." Daisy scurried away.

Josh looked at Detective Paluzzi. "I don't suppose you could conduct the questioning here at the house?"

"No, sir," Sal replied. "We'll be recording."

"I see."

Daisy returned with his wallet and phone.

"What do you want me to do?" She slid her eyes to Violet with a quelling look.

"Call Austin, and let Katia know that I'm not sure when I'll return."

"I will," Daisy said, and went to the front door. She held the knob.

Josh glared at Violet. "I guess one arrest wasn't enough for you, Officer Hawks?"

"This isn't an arrest, Jo... Mr. Stevens. We simply have some questions."

"Trust me, Officer Hawks. There's nothing 'simple' about any of this."

She narrowed her eyes as she returned his glare. "Of that, I'm quite certain."

Surprisingly, Josh was able to walk out of the house and up to the squad car. At least they hadn't turned on the lights and alerted the neighbors to the "event" taking place at his best friends' house. He'd have to apologize to Austin and Katia for dragging them into his drama.

And drama it was. Miguel had always been about chaos.

Now Josh was in the middle of it.

CHAPTER TWENTY-NINE

THE LOSS OF love in Josh's eyes shredded Violet's heart. All her life, she'd made her career priority. And it had been.

Until Josh Stevens walked into my life.

Every tenet she'd held since childhood and all through the police academy was now under scrutiny. Her view of life had always been black and white; now everything was gray. She saw two and even three sides to situations.

She'd always thought of herself as the good guy, the protector of the innocent and weak. The one who knew right from wrong, and anyone in the wrong was guilty. She could recite state laws and articles without looking for affirmation. She'd thought herself noble.

She followed her superior officer's orders, sure. But she'd volunteered to stay close to Josh, and she hadn't removed herself when she realized she was developing feelings for him. She'd known his feelings for her were real, and she'd allowed her heart to open to him. If anyone had been entrapped, it was her.

She might have been the bait for her task force to gather intel and possibly arrest Miguel Garcia in the process, but she'd known what she was doing. She'd known right from wrong.

In the end, she'd betrayed the man she loved.

Violet followed Sal Paluzzi and Josh into the interrogation room at the police station. She was aware of eyes on her as Trent Davis walked out of his office toward them. She saw Trey give her a thumbs-up. She didn't feel victorious in the least.

"Thank you for coming in, Mr. Stevens," Trent said, holding out his hand.

Shockingly, Josh shook the detective's hand. "I'm happy to help."

"This way." Trent gestured with his left hand.

Violet noticed that Josh's eyes slid to her and then back again to Trent.

Bob Paxton was already in the room, setting up the video camera. He shot to his feet as Josh entered the room. Trent, Sal and Violet followed him in.

Bob nodded toward Josh. "Mr. Stevens. If you'll sit right here." The detective scurried around to the chair and pulled it out. He pointed to the chair and then went back to his camera.

Violet stood against the wall next to the

closed door. She was present only as a witness. She was not one of the investigators due to her relationship with Josh. All she could do was listen.

Sal walked around to the other side of the room. This was done so that each investigator could view different angles of the witness's face. They were looking for ticks and gestures indicative of lying. They looked for subtleties in voice, eye movements. Hand gestures.

What the camera didn't recognize, one of the team members would.

Violet didn't know how much of this Josh picked up on, but she also knew he was very comfortable in front of a camera. Any camera.

Trent sat across the table from Josh. "Would you like some coffee?"

"I was just having breakfast when your—" he looked directly at Violet with eyes so scathing, she felt seared "—er, team arrived. Maybe later."

"Fine. Then let's get started," Trent began, and lifted a pen to take notes.

Josh splayed his palms on the metal table. "How about we cut to the chase, huh? You want to know about Miguel."

"I do," Trent answered.

Violet's hands were shaking. At this moment

she wanted to be away from here. She wished none of this was happening.

Josh didn't look at her. He kept his eyes on Trent as he spoke.

"It's my guess you know just about all there is to know about Diego and me. Maybe more, considering how effective and thorough Officer Hawks and the fine members of your team are at intelligence gathering and discovery."

Trent put his pen down and leaned back in his chair. "We do. We also know that Diego Lopez, now Miguel Garcia, has made a formal bid to take over the remnants of the Le Grand gang that we busted up two years ago."

Josh pursed his lips and blew out a deep breath. "I didn't know that part."

"Garcia is smart. He's managed to elude us at just about every turn. He faked a meth lab on the outskirts of town, close to where Officer Hawks arrested you for speeding."

Violet would have cringed if she hadn't assumed a stiff-shouldered stance.

Trent continued. "We've been on stakeout around that farmhouse for weeks. We executed a surprise bust at that location recently and arrested three of Garcia's gang."

"But you don't have Miguel," Josh surmised.

"We don't. And that's why we need your

help. Officer Hawks reported following you to an area near Indian Lake—"

Josh interrupted. "The stone bridge."

"Yes," Trent said.

Josh looked into the camera lens. "Miguel and I have been estranged for years. Two years ago he got busted in Chicago for minor possession. He called me out of the blue and asked for bail money and the name of my attorney to help him. I wired the bail money and even arranged for my attorney to defend him. Paid Paul's fees as well. I knew that Miguel was a user and an all-around liar, but I didn't know until that time his level of, er, interest in the drug scene. Of course, your information astounds me. I figured he was small-time and he could get out. I drove to Chicago in my new Maserati..."

"Your Maserati?" Violet burst out.

Josh's eyes met hers. "Yes, Violet. Mine." He turned back to the camera. "I took him to lunch. I gave him a couple thousand dollars in cash. I begged him to go straight. I told him I'd pay for rehab. Miguel claimed he wasn't using. That's when I realized the marijuana he had wasn't his to use, but to sell. We had a couple drinks. We talked about the old days. As we reminisced, I discovered how jealous he was of me. Not just now, my accomplishments and fame, but even then. I had no idea. He said I got off easy. I felt terrible. I told him that if he'd go straight, no more drug deals, and get a real job, an apartment of his own and show me that he was trying, I'd give him the Maserati."

"And did he?" Trent asked.

Violet noticed that everyone in the room was hanging on Josh's every word.

"Yes. He did exactly as I'd asked, so I gifted him the Maserati. I paid for the insurance for two years so he wouldn't have to worry. I no sooner handed him the keys than I stopped hearing from him. He didn't answer my calls. He changed his cell phone number. He moved. I didn't know where he'd gone. Frankly, I was busy working overseas so much of the past eighteen months, I didn't think anything of it. Then, he showed up here in Indian Lake. He texted me and asked to talk. Said he'd seen an article about me and the foster child center. I mean, the guy texted me from Austin's front curb! I couldn't believe it."

Violet moved a step forward. "But why did you take him to the stone bridge?"

Josh didn't look at her. "Officer Hawks had shown me that area a few days prior. I knew no one would see us there. I thought I had a chance to get through to him. Get him to turn over a new leaf. I suggested he turn himself in, but he refused. He said he needed this base in Indian Lake. That he intended to expand to Kentucky and to Cookeville, Tennessee. I was hoping to get more information from him. I know he's connected to a Mexican cartel now."

"Not just Le Grand's gang?" Trent asked.

"Right. I hoped to get the name of the Mexican drug lord from him, but didn't."

Trent said, "And turning himself in?"

"He refused. He said that in a year he'd have more money than I'd ever make. He told me he still wanted the Maserati. In time, he said he'd pay for it, but it was important to him. He felt he was entitled to it. When he drove me back to town, I told him to drop me off and I'd walk home."

"And that was the end of it?" Violet asked.

"Yes."

Trent drew a deep breath. "Frankly, Mr. Stevens, we were hoping you knew his exact location. His arrest now would break up the Le Grand gang for good. Stop any expansion. And...we'd arrest the remaining gang members, as well."

Josh leaned back in his chair. "That's what you need?"

"Yes."

"Believe me, if I had Miguel's address I'd give it to you." He drummed his fingers on the table. “What I do have is his new cell number. The one he used to text me on.”

This time he turned and looked directly at Violet. “What if I were the bait for you to trap Miguel?”

“You would do that?” Trent asked.

“I would.”

“It could be dangerous.”

Josh’s eyes didn’t waver.

Violet felt her heart drop to her stomach. She knew she’d hurt Josh, but she didn’t know how deeply or if her sin was irreparable.

“Danger? Nah.” His eyes were piercing as he looked at her. “Not much can hurt me anymore.”

CHAPTER THIRTY

VIOLET DIDN'T BLAME Josh for not returning her calls or texts. She'd tried to tell him she was sorry and that she didn't blame him for being furious with her. Twice during the following four days since his interrogation, she'd started to walk to Austin's house to see him and explain, but the truth was there was no excuse for her. No forgiveness would be forthcoming.

His silence told her that his anger was best left restrained. She didn't blame him if he never spoke to her again.

That was why she was stunned when he walked into the station a week later with both Trent and Sal. He breezed past her desk with a "Hi, Violet," and then just as calmly went into Trent's office and shut the door.

Clearly, Josh was dealing only with Trent. Another sign that her betrayal had sliced him deeply.

Violet's hands slid off her computer keyboard and landed in her lap. She couldn't breathe. She couldn't think. She stared at the closed door.

Trey walked up with a box of fresh doughnuts. "You gonna break your fast and try one?" he asked.

She barely knew Trey was talking to her.

He snapped his fingers in front of her eyes. "Hey. Doughnut?"

"No. Thanks."

"Suit yourself." Trey left and went to the break room.

Violet was still staring at Trent's closed door when Bob Paxton said to her, "Hawks, let's go. I'll drive."

"Drive?" She blinked at him and brought his face into focus. "What?"

"You okay? You look pale. Blood sugar drop, huh?"

"Uh, yeah."

"I got two doughnuts. You can have one of mine. Let's roll."

She was so out of it she'd forgotten that Trent had instructed the team that they were on alert for a meeting between Josh and Miguel. She just hadn't expected to see Josh at the station. Apparently, he was following through with his promise to Trent.

Her heart tripped in her chest. Josh wasn't a

cop. He didn't know how a bust like this could go wrong. He could get hurt. Or killed.

She wanted to stop everything.

Trent's door opened slightly, and she could see Sal holding the door while still talking. She heard Josh say something, but she couldn't catch the words.

Clearly, it was too late. The die had been cast.

"Hawks," Bob urged, "get it together here. C'mon."

"Sure." She grabbed her cell phone and followed him out the front door just as Josh walked out of Trent's office.

Josh didn't call out to her. No words of any kind. He didn't approach her from behind, but she could feel his eyes on her back.

She remembered all too well how loving those eyes had felt only a week ago. She hadn't slept in days, thinking about Josh's kisses and how his face had lit up when she told him she loved him. It was all she could do to keep walking, get in the squad car and ride away from the station with Bob.

Looking in the side-view mirror, she saw Trent and Sal get into Trent's unmarked car. When Josh started to get into the backseat, he stopped and turned to watch Bob's car leave the lot. Violet sucked in her breath. For a split second she almost believed that Josh had wanted to talk to her.

She wanted to apologize to Josh, tell him that she should have handled everything between them differently and tell him once again that she loved him.

It was too late. He wouldn't believe her.

JOSH HAD NEVER worn a wire before. It felt incredibly invasive, but now that he had read all the reports from the Drug Task Force, including Violet's, he realized that Miguel was no longer the kid he'd grown up with. A Chicago detective, Richard Schmitz, had found even more information on Miguel in the past week, verifying that he was so deep into the Mexican drug traffic system that Josh believed nothing he could ever say or do would persuade Miguel to leave the underworld. Until recently, Miguel was a petty dealer. Now he was gunning for the top position. Josh's decision to help the cops as bait was drastic. But it had to be done.

The one thing Josh knew about Miguel was that in addition to his jealousy of Josh, Miguel's reigning motivation was greed.

Josh's only play was the Maserati.

He still held the title to the car. He'd texted Miguel that he realized they lived in two different worlds. Josh told the truth when he said he didn't want anything more to do with him. Nor did he want the Maserati, as it would always remind him of Miguel. He arranged to meet his childhood friend at the stone bridge and give him the title.

Miguel had wanted to meet at night. Josh retaliated with a midday time. If Miguel didn't comply, Josh reminded him that his contacts in the automotive world would find him the best "repo men" money could buy. Josh would get his car back.

Josh stood on the stone bridge, the dappled sunlight through the trees glinting off the water below when Miguel drove up in the Maserati.

Miguel got out of the car and motioned for Josh to come closer to the vehicle.

Josh wasn't sure where Trent and the team were positioned, but he knew they were close. As long as he stood close enough to Miguel to get his confession on tape, Josh would have done his job.

He took a couple steps and halted. Every fiber in his body raised a caution flag. He braked. He pulled the title paper out of his white windbreaker jacket pocket. "It's all yours, Miguel."

The man hesitated, shrugged his shoulders and walked toward Josh. Miguel was tall, the same height as Josh, but thinner and not as muscular. His black eyes tracked around the foliage and to the other side of the bridge, looking for lurking cops. Josh wasn't sure if he was still doing drugs or if the stress of his lawless lifestyle contributed to his high-pitched jitters, nervousness and innate paranoia.

Josh held out the title. "Drive it in good health," he quipped.

"Thanks, man."

Josh pulled the papers back. "One last thing, since I'll never see you again. I just want to know—is it worth it?"

Miguel burst into laughter. "Are you gonna preach to me?"

"I'm curious. How much money? Say at the end of this year? What's your personal take?"

Miguel lifted his bushy eyebrow. "What? The racing business drying up for you, amigo?"

"I never know."

"Over two million."

"And next year?"

"Triple that. Then I get into your league."

"Amazing. Who'd ever have thought a little town like Indian Lake could bring that kinda dough."

Miguel shook his head. "This isn't the big time. This is the way station." He puffed out his chest. "My network's primed to go to Ohio, Kentucky and Tennessee. And Canada. Aw."

He pinched his fingers together, held them to his lips and kissed them. "Sweet."

Josh handed him the title. "Well, I just want to say I'm not proud of you."

"I could give a—"

"Halt! Police!" Trent's voice boomed across the parking area and he, Bob, Sal and Violet converged on them. Guns drawn, they were ready for anything.

Miguel rolled his eyes. Then looked at Josh. "You son of—"

Trent circled quickly and handcuffed Miguel. Violet began reciting the Miranda rights.

As Violet walked with Trent and Miguel to Trent's car, Josh stood on the edge of the bridge watching them leave.

Sal turned to Josh. "You want to take off that wire now?"

"Sure," Josh replied.

"I'll drive us back to the station," Sal said.

"Thanks. Could you drop me at the McCrearys'? It's time I packed up and went home." The second he said the word, Josh felt his heart pinch and the pain lingered. For weeks he'd built a vision of a new life in Indian Lake.

With my arms around Violet.

He'd rushed into the romance like a teenager, not caring if he had blinders on. Even the fact that she'd kept her investigation a secret hadn't caused him to stop trusting her completely. Not until she'd lied to him had his heart skidded right into this crash.

"Home? To the McCrearys'?" Bob asked.

"Home is Indianapolis," Josh said sadly.

Bob peered at him. "You were great. Not many guys I know would take such a risk. If I didn't know better, I'd say you felt something for this town. And some people in it."

Josh looked up at the tall maple limbs shutting off his view of the sky. "I feel a lot of things."

"You know what they say? The heart knows what it needs. Maybe you should listen." Bob slapped his back.

Josh heard an owl hoot. Had he been listening to his heart enough? Or had he been reasoning away what others would think was misplaced trust? Was it over between him and Violet? Was there still a chance?

Sal Paluzzi walked over and put his hand on Josh's shoulder. "We appreciate everything you did. Indian Lake owes you a debt of gratitude."

"Thanks."

"You really leaving town?"

"I should."

"But you don't want to." Sal glanced at Violet as she closed the door to Trent's unmarked car. "Takes guts—those big decisions."

"Yeah." He looked down at the gravel under his shoes. This had been Violet's secret place she said she'd never shared with another person. She said she'd wanted it to be theirs.

"You'll be missed," Sal said.

"Yeah? Well, I don't think so. I'll be movin' on," Josh said as Sal walked away.

Josh walked to one of the squad cars and got in. He watched as Violet drove away in the passenger seat of Trent's car. Then Bob and Sal got in the front seat.

Josh had never been so aware of the chasm a short distance could be. As Violet and Trent's car disappeared down the lake road, he realized he was alone again as if his time in Indian Lake had never happened.

And the love he'd felt had only been a dream.

CHAPTER THIRTY-ONE

VIOLET OVERSAW EVERY aspect of Diego Lopez/Miguel Garcia's booking, interrogation and internment as was required by her duty as an officer of the law for the Indian Lake Police Department. The arraignment was set for nine the following morning.

She typed her report and participated in a closed-door meeting with Chief Williams, Trent Davis, Sal Paluzzi and Bob Paxton. Several times she was given kudos for her work.

Each time Chief Williams or Trent mentioned Josh's name, she felt a stab to her heart. She'd made so many mistakes with Josh, she knew he'd have to be superhuman to forgive her.

"That about wraps it up, team," Trent said. "I want everyone here early. We'll go en masse to the arraignment. Judge Clement is presiding."

Violet's eyes widened as they rose from their chairs. She was the first out the door. She turned to Sal. "Isn't Judge Clement the one whose..."

"Son overdosed two years ago. Yeah."

"A hanging judge if ever I knew one," Bob whispered. "See you in the morning."

Sal reached for Violet's arm and pulled her toward his desk as Trent waved to them. "Can I have a word with you?"

"Sure."

"Are you going to see Josh before he goes?"

Violet's mouth was instantly dry. "Goes?"

"Yeah. He said he was going back to Indy. I thought you knew."

"No," she replied lowly, feeling an immeasurable sadness grip her chest. *He was leaving?*

"I was hoping you'd tell him how grateful we all are..."

Violet tore away from Sal, grabbed her cell phone and keys from her desk. "I gotta go!"

Violet ran from the building, did not take her car from the lot but shot across the street and down the sidewalk. She ran up the drive to the back of Mrs. Beabots's house. She unlocked the back door and took the stairs two at a time, unbuttoning her uniform shirt as she sailed up the steps.

She needed to come up with the apology of all time, and she had to do it as quickly as possible. She could only hope that Josh hadn't left town already.

JOSH KNEW THERE was no arguing with women as Daisy and Katia glared at him with their hands on their hips.

"You can't drive to Indy by yourself," Katia said. "The doctor…"

"I hired a driver," he said.

"Well, you can't leave on an empty stomach," Daisy said. "I made all your favorites."

"I'm fine."

"Honest to Pete, Josh," Katia said. "You are so stubborn. And after the day you've had…"

"That's right," Daisy added. "Saving the world is one thing, but I know it takes energy. You've barely eaten a full meal since you broke up with Violet Hawks."

"We didn't break up."

"Oh? What was it then?" Katia countered.

"Katia, in order to break up, you have to be a couple first. Apparently, I was a pawn in her bid for a promotion in her career."

"Josh Stevens, that is not true," Violet said, walking onto the terrace dressed in a gauzy pink and lemon floral blouse, white skirt and white sandals. She'd brushed out her hair and taken the time to put on makeup.

Austin walked up from behind Violet. "When I drove up, I saw her walking to the door. I figured you'd all be out here."

Austin motioned to Katia and Daisy with

a jerk of his head. “Daisy, why don’t you get some drinks for our guests? Katia, sweetie, I’ll help with the bruschetta.”

Katia smiled and went to Austin. She kissed him and took his arm. “Good idea.”

Josh never took his eyes from Violet.

The others had left the terrace, but their departure was a blur to him, like the cars that shot past him in a race when he knew he needed to slow down in order to make a decisive move.

But right now, he didn’t know exactly what to say or how to say it. It was as if he’d been zapped back to that time when she’d worked magic on him, when she’d allowed him to believe that she cared about him. Josh. The guy who’d come to realize that most of life had passed him by. Until Violet.

And then he’d discovered that she’d been using him all along.

“It’s not true?” he asked.

She took a step toward him, the summer breeze lifting the ruffles around the neckline of her blouse. Clouds scampered across the early-evening sky, promising pink and delivering amber. He’d been angry with her for days, but right now, he wanted to hear what she had to say.

“I know it looks like I was out for myself, but there’s more to it than that.”

"But you admit that some of it was true."

"Josh, everything I told you about my dreams and ambitions was true. I want to protect people from drug dealers like Miguel. I would be lying to you if I said that wasn't me. It was me."

She came closer. He could smell flowers and spice. The scent of Violet, he thought. He took a small step toward her. It wasn't much, but he felt it was good.

"You have to know that I would lay down my life to protect you. Protect my family. I don't care—"

"I saw that."

"I know who I am. But at the same time, I can't let you leave Indian Lake thinking that I'm your Judas."

"I did think that."

She took another step. He thought he'd drown in the sincerity in her eyes. "Go on," he said.

"I'm sorry for everything that happened. I'm sorry that you were put through any of this. You have been nothing but generous and kind to me. To just about every person you've met in Indian Lake. What you did, rather, are doing for Mrs. Beabots and Gina Barzonni with the foster child care center is nothing short of... of...astounding. I've never met anyone like you. You didn't blink an eye when you volunteered to help." She fluttered her hands in the air. "You told the truth and were innocent of wrongdoing all along, even when I and the rest of the ILPD suspected you. And then on top of all that, you risked your life to help with our arrest of Miguel. Josh, for heaven's sake! You could have been killed!"

"But I wasn't."

She peered at him. "This guy was packing and we knew that."

"So did I."

"How could you do that? You're not a trained cop!"

He shuffled his left foot and touched his sling. "I had faith."

"In a drug dealer?"

"In the kids he and I once were. It was a crazy notion, but it worked."

"And what if it hadn't?"

He shrugged his good shoulder. "I woulda lost."

"Don't joke about something like that."

"I wasn't joking. It was the same kind of feeling I have when I race. If I'm meant to win, I will." He paused. "You on the other hand, were a different risk."

Violet dropped her eyes for a moment and when she lifted them, he knew he saw tears this time. One fell to her cheek. This time he guessed they wouldn't dry.

"Violet..."

She held up her palms. "Don't... Josh. I could use the excuse that I was under orders to follow you, meet with you and to stay by your side—"

"And tell me you love me?" he interrupted.

"No. Not that. I never deceived you, and I *will* never deceive you. I loved you."

He stopped cold, feeling his heart turn to ash. "You don't love me now?"

"I didn't say that," she replied. "I meant that I loved you with all my heart when I said that I did. Even if you leave here now and you never want to see me again, I'll always love you." She hesitated. "I found out that's how love works. I can't turn it off."

One more step and he'd reach her. If he touched her, he knew there would be no turning back for him. "Violet." He put his right hand over his heart. "I hurt. In here. And that's never happened to me before. I've been so mad at you. You can't imagine how angry I was. But when you drove away from the lake last night, I don't think I ever felt so alone. I realized that being angry with you was about the dumbest thing I've ever done. And I found I can't stay mad at you for long, it seems. Apparently, my love for you is strong and stubborn."

Her tears were flowing down her cheeks now, but she didn't seem to know they were there. "I know what you mean." She looked at him with eyes so caring, he wanted to comfort her. But he had things to say.

"Violet, of all the people I've known, you were the only one who saw me. I wanted an 'us.' I knew that taking you to the car museum and telling you I loved you in that antique car..."

"Was magical," she sobbed.

"It was for me, too."

She nodded.

"That's what falling in love with you has been for me. Magical. I don't want us to end. I don't. Please just tell me..."

She stumbled into his arm and threw her arms around his neck. Her lips were against his. "I love you. With all my heart. Forever."

"Promise?"

"Yes. I promise. If..."

"If what?"

"You'll forgive me," she whispered as her lips grazed his.

"Sweetheart, I forgave you before I agreed to be wired and see Miguel."

Her eyes widened. "You did?"

"Uh-huh. I knew you'd still hold a place for me in your heart no matter what happened. How could I not forgive you?"

She kissed him with a longing and eagerness Josh hadn't felt from Violet before. He kissed her back with all the love in his heart. He stretched his right arm around her, pulling her as close as he could with his arm in a sling.

She pulled away slowly. "Josh, I want you to know that even if I hadn't seen you today, I wouldn't have a place in my heart for you."

"What? Why not?"

A smile curved her lips as she moved in for another kiss. "Because, silly, you hold my whole heart."

EPILOGUE

LATE SUMMER BREEZES lifted the undersides of silver maple leaves as rainbows of sunflowers from lemon yellow to deep rust and burgundy bloomed around Indian Lake. The harmony of happy voices chatted about the wedding of the year between celebrity Josh Stevens and hometown policewoman Violet Hawks. Scott Abbott had written another scintillating piece about Detective Trent Davis and his Indian Lake Drug Task Force team that brought down elusive Miguel Garcia and the last of the Le Grand gang.

Officer Hawks was mentioned twice in the article. Josh Stevens's name was never brought up.

But those in their circle of friends knew the truth.

Violet stood in the master bedroom of Katia and Austin's house and stepped into the peau de soie wedding gown she'd found at a Chicago discount bridal shop that only Katia would have known about.

Daisy brought in a silver tray of flutes filled with champagne. "For toasting the bride!"

Isabelle, dressed in a soft saffron-colored sheath dress, grabbed a glass. "Mom? You want one?"

Connie Hawks, the mother of the bride, dressed in a short-skirted beige dress with a jeweled jacket replied, "Absolutely! My daughter's wedding is a day never to forget."

Violet pulled the strapless dress up over her white underwear. "Oh, Mom. You're an old hand at this. Isabelle's wedding…"

"I know, honey, but I thought…" Connie started to cry. She blew her nose.

"You thought because I was a cop, it wouldn't happen for me?"

"No. I didn't think you'd find anyone so… wonderful! He's like one of you kids to me. Part of the family."

Violet grabbed her skirts and trundled over to her mother. She threw her arms around her. "Mom, I love you. I love him. I love everybody."

"Oh, honey. You're going to make such a good wife. And an incredible mother."

"I don't know anything about kids," Violet choked out.

"Sure you do, honey. You just love 'em. Without judgment. The rest will come to you."

"I can do that."

Isabelle sniffed and dabbed her eyes with a tissue. "You do exactly that with my kids. With your own and Josh's, it'll be a breeze." She sniffed again.

"Why are you crying?"

"I'm so happy for you!"

Just then Violet's sister Sadie raced into the room holding an enormous box. "It's a disaster!"

"What is?" Violet nearly tripped on her unzipped dress.

"The bouquets. They're sunflowers. I thought you wanted roses. And look at these screwed-up funny-looking things." She pointed to curled-up white flowers that looked a bit like trumpets.

Violet started laughing. "Oh, Sadie! They're perfect."

Isabelle and Connie inspected the bouquets. "They are?"

"Uh-huh." Violet beamed. "There's a reason my ceremony is a night wedding."

Katia knocked on the door and simultaneously opened it. "Violet, everyone is here," Katia gushed, and swept into the room. Katia was the only woman Violet knew who *swept* into rooms, drawing attention to whatever designer gown or dress she wore. As one of her bridesmaids, who all wore their choice of lemon, saffron or daffodil yellow, Katia's gown was a long, off-the-shoulder chiffon.

Mrs. Beabots followed Katia inside and shut the door.

Violet eyed the octogenarian, who was wearing a long sunflower-yellow silk dress with a capelet. Long gold and topaz earrings dangled to her shoulders. Violet peered at her landlady. She'd heard stories about the ensembles and jewels that Mrs. Beabots kept in her *somewhat* secret closet. Isabelle had seen its interior, which she said was the size of a normal bedroom, but Violet had never seen it. Judging by the dress Mrs. Beabots wore, which outshined the bride, she wondered if she'd ever get the opportunity to see those treasures.

"Did my brothers pick you up like they promised?" Violet asked.

"Such handsome boys. And all single."

Violet stared at Mrs. Beabots, who was well-known for putting her finger in the matchmaking pie. "What are you up to?"

"Nothing at all. It's just that weddings are interesting places for couples to meet. You never know what can happen at one."

"Including tornadoes and thunderstorms," Katia added with a wink.

Violet glanced out the window. The sun was

nearly down. The sky was clear. No tornado would dare disrupt her wedding.

"How's Josh?" Violet asked Katia anxiously. Suddenly, she was focused only on him. She'd seen him last night at the rehearsal dinner, which also had been held at Austin's house since Josh had no family. Austin and Katia had been more than gracious to offer their home for the wedding and the rehearsal dinner.

Josh had told her he wished the rehearsal was the real thing. "Then we'd be married. I've waited long enough through slings and rehab to hold you in both my arms," he'd teased. At least she thought he was kidding.

All she remembered was his kiss. Sweet. Moving and loving. She was amazed that her love for him grew with every day. Her reliable intuition told her that it would always be this way for them.

Katia beamed. "He asked me to ask you the same thing. He's a bit nervous, I think."

"Really? Why? Does he have cold feet?" Violet started across the room to Katia as Connie struggled to zip up her dress.

"Vi. Really, you can't go down that staircase half-dressed!" Connie exclaimed.

Katia took both Violet's hands in hers. "You're shaking."

"I'm worried he could be having second

thoughts. After all, he's the one giving up his racing career to move here to Indian Lake." Violet knew that Josh had arranged for all his pit crew to work with Crash Crain now that Crash had won the Indianapolis race. The reality was that Crain would probably win more races now that Josh was out of the picture. Harry and Paul would always be needed for his commercial and merchandising work.

Katia smiled broadly. "He told us he's thrilled about working with Austin. He's got amazing plans for the car museum. And there's the center for the foster kids. He's so involved in that, too. You've seen how he is now over these past months. He's happy. Serene. All that awful pressure to perform is over."

"You're right. He said he's never known life could be—" Violet felt her blush rising from her toes "—so sweet."

"Thanks to you."

Katia squeezed Violet's hands. "Oh, Violet. I haven't seen a guy that much in love since Austin."

Isabelle coughed, holding her hand to her mouth.

Katia corrected herself. "Uh, since Scott and Isabelle."

Mrs. Beabots grabbed a champagne flute. "Sweethearts, let's not forget Beatrice and

Rand, who just married. And then there's Liz and Gabe. Sam and Gina. Olivia and Rafe. Grace and Mica..."

"I know!" Katia exclaimed. "Isn't it wonderful? Maybe we have a thing going in Indian Lake. This is where true love ignites and remains for a lifetime. Like music that is played for centuries."

"Oh, Katia!" Violet groaned. "You are *so* overly romantic."

Katia hoisted Violet's left hand to her face and turned it so that Violet was looking squarely at her engagement ring. "Look who's talking. You have a moonstone surrounded by diamonds because you and Josh have a thing about moonlight and stars. He told me. And those funky looking flowers in your bouquets are moonflowers that only bloom white after the moon comes out and the sun is gone. So, yeah. Sunflowers and moonflowers. And you're not romantic?"

"Guilty. Okay?" Violet sighed heavily. "I was afraid it would hurt my police image."

"Never," Mrs. Beabots said with a winning smile of approval.

Strains of Debussy's "Clair de Lune" wafted up the grand spiral staircase played by the string quartet Katia had positioned in the hall in the curve of the stairs.

Violet inhaled. "That's my cue."

She took her bouquet from Isabelle as her sisters and Katia took their places at the head of the stairs.

Connie kissed Violet's cheek. "I love you, sweetheart. I'm so proud of you. And so very, very happy."

"Thanks, Mom. I love you, too."

Connie hurried down the stairs to take her seat.

Violet watched as her bridesmaids walked down the staircase and into the living room, which had been set up with white folding chairs. Violet's brother Christopher had actually exchanged his ever-present EMT uniform and vest for a black tuxedo to walk her down the aisle.

"You're beautiful," he said, kissing her cheek. "And you took a shower. A miracle."

"Hey, I'm off duty." He took her arm.

Judge Clement stood in the center of the fireplace wall with Josh to his left, Austin as best man next to him.

The moment Violet came to stand in the huge living room doorway, Josh's face illuminated with happiness. Violet knew she wouldn't ever tire of his smile.

Violet didn't know what went through the heads of other brides when they walked down the aisle, but as she looked at the radiant faces of her friends, she noticed that not one was missing. Gina Barzonni Crenshaw and Sam Crenshaw sat in the front row to be with her mother. Since Josh had no family, her brothers Ross and Dylan had shown up in white dinner jackets and black tuxedo pants and took up the groom's first row. She saw Gabe and Liz Barzonni and their three-year-old son, Zeke. Zeke was playing with his cousin, two-year-old Jules, who'd flown in from Paris with his parents, Mica and Grace Barzonni. Maddie and Nate Barzonni and Olivia and Rafe Barzonni sat on the bride's side. Sarah and Luke Bosworth with Annie, Timmy and Charlotte sat with Mrs. Beabots. Sophie and Jack Carter were next to Cate and Trent Davis, and their son, Danny, who sat next to Sal Paluzzi and Bob Paxton. Isabelle and Scott with Bella and Michael sat with Beatrice and Rand Nelson and their adopted kids, Chris and Eli.

And through my work, I've helped to keep each of them safe, Violet thought.

When she raised her eyes to Josh she knew the tingles down her spine were a sign from her intuition that everything in her world was right and good.

Rather than wait for Violet to walk to him, Josh broke ranks and met her halfway. He took her arm and looped it through his. "I couldn't wait another second," he said.

"Always have to be first over that finish line, huh?" she teased.

He kissed her as they continued walking up to the judge.

Judge Clement leaned toward them. "You're supposed to wait till the end to kiss her."

Josh didn't take his eyes from her. "I won't apologize. I couldn't wait. I do."

Violet laughed. "That's not how it goes."

"I'll do the formal thing, too. But I wanted you to know I love you. In case you were worried."

Dropping her smile, she whispered, "Katia told."

"Uh-huh." He touched her cheek. Sincerity blazed deep in his eyes. "I'll always love you. I'll never leave you. If I had my way, you'd be by my side every day and every night. No matter what. Being with you has given me life."

"I meant it when I said I'll love you forever, Josh. There's nowhere I'd rather be than with you."

Judge Clement slowly closed his Bible and said, "That's not what we rehearsed, but those are the most heartfelt vows I've ever heard. I don't suppose you want to skip the rings?"

Austin tapped him on the shoulder and

handed him a band of diamonds. “This what you want?”

Josh chuckled and took the ring.

Katia took Violet’s bouquet and gave her Josh’s platinum band.

They exchanged their rings and repeated the judge’s words.

When Josh lifted her hand and kissed the ring on her finger, she couldn’t stop her tears. They kept falling as she put his ring on him.

Josh whisked her tears from her cheeks with his fingertips as Judge Clement said, “By the power vested in me by the State of Indiana, I now declare you husband and wife. You may kiss the bride. Again.”

Violet flung her arms around Josh’s neck and kissed him. Though her eyes were closed, behind her eyelids she saw flashes of lights as cameras captured the moment. But Violet knew she didn’t need a photograph to freeze this moment for her.

She and Josh would make a lifetime of thrilling memories, and each of them would make her heart race.

* * * * *